Sugar

Sugar's mind turned over the glitter and laughter of the evening, trying to sort it all out. She'd liked the attention, liked the appreciation of her work, but how much of that was party and fluff, and how much of it had been real? How much of what she was feeling for Emily was based on fleeting attraction, and how much was something more? What was "something more" anyway?

"Here they are," Emily said as she entered the lounge. "When was the last time you had a drink?"

"An hour, maybe two. Before we were dancing."

"I don't want you to drive out there if you're not sober." Emily had taken off her shoes, and her feet made no sound as she padded across the soft carpet to join Sugar in front of the fire.

"Alcohol isn't why I'm feeling dizzy."

"Why, then?" Emily's hand cupped the back of Sugar's neck. "Is it because of this?"

The brush of Emily's lips over her own drew a small moan out of Sugar. "Yes," she breathed, and then Emily's lips were on hers with increasing pressure.

They stayed like that for a long while, the brush of lips mixing with smaller nips and longer kisses. Their bodies were a slow, yielding melt of hips and thighs finding the way that fit best. When Sugar filled her hands with Emily's silky hair, it was Emily who moaned.

WRITING AS KARIN KALLMAKER:
Sugar
One Degree of Separation
Maybe Next Time
Substitute for Love
Frosting on the Cake
Unforgettable
Watermark
Making Up for Lost Time
Embrace in Motion
Wild Things
Painted Moon
Car Pool
Paperback Romance
Touchwood
In Every Port

WRITING FOR BELLA AFTER DARK:
All the Wrong Places
Once Upon a Dyke: New Exploits of Fairy Tale Lesbians

WRITING AS LAURA ADAMS:
Christabel

The Tunnel of Light Trilogy:
Sleight of Hand
Seeds of Fire

Daughters of Pallas:
Night Vision
The Dawning

KARIN KALLMAKER

Bella
BOOKS

2004

Bella Books, Inc.
P.O. Box 10543
Tallahassee, FL 32302

Printed in the United States of America
First Edition

Editor: Christi Cassidy
Cover designer: Sandy Knowles

ISBN 0-7394-5093-X

For Maria,
and the wonderful recipe we've discovered along the way

In memory of Julia Child
Life is the proper binge
Above all,
save the liver

Sixteen candles and no end to the light

About the Author

Karin's first crush on a woman was the local librarian. Just remembering the pencil through the loose, attractive bun makes her warm. Maybe it was the librarian's influence, but for whatever reason, at the age of 16 Karin fell into the arms of her first and only sweetheart.

There's a certain symmetry to the fact that ten years later, after seeing the film *Desert Hearts*, her sweetheart descended on the Berkeley Public Library to find some of "those" books. The books found there were the encouragement Karin needed to forget the so-called "mainstream" and spin her first romance for lesbians. That manuscript became her first novel, *In Every Port*.

The happily-ever-after couple now lives in the San Francisco Bay area, and became Mom and Moogie to Kelson in 1995 and Eleanor in 1997. They celebrate their twenty-eighth anniversary in 2005.

All of Karin's work can now be found at Bella Books. Details and background about her novels, and her other pen name, Laura Adams, can be found at www.kallmaker.com.

Chapter 1

Honestly, Sugar Sorenson thought to herself, she'd had no idea oven insulation was flammable.

She did know, from repeat experience, that charred sucrose, glucose and fructose smelled for days. The acrid aroma could ruin clothing, other baked food and linens. It snuck into flour and tainted spices.

More than sugar had burned today. Looking at the sodden remains of her one-room living quarters, Sugar was pretty sure nothing in the so-called "garden cottage" would ever smell clean again—the stench of burnt converted garage was worse than anything she'd ever managed. Even though water dripped from every surface in the kitchen area, some things—like the pile of cookbooks she hadn't been able to rescue—were still smoking.

Outside, on her landlord's lawn, were the few cookbooks she'd saved. The haphazard pile was surrounded by several lingering firefighters, talking quietly amongst themselves. Their poses were curiously relaxed, making it hard to believe that thirty minutes ago they'd been smashing her car windows so it could be pushed farther from the blaze. When she'd bolted outdoors, getting her car keys had been the last thing on her mind.

That was it. All there was. Poof, flash, crackle . . . ashes.

It was all over so quickly. She'd called 911 less than an hour ago. That had been a scant minute from the moment she'd realized her little fire extinguisher wasn't going to stop the rising flames. The fire station was only a block away and reassuring sirens had begun even before she'd hung up her cell phone.

She'd hated the sleeper-sofa and it didn't belong to her, so, all in all, its fate was a blessing. But her little red Honda hatchback she had loved. She hoped missing glass was the worst of its woes once it dried out.

She moved slowly toward the smoldering pile of cookbooks. Perhaps the ones in the middle could be saved. She pulled open the drawer where she kept the oven mitts, but a large puff of smoke bellowed into her face and she couldn't help a startled cry.

"Hot spot!" Heavy footsteps pounded behind her and someone with a very strong arm muscled her out the front door and into the fresh air. "Please stay out of here, ma'am!"

"I was just hoping there'd be something left, that's all." Sugar's protests seemed to fall on deaf ears.

She had to admit the firefighters were doing their firefighter thing with efficiency. The "cottage," as her landlord had advertised it, was an illegal rental, and Robert was going to be very unhappy about the ruin. She supposed she should call him. She wondered if firefighters were required to tell county inspectors that there had been living quarters here. Maybe she should quietly disappear— but where could she go? Noor would put her up for a night or two before familiarity bred contempt. She wouldn't last that long with any of her other exes. Her sisters would make space for her, but only after she'd agreed to live her life according to their relentless perception of her as the baby of the family. So what if she was youngest? At thirty-four she had a right to self-determination.

With a sinking heart, she realized the only person who'd welcome her with open arms was Grannie Fulton.

No way, Sugar thought. Grannie Fulton's arms might be open but her mind was not. She'd have a killer brownie in one hand and the Good Book in the other. "Come in, my prodigal," she'd boom. "Come in and find your salvation!"

Gran's brownies were a religious experience, but all that talk of hellfire and brimstone ruined the epiphany.

Sugar belatedly realized one of the firefighters was gesturing at her from the cottage doorway. She walked in that direction but the firefighter bolted toward her in response. She hesitated and let the imposing figure reach her.

"You need to get at least as far away as that fence, ma'am!"

The voice and visage were muted behind the safety gear, but Sugar could tell the speaker was female. Looking up and doing the math, she figured the woman for six-two, a good eight inches taller than she was. "Why?"

The because-I-said-so exasperation was plain. "It's for your safety."

"What about yours?"

"I'm the professional."

Having no tart response to that, Sugar retreated to the fence that separated her imputed lawn space from her landlord's. The off-kilter pickets divided his tended lawn and garden from the lumpy broken part she was supposed to care for. It was what she had signed on for, she reminded herself. Living in a converted garage with nothing but her own resources to carry her forward in life, that was the goal. She'd given up slaving in restaurants for other people. What a waste of ten years that had been. She needed nothing and no one.

Well, except a place to live.

Not that anyone had asked to take care of her forever. Not that she wanted to be taken care of, either. Not that she'd had more

3

than a passing coffee with an eligible woman since Noor had said, "This isn't working for me." Not precisely heartbroken, Sugar hadn't gone right back to dating simply because she hadn't had much spare time. It wasn't as if anyone had sought her out once word got around that she was single.

Did she care? Of course not. She could live on her own. Of course she could.

The warm spring breeze shifted and the smell from the house did *not* make her think of the status (burned up) of her life. The skyscraper of a firefighter turned around as if to warn her to move farther back, but Sugar was saved from another admonishment by the arrival of an ordinary sedan in the tiny side driveway that led to her "garden cottage." It was the kind of car you'd forget seconds after seeing it. The King County seal on the driver's door caught her attention then. That was quick, she thought. Was it a building inspector or arson investigator? Someone from the tax board coming to demand payments of some kind from the landlord for the illegal rental?

Even worse, could it be a health inspector finally realizing that Cake Dreams by Sugar was operating at a new address, and had been for longer than allowed without updating her business license and inspections? She'd known all along the cheap rental was temporary. Now, fate had decided it was time to get legal again, it seemed. She wasn't missing *that* message in all this chaos. How would she afford a new place with the right zoning to get her inspections back up to date?

The woman who climbed out from behind the wheel did not have a clipboard. In Sugar's experience, all inspectors carried clipboards. Nor did she look the least bit like an accountant. Of course Sugar didn't know exactly what an accountant might look like, but the black lace-up Doc Martens, calf-length leggings and flowing overshirt of blue, green and purple patchwork didn't fit the stereotype in her head. Neither did the brilliant emerald crocheted bag tucked under one arm. If tax assessors looked that good then no one would be anxious to talk to one, she realized.

Two realizations hit her at once: the newcomer was stepping over fire hoses with the aplomb of someone accustomed to doing so, and, after an exchange of curt nods, it was clear that the tall firefighter knew her.

"I'm Gantry Racine from Victim Services." She held out an elegantly pale hand tipped with short but gleaming nails. "Do you need anything? I have fresh bottled water in the car and an armful of resources we can call to get you shelter for a while if you need it."

"Oh. I'm a victim?"

"Of a fire, yes, but we don't have to worry about if the label fits." Gantry had black eyes that snapped and sparkled.

I must be in shock, Sugar speculated, not to have taken in right away that she's likely the most beautiful woman I've ever seen in the flesh. She'd heard of porcelain skin but never actually looked at it except in paintings.

"Drink this," Gantry said firmly. She produced a foam cup from her bag, along with a Thermos bottle. "Tea. Would you like sugar?"

"Yes." Tea sounded really good, now that she thought about it. "That's my name."

"How rude of me." Gantry handed over the cup, then tipped the contents of a sugar packet into it. "I didn't ask your name. I sincerely apologize."

"It's okay." Sugar rushed to reassure her. "Sugar Sorensen is the whole name."

"I wish we were meeting under better circumstances." She nodded at the cup in Sugar's hand and Sugar dutifully sipped. Hot, a bit strong, but the act of sipping was calming.

The firefighter, who had watched their exchange behind the passivity of the safety mask, spoke so suddenly that Sugar nearly jumped. "Hey, Gantry."

"How's life been treating you, Charlie?" Gantry pushed her thick, blonde hair over her shoulder, but there was no flirtation in the gesture.

5

"Same old, same old. Are you going to be at Dee's shindig?"

"I'm on call, so who knows?"

"Me, too."

There was a loud shout of "all clear" from inside the house. The firefighter, Charlie apparently, pulled off her safety mask. Sugar took note of the two light brown eyes set in a face too evenly café au lait in shade to be the result of a mere temporary tan. Close black curls were glossy with perspiration.

I must be in shock, Sugar thought again. All the women were looking like models. She stifled a giggle. If she looked in a mirror maybe her freckles, chipmunk cheeks and unruly, mousy brown hair would be gone. Instead, she'd see Meg Ryan at thirty-four. That wouldn't suck.

The other two women were talking in fits and starts about Dee's shindig, which appeared to be a wedding of some sort. Sugar was staring morosely at her poor windshieldless Honda when yet another car arrived.

Whoever it was didn't work for any government agency. The Jaguar's door opened and the first thing Sugar could see clearly was a tapered black pump, exactly the kind that made her feet hurt just looking at them.

Deep down there was a thought that she ought to know who this person was, but nothing came to her as the quiet click of the heels on cement proceeded toward them. The woman's brow was furrowed with concern, but she still stepped forward with confidence. Her red hair was caught in a French braid that shimmered in the sunlight. "Sugar? Sugar Sorenson?"

"That's me," Sugar replied brightly.

"The fire truck is blocking the street." The newcomer glanced open-mouthed at the ruin of Sugar's car and then at the smoldering cottage. "My goodness, what's happened?"

Producer—she had to be the producer for *Best of Seattle*. The producer who might want to do a spot on Cake Dreams by Sugar. The producer who was supposed to melt off the chair with a casually offered slice of fruit and chocolate mousse torte. That torte, had it survived the drenching from the fire hoses, would have tasted like burnt house, Sugar realized, so the deluge was just as well. Under the circumstances she was fairly certain her hospitality wasn't under scrutiny.

Charlie answered seriously, "A single-unit domestic fire. Seems to have started in the kitchen wall from an electrical source."

"Oh, my lord." For the third time in minutes, Sugar found herself appraised by a lovely pair of eyes. These were the blue of four drops of food coloring into a quarter-cup of sugar. I've cracked up, Sugar thought. "What a shock that must be."

"You look very familiar to me, but I don't think we've met." Gantry regarded the producer for a moment. "Was your picture in the *Advocate*?"

The perfectly lipsticked mouth opened in slight surprise. "Yes, it was. They did a piece on women in television. I'm here to set up a segment on Sugar's culinary business and discuss the desserts category of the Seattle Eats cookoff coverage."

Sugar considered that she hadn't been this close to this many lesbians all at once in quite some time. The last time was at the Grrlz Dance Party, and she wasn't really a "grrl." On the other hand, she hadn't been the only over-thirty lesbian there, either. Why was she thinking about a party from months ago when her house had just burned down? She looked closely at the producer, now thinking those incredible blue eyes were familiar. Surely she was losing her mind. But how did she ask? Did she say, "Did I meet you at that dance-mostly-naked, step-out-back-if-you-want-to-do-more party? Didn't we bump hips and other body parts for a while on the floor?" It had been in March, in honor of Noor's thirty-fifth birthday. Pathetic that the only party she'd been to in ages had been for an ex. She couldn't bring it up. It would sound like a come-on, as if she'd burnt her brains along with her house.

Even if they had met—maybe even briefly danced—she didn't want the producer thinking she was a compulsive party girl. She was hardly the good-time girl her family thought she was. Rose took those honors.

She'd never had the luxury of the time or money to drink bitter coffee and plan her next body piercing. Her small circle of friends was comprised of sous chefs and wannabes, which meant they were free for two hours a month. There were a few women in the greater Seattle metropolitan area with whom she had shared a misguided night that had turned into an awkward breakfast, but only Noor counted as an ex. They'd dated for almost three years, ruined that by moving in together and broken up a few months later.

Now that the house had burned down, however, there were three awesomely attractive lesbians all looking her over. And all she was to them was a victim.

"Yes, well, it certainly is." Emily Dorsett, Sugar thought. The producer was Emily Dorsett. She turned that bright blue gaze in Sugar's direction again. "We'll reschedule this, Sugar. I'm just devastated for you. You've got my card, right?"

"Actually . . ." Sugar swallowed as her voice cracked. "I'm not sure I do anymore."

Gantry was the one who moved first, but it was Charlie who caught Sugar before she hit the ground.

"What was I thinking?" Gantry's face swam in Sugar's vision for a moment. "Standing her out here in the sun after a shock."

Just before Sugar blacked out she thought that they all had angels' faces, looking down at her in concern, like a trinity of lesbian beauty, compassion and strength. Angels of cocoa, cinnamon and vanilla . . . If she'd known they were coming, she'd have baked a cake . . .

Sugar . . . sugar bear. Sugar, give me some sugar, darlin'. Sugar, ah honey honey, you are my candy girl. Sugar . . . sugar pie. Wake up, sugar pie, honeybunch. Sugar in the morning, sugar in the evening, sugar in the afternoon . . . sugar . . .

"Sugar. Come on—she's coming around."

"Sorry." Sugar turned her head away from the hand patting her cheek. "I don't know what hit me."

"Shock."

She was in the passenger seat of Gantry's car. Given that she smelled even more strongly of smoke, she was willing to guess Charlie had carried her there. If she'd known some hunky fire-fighter would have to pick her up she'd have worked harder to lose the fifteen pounds self-employment had put on her body.

Charlie was speaking into the radio on her shoulder. "She's conscious, so the paramedics can—"

"No, please," Sugar protested. "I don't need paramedics. I just fainted."

"Sorry, it's procedure."

"You did lose consciousness, Sugar," Gantry said quietly.

Without looking at Emily, Sugar admitted, "My health insurance deductible is huge. Please, if you can cancel that call I'd appreciate it. I won't let them work on me."

Charlie sighed, then shrugged. Turning away, she spoke into her radio again. The back of her black- and yellow-striped jacket was emblazoned with *C. BRONSON.* Sugar remembered having seen the name around the neighborhood. Some mornings when she went out for the paper, she'd seen letters in bold red across the shoulders of a sweat-soaked T-shirt as the early-morning jogger zipped past the house. She'd even giggled to herself and thought, "Must be Ms. Majestyk."

"I'm glad you're feeling better." Emily glanced at her jeweled watch, but Sugar didn't sense she was unduly impatient. Yet she must be a busy woman, and her trip to the suburbs had been point-less. "I think I should leave you in peace. Please let me know when you're settled. I was really looking forward to doing this segment about you and your work. The photographs you sent were amazing."

Sugar brightened, realizing that Emily did have a copy of her portfolio and a number of photos. "I will be asking for those back sometime soon, I hope, to make copies. It's possible my computer survived. It was farthest from the kitchen. And my digital camera might still be okay." She looked after the imposing Charlie, wondering when she might be able to go back into what was left of her home. She had no idea how far the water had spewed from the original blaze.

As if reading her mind, Gantry said, "You'll probably be okayed to go back in tomorrow. At least you got a few things out. And some of your appliances will have survived the water."

A screech of tires startled them all. Sugar started to get out of Gantry's car but found that Gantry's hand clamped on her shoulder held her in place with no effort at all. Sugar marveled for a moment at her unresponsive arms and legs. Wow, limbs could actually be so weak they trembled.

"What the hell did you do?"

Christ, it was Robert, her landlord. Large, loud and certain he knew what was best, Robert planted his feet, ignoring everyone but Sugar. The man was an idiot, Sugar thought, to ignore two beautiful women in order to look at her.

"I didn't do anything. The fire started in the oven."

"Some concoction of yours? How are you gonna pay for all this damage?"

"Are you the homeowner?" Emily's tone snapped Robert's attention to her. "Your own insurance will compensate you for damages and of course Ms. Sorenson for her lost property. And if they don't, you will."

Robert must have noticed how gorgeous Emily was because his tone became moderately more civil. "I'm not paying for anything of hers. She was supposed to get her own insurance."

"Your own insurance company is aware that you have a . . . *dwelling* . . . in your garage?" Emily's right eyebrow quirked.

Robert slowly turned purple. Sugar wondered if he'd like some tea now, too. "I don't see that that is any of your—"

"But it is mine," Gantry cut in. She flipped out a business card. "I will be reporting the illegal rental to other county departments. They will be quite interested to learn of it."

It crossed Sugar's mind that Elliot Ness hadn't been the one to get Al Capone. The credit went to the I.R.S., and Robert would likely be getting a call from them, too. He had been an ass to her the last eighteen months, over everything from "excessive" use of the driveway to whether her newspaper was too close to his after they were delivered. Now that her cheap place to live was no more, she was rooting for the Feds. Careful, she warned herself, with visions of health inspectors in her head. You're not exactly squeaky clean in all this, either.

"She was operating a bakery out of the cottage," Robert accused. "Whatever happened was because she started it!"

"I did not!" Sugar really had had enough. All her hopes and dreams had gone up in flames. She didn't even have flour to her name and her only order due in the next week might be lost. She'd forked out good money to enter the Seattle Eats competition a mere two weeks away and there was no way she'd have anything worth submitting now. She struggled past Gantry's restraining hand. "I was making one cake a day, well within the capability of the oven."

"You report me to anybody and I'll report you!" Robert stepped toward Sugar but held up when Emily and Gantry moved in as well. "We have a contract!"

"A contract to further an illegal arrangement isn't valid." Emily waved one hand as if the truth of her words was something a first-grader would know.

"I'll sue you for everything you have!"

"Oh, like that'll make you rich." Sugar dashed angry, helpless tears from her cheek. "It wasn't my fault."

Robert cracked his knuckles. "You'll never prove that."

"She won't, but I will." The cool voice coming from behind Sugar brought Robert up short. Well, it was either the voice, Sugar thought, or the fact that Charlie was four inches taller than he was. Her lesbian trinity closed ranks. Charlie's tone was scathing. "The oven was installed on a combined one-ten electrical connection, and two one-tens don't make a valid two-twenty. There was also no ground and the circuit box was overfused. You endangered her life, your own, and that of your family and neighbors."

11

"Your insurance company is going to be very, very unhappy," Emily added.

"Even lacking intent to commit a physical crime, I wouldn't be surprised to find that your entire rental fraud was criminal in nature," Gantry speculated.

Robert's mouth opened and closed and Sugar said the only thing that came to mind. "My big sister is a lawyer!"

Charlie cleared her throat, and while she never broke a smile, Sugar saw one in the light brown eyes.

Robert gaped just once more, then hurried for his back door, slamming it shut behind him after a wild look at the four women, none of whom had moved.

"And the horse you rode in on, asshole." Emily's vivid blue eyes crackled with animosity. "I hate bullies."

"Hear, hear," Gantry said. "That type doesn't think beyond the next buck. Even now he doesn't care that someone might have been killed."

"Oh, oh—I know." Charlie was smiling broadly now. "Let's all get on our cell phones. You know he's watching, and he'll croak."

Sugar felt like a spectator at a well-choreographed play. Three phones, three chirps, three women separating themselves by polite distances. Their conversations flowed over Sugar as if she wasn't even there.

Emily said without preamble, "We'll need to postpone the Cake Dreams feature . . ."

Gantry was more roundabout. "It's me. Just checking in. How are you feeling?"

Charlie, after listening for a bit, said only, "Oh, hell, my mother called."

Another cup of tea settled Sugar's nerves more, and her sodden purse was brought out to her. It was typical of her, Sugar mused, that she'd rescued cookbooks but not her checkbook. Her cell phone was damp, but turned on for a minute before the battery went dead. She'd been meaning to charge it.

"Who can you stay with, dear?" Gantry patted her arm. "I will warn you that it's not unusual to sleep badly the first several nights after a big shock."

"It's not like I have a girlfriend who'll care," Sugar muttered.

"Every woman needs a girlfriend," Charlie remarked from her position, leaning on the hood of Gantry's county car.

"I have girlfriends, but not a girlfriend," Sugar said. Charlie's mouth twitched in what might have been a relieved smile. Sugar all of a sudden wanted to blush. The woman had amazingly suggestive eyes. That or she was still in shock. Yes, that was a far more likely explanation.

Emily lightly touched Sugar's arm. "I really must go, but as soon as you feel up to it, I would love to do the feature. We have a studio kitchen we could shoot in, change it a bit to look like it might be yours." She frowned for a moment, as if ticking off a mental checklist. "I think we'd have done that anyway, given how small your real kitchen is, er, was. Here's my card again, and please—I meant it—call."

"I will," Sugar said sincerely. If she ever hoped to get on her feet again the feature would be a real boon.

Emily hesitated. "I'm really sorry about all this. I had hoped . . ." At Sugar's inquiring look, she hurried on, "A friend of mine is having her fortieth birthday this weekend and I've left organizing things late. I was hoping I could persuade you to take a rush order for about twenty people. I even brought photos of her cat."

"Oh." Sugar quickly ran through the necessary calculations. A lookalike cake for twenty had been priced on her Web site at two hundred dollars, something Emily had to know, and she could certainly use the money. It might cover half of a new windshield. She brightened. Her Web site, which was hosted on a paid server site, would still be up. She'd still get orders. All she needed was a kitchen. She had enough savings for supplies.

Grannie Fulton had a large, utilitarian kitchen capable of producing a Thanksgiving meal for thirty. Damnation.

"I think I can stay with my grandmother," Sugar said slowly. "When did you want the cake delivered?"

"You really think, given all this—" Emily waved a hand at the smoldering, smoking cottage. "You think you could still do it?"

"I think so, yes."

"Wow, okay. Well, here's the photos."

"Excuse me," Gantry interrupted. "But why does she need photos of the cat?"

Emily flashed Gantry a smile. "Sugar does the most fabulously realistic three-dimensional cakes, to order. The only other place I know of in the country where you can get one like it is New York."

Sugar eyed the calico's markings. They were intricate, with at least five different shades of icing and a lot of pastry brush painting to simulate fur. The yellow eyes and jeweled leather on the collar would be fun. But if she kept the pose simple, it was doable. "Would she like one of the cat on her back, like this? Wanting a tummy rub?"

"Oh, that would be delightful, yes." Emily grinned. "Okay. Well. Here, let me write my home phone on the back. If you realize later you can't, please call me, okay? I can always order something from the grocery."

It was unthinkable that she might lose the order to Safeway or Costco. Somehow Sugar found some basic business sense. Running a business wasn't her strength to begin with, so finding a moment of practicality under the circumstances was a bit of a miracle. Grannie Fulton would say the Lord had worked in His mysterious way. Right, burn down the house to make a good business contact. "Chocolate cake with a ganache, or vanilla with something like a lemon?"

"Chocolate. It's an all-dyke event."

Sugar nodded with a knowing smile. "And you know how much I charge for one of these?"

"Yes." Emily handed back her business card. "She's my best

friend and it's her fortieth. I really don't want an ordinary cake. One of yours will make the freezer-to-oven easy hors d'oeuvres forgivable."

"As you wish," Sugar murmured, her mind whirling through the ingredient list. She longed to go back into the house and at least get her metric scale and favorite measures. Her cake ingredients were calculated by weight, not volume, which allowed vast flexibility in sizing recipes along with precision in measuring. "I know I can get this done."

Resigned, she knew that she would have to put up with Gran and the lectures about being single, missing church and preferring cookbooks to the Good Book. She would do nearly anything to avoid going back to restaurant slavery. Anything not to have to ask a single sister for money. Again. At Gran's she could pay her way. At least Gran thought trying to make a living by baking was laudable.

Charlie joined them quietly, holding a large box as if it were a feather.

"The other thing I was going to talk to you about," Emily said cheerfully, "is your entry for the Seattle Eats competition. I saw your company name on the competitors list. We're covering it, and I was hoping we could tape your preparations as one of the competitor background stories."

It was abruptly too much to think about. Sugar felt the blood drain out of her head again. Gantry put an arm around her shoulders. "I really think it's time to move you to your grandmother's."

"I'm so sorry, babbling on." Emily held the passenger door open for Sugar. "Call me. We'll get everything sorted out when you're ready."

Gantry's arm was very comforting and Sugar found herself wondering how old she was. Anywhere between thirty-five and forty-five, she thought.

"Hang on a minute!" Sugar looked up dazedly to see Charlie offering her the box. "I thought you could use these. And we'll leave warning tape on the doors and windows. I hope that keeps the jerk out of your stuff. Someone will be here tomorrow at ten a.m. to check if it's safe to enter. If you're here with a truck, you might salvage most of your equipment."

Sugar peered into the large box, wondering where on earth Charlie had found such a large carton. It wasn't full of clothes, which would reek of smoke, but the durable items from the counter and primary baking drawer. Her scale, stainless steel bowls, whisks, copper measuring cups, even her favorite metal scrapers and spatulas. Her cell phone charger and portable CD player were also inside. She blinked back tears. "Thank you. I— that was very kind. And what I'll need most for the next few days."

Charlie shrugged. "I guessed."

The box was settled on the seat behind them, along with her squishy purse and the meager items Sugar had already removed from the house. Emily took her leave to back out the Jaguar. Gantry followed suit and the last Sugar saw of Charlie was as she walked back toward the cottage with a roll of bright yellow warning tape in hand.

"Sugar, my child! You look back from the shores of hell itself!"

"Something like that," Sugar said, then she was enveloped in Grannie Fulton's attar of roses with a hint of vanilla scent. It was an aroma right out of her childhood and suddenly Sugar found herself in tears, crying helplessly in the safety of Grannie Fulton's arms.

Gran had her and Gantry both in seats at the kitchen table with slices of banana bread and steaming mugs of coffee before Gantry could finish explaining what had happened. Sugar blew her nose and took a nibble of the treat. It was wonderful. Dense and moist, it tasted of banana and pineapple, even a hint of coconut. She would have to get the recipe, she thought.

Then she recalled that her recipe boxes were now a fused pile of paper pulp and ink. She'd been meaning to scan them for, well, years. Tears trickled down her cheeks. Gantry offered a small packet of tissues, which Sugar accepted with a grimace she hoped looked as grateful as she felt.

"Have another bite, Sugar Bear," Gran urged. "There's nothing that can't be helped by food in your stomach." She turned to Gantry. "Could I bother you to fetch that basket of preserves? My old legs aren't what they were."

Gantry rose to get another artifact of Sugar's childhood. "Goodness, I haven't seen a jam cozy in ages. What a beautiful handle, and it holds six tall jars. My grandmother's held four standard-sized."

"I used to have quite a crew to feed in my younger years. Now, every jar in there is all my own fruit," Gran said proudly. "You haven't tasted anything like my peaches in ages, either. Gantry, now that's an unusual name."

"It's a family name." Sugar watched Gantry's eyes light up as Gran proffered a jar of preserves. Gantry was earning big points, having the etiquette to use the jam spoon to put two dollops on her plate, not on the banana bread. Crumbs in the jam were verboten. "My father's middle name and his father's first name. If I'd had any brothers I might have escaped. Most of my friends call me Tree."

"Gantry has a fine, strong ring to it," Gran Fulton observed. "It seems to suit you as much as Sugar suits my granddaughter."

Sugar blew her nose to avoid meeting their combined gazes. "I don't know about that."

"You were the sweetest of the litter." Gran patted her hand. "And you know you can stay as long as you like. My door has always been open to you. I'd certainly like to meet any gentlemen friends you may have, too."

Sugar caught herself before she rolled her eyes, then stole a glance at Gantry, er, Tree. She responded to Sugar's very slight shrug of chagrin with the most subtle wink on record. "I don't have time for dating, Gran."

"You're the last grandchild not married, so I worry about you. Go forth and multiply," Gran quipped.

"Mom and Dad did enough of that, and Patricia and Quinn did

their part. I don't need to add to the population," Sugar answered back. She glanced at Tree. "I have three older sisters. That makes me the baby of the family."

"You still are," Gran said serenely. "Now, the guest room is all yours, and if you bring me the phone, my friend Judy has a daughter your size, and I'm sure we can get you a few things to wear. You'd best take a shower, dear. I can't say you smell all that good."

"I know."

"I'll be going," Tree said quickly, after bringing the phone from the counter to the table. "You have my card, Sugar. I'm glad to get you settled."

"Thank you. You've really been *very* kind."

"Not everyone is so lucky." Tree gave her a steady glance.

It wasn't ideal, Sugar knew, but Grannie Fulton was a darned good safety net. She nodded. "I know."

"Sugar, dear, would you go in the pantry and fetch a jar of last year's peach preserves? It was an uncommonly fine year, all the early spring rain. For Gantry to enjoy all on her own."

Sugar found the jar easily enough. She knew her way around Gran's kitchen and pantry. There was a stockpile of baking ingredients, too. She could start on Emily's cake tonight, if her nerves steadied. Right. Every woman looked like an angel to her and she cried at the smell of vanilla. She could bake tonight, sure.

"I really can't accept it," Tree protested. "There's a rule."

"A jar of fruit, what harm is that?" Gran pressed the gift firmly into Tree's hands. "I insist. Kindness is in short supply in this world. That's all I have to say."

Tree relented with a grin. "Well, having tasted some already, I'd be a fool. And my mama didn't raise no fools."

Gran patted Tree's hand. "It'll make tea tonight that much better."

Naturally, but clearly, Tree said, "My partner adores peaches. Thank you, really."

Sugar waved good-bye from the door and steeled herself for Gran's inevitable question.

"Now, what do you suppose she meant by 'partner'? Do you think she's one of those gay women?"

I could have died in the fire. Sugar thought about that for a long moment, and the reality of life's fragility swept over her. She'd always thought it wasn't worth the trouble of coming out to her Bible-thumping, church-going, loving but homophobic grandmother. At that moment she no longer had the energy for the secret. "I do think she is, Gran. And so am I."

Grannie Fulton gazed at her for a long, tense moment. After a sigh, she said quietly, " 'Whatsoever things are true, whatsoever things are honest, if there be any virtue I have learned to be content.' "

She dialed the phone, leaving Sugar to make her way bemusedly to the shower. Maybe the world would make sense tomorrow.

Chapter 2

"Why, you knead that just like bread dough. My, my."

"Nearly," Sugar admitted. "You taught me the basics, remember?"

Sugar wasn't put off by Gran's intent study of her methodical scrape-fold-press motion with a metal spatula and one plastic-wrapped hand. It was calming to be doing something so familiar after her panicked awakening. She'd thought she'd smelled smoke, then couldn't remember where she was. It had lasted only a moment or two, but her heart hadn't stopped pounding for ten minutes.

Kneading fondant, which would serve as her molding material when she iced the cake, was something she could do in her sleep. Just this past Sunday, for Mother's Day, she'd had three cakes to ready all at the same time and that *had* felt as if she were kneading fondant in her sleep.

Business plan item number nine—hiring assistant bakers—was now even farther down the list.

She'd already had two batches of the malleable, creamy white sugar solution chilling in the refrigerator that had been included in the rental, for all the good they did her now. Unlike the car, they weren't insured. Thank goodness she'd gone for more than minimum coverage. A glass-repair guy was supposed to meet her around noon and drop a new windshield and windows into place, and it wasn't costing Sugar a dime. It was a huge relief.

You've worked hard, she told herself. You've got a nest egg for the business and you won't be spending it on employees anytime soon, so it's time to decide what you need most now. New place to live?

She'd think about it tomorrow, she decided, then felt better for having made a decision, even if it was not to decide.

"Don't forget the time, Sugar. I'll get the layers out of the oven, no problem." Gran peered at the timer. "It's going to be hard not to sample. That's a heavenly aroma, your chocolate sponge."

"Thanks." Sugar blushed, feeling a pleasant thirteen again. "I really think it's the barest hint of cayenne. It wakes up the chocolate aroma and flavor. Time-wise, I'll just make it. Thank you so much for watching the clock for me."

"The way your landlord sounds, you don't want to leave anything to him."

"Not a good idea," Sugar agreed. She wanted to be there when the fire department cleared the remains of her belongings. Gran's ancient but well-maintained Olds '88 would hold a lot of her things. She already missed her marble slabs. She lightly misted the fondant. "I think it's a little less humid here in Redmond. This is drying more quickly than I expected."

"Now, I've always thought this slope caught a tad less of the ocean moisture, but you can't get the weather folks to admit it." Gran moved heavily from the sink to the table, sinking down in a chair. "Old bones, old bones," she muttered.

Sugar hid a frown of concern. She hadn't seen Gran since Christmas and Gran's old bones were moving far more slowly. "Have you been to the doctor?"

"I have, and there's no room in my life for hip replacement. I can't be laid up like that."

Sugar made a noncommittal noise. Hip replacement was something she knew absolutely nothing about, but Gran was obviously in discomfort. "What kinds of things would you need doing?"

"Well, there's my canning, beginning with the apricots, and baking for the shelters. Church events—nobody is going to see to the Harvest Fair. It can't wait until the last minute. It takes the whole summer to get people to commit to having a booth and so forth."

"Surely someone would step in." Sugar remembered Gran organizing the Harvest Fair from years ago. "Time someone else did."

"Not someone I'd trust to do it right. Or let me have my say once I was back on my feet."

Ah, well, that made sense. Sugar supposed that if Gran had ever really wanted someone else to do the work, she'd have let go when she turned seventy. She patted the mound of fondant. It was a miracle of chemistry that a boiled sugar solution would knead into such a delicious, versatile substance. "That's done, then."

Hands washed and hair brushed, barely, she put on the jeans and T-shirt that Gran's friend had dropped off. The tee was a little tight. Likewise the jeans, but a look in the mirror said the shape suited her. Her license and credit cards tucked in her back pocket and cell phone hooked on her belt, she carefully steered the mammoth car toward her old home. It wasn't far from Redmond to Issaquah, but typically Lake Sammamish Parkway was congested on weekdays.

She'd slept poorly and still hadn't beat Gran to the kitchen this morning. Over coffee and a discussion of their baking day—Gran supplied quick breads and fruit cobblers to a halfway house and a women's shelter—Sugar had braced herself for a lecture on her pronouncement of the previous night. But Gran had never alluded to Sugar's declaration. She hadn't even sighed or looked pained and worried aloud about Sugar's single status.

What had Gran said last night? That if Sugar was honest and virtuous, Gran would be content? Well, she'd finally been honest about liking girls. Virtue, well, zero opportunities accounted for that—at least in the last few years. It had been a while since she'd even had a chance to be naughty.

Gran's lack of response was somehow disconcerting, but thoughts of that went out of her head at the sight of not only a fire department SUV but a sheriff's cruiser in front of Robert's house. She nearly kept going, but then she spotted a tall, familiar figure in a white King County Fire District T-shirt talking to the cop. Robert stood on his porch, his arms crossed defiantly.

"Ah, here's the property owner now," Charlie said to the cop as Sugar warily approached.

"I'm not the owner, he is," Sugar said. She thought Charlie had understood that.

"There's been an alleged burglary," Officer Tuhrez informed her.

"You owned some of the items in there, right?" Charlie looked indignant. Sugar saw that another firefighter was circling the outside of the blackened building, and that the yellow warning tape over the doorway was torn.

"Oh, yes. Some of them."

"Laptop, copper bowls, knife set, heavy-duty Calphalon? All stuff that was there yesterday?"

"Yeah, I was hoping some of it survived."

"It's been cleaned out." Charlie looked accusingly at Robert. "The tape was breached. Somebody did some breaking and entering."

The sheriff shifted in his black boots. "Technically, if entrance was through an unlocked door it wasn't breaking."

"What about stealing?"

"I didn't take anything of hers. It would have all been worthless." Robert didn't leave the safety of the porch.

"I don't suppose you'd let me take a look in your garage, would you?" Officer Tuhrez, who, in Sugar's opinion, could have taken butch lessons from C. Bronson, Firefighter, gestured at the closed garage door.

"Not without a warrant." Robert crossed his arms smugly.

Looking at the smoldering remains of her ambition, Sugar felt that same disbelieving numbness she'd experienced yesterday afternoon. Then it shattered in a flash of white-hot rage. Her *knives*! The bastard had taken her *knives*. How unbelievably petty. How cruel, too, to take advantage of her loss by stealing from her!

"Are you okay?" Charlie started toward her in concern.

Sugar waved a hand. With a deep breath she bellowed, "I don't need a warrant!" and bolted for the closed door.

"Stop her," Robert screamed.

"Miss, don't do that," Officer Tuhrez ordered. If Charlie had given her an order, she might have obeyed, but the cop just didn't have the same command.

The two-car-wide door was wood, old and heavy. She'd watched Robert's wife struggle with it many times, but Robert was too cheap to get an automatic opener. In her anger she flipped it open as if it were cardboard. The footsteps right behind her belonged, thankfully, to the two people in uniform. Robert skittered to a stop at the corner.

Sugar had the satisfaction of watching him turn a deep purple. The hue of shame, Gran would say.

"For the record," Charlie said conversationally, "that pile of stuff looks exactly like the things I took note of yesterday in the dwelling."

He'd even taken her plasticware, some of which had been warped by the heat.

"Would you like to explain?" Office Tuhrez had a we-are-not-amused look on his face as he turned to Robert.

"You don't have a warrant. You can't look!"

"You asked me to stop her. Now I see stolen property in plain sight. I can get a warrant to search the *entire* premises at this point."

"Then, then," Robert spluttered, "then arrest her!"

"For opening a frickin' door?" Charlie burst into laughter.

24

"Look," Officer Tuhrez said with exaggerated patience. "You can give the lady her things back and see if she feels generous in forgetting all about this, or I can tag it all as evidence and call the crime scene people."

"She can have her crap back," Robert snapped. "It's all worthless, anyway."

Sugar said indignantly, "For your information, those knives probably cost more than your truck. They were a gift from my entire family when I got out of culinary school and my *name* is engraved on each blade." Sugar couldn't stop her voice from shaking. Even now she didn't know if they'd survived, though the protective roll that housed them seemed to be intact. "I could slice your testicles into pieces so thin you could see through them—"

"Enough," the sheriff said firmly. "He's willing to give it all back. What do you say?"

"She threatened me! You heard her!"

"You, sir, are looking at charges for a high-level misdemeanor at the very least, which can have a hefty fine. I wouldn't make waves right now." Officer Tuhrez turned back to Sugar.

"If I don't take my stuff now, when would I get it back?"

"Could be weeks, months." He shrugged.

She was sure the laptop was toast. The cookware she could get by without. The knives, if the handles had survived, were irreplaceable. She didn't want to let Robert the slimeball off the hook. He didn't deserve mercy.

"I just took it all for safekeeping."

"Then why did you deny you had it?" Charlie demanded.

"I realized it looked bad," Robert said sullenly.

Sugar didn't believe him for a minute, but pressing charges would be one huge waste of time. It wouldn't resurrect her recipe files. "One condition—nothing moves until I make some sort of record of what was . . . moved." It would give her some sort of hold over him and maybe his insurance company. If he had installed the oven wrong then maybe she could get some kind of settlement for her laptop and printer and things like that.

25

She pulled her digital camera out of a box with a sour look at Robert. She pressed the On button while holding her breath, then sighed in relief when the greeting chime and display operated normally. "This will save time and bother," she announced, and started taking pictures before Robert could do more than make a strangled sound. He watched thereafter in stony silence.

"All done?" Charlie leaned over the largest carton, heaped high with Sugar's anodized cookware. Over her shoulder she said cheerily to Robert, "Hey, thanks for putting most of it in these boxes. Makes it easier to put them in Miss Sorenson's car." Under her voice, she added, "You moronic, selfish, male chauvinist bastard excuse for a human being."

Sugar smothered a laugh. Robert started to say something but glared instead.

Reaching into a box, Sugar rescued and unrolled her knives, fearing the worst as the plastic outer wrap broke into brittle pieces. The fabric underneath looked singed. A wave of relief washed over her as the first handle emerged—it looked fine. She slid the knife free of its pouch and hefted it.

"Whoa! Don't slice me, I'm helping!"

Startled, Sugar turned to Charlie. "Oh, sorry, I didn't know you were there." She sighted along the blade of her favorite twelve-inch utility knife. It was perfect. "I don't get to use these much, but they're very precious to me."

Charlie made a show of giving Sugar a very wide berth. Feigning a patronizing smile, she said soothingly, "Of course they are."

Sugar grinned as she slipped the blade back into its pouch. "The holder is toast, but the knives . . . that's a relief."

"You could put seven dead bodies in here," Charlie said of the Olds' trunk when Sugar opened it.

"My grandmother's," Sugar explained. She caressed the glossy sea-green paint. "It seats about twenty."

" 'Remember to bring your jukebox money.' " Charlie snapped her fingers along with her words. " 'Cause the love shack, it's a little ol' place where . . . ' " Charlie studied Sugar's expression. "Don't know that one, huh?"

"I don't get out much."

Charlie looked skeptical, but all she said was, "The car's a beauty." She gave it a loving look as they trudged back to the garage for more boxes.

"Thank you for helping. And for . . . everything."

"I hate bullies. You were inspired."

"I got mad. And I knew he never locked the door. He'd park up to it at night."

"I meant the image of thinly sliced scrotum."

Sugar spluttered with laughter. "When you work in a restaurant around men, meat, fire and knives, you learn effective threats."

"Sounds like restaurants gave you the same education I had to hang out in a firehouse to get."

Sugar looked the question at Charlie as she picked up the last box.

"I'm following in my father's footsteps. Hung out in the firehouse after school for years. That's how I recognized those commercial Sabatier knives. They had just one of those, for boning fish, and heaven help me if I touched it."

"You must have had some great meals." Firehouses, by legend, had some of the greatest amateur chefs in the country.

"It was just Pop and me, so any meal he didn't have to cook for the two of us was good eats. Hey, why don't you back this barge up to the front door and we'll start grabbing stuff."

"Let me move my Honda to the street. A glass guy is supposed to be here in an hour or two."

"Sorry about the car, really," Charlie said. "No way were we looking for keys in a burning building."

"I understand." Sugar plodded off to start the Honda. The interior was still soaking wet in places and the seats covered with glass, but it wasn't as bad as she had thought it would be. The ice scraper from the glove box proved useful for flipping glass off the seat, and the engine eventually turned over with a little coaxing. She found a parking place on the street and realized with chagrin there was absolutely no reason to lock it.

When she got back to her grandmother's car, Charlie was waiting, her legs looking impossibly long in close-fitting Levi's. "Where do you want to start?"

"You don't have to help me—"

The light brown eyes were smiling at her. "I know. Meet you inside."

Officer Tuhrez was having a sotto voce conversation with Robert, which suited Sugar just fine. It took three back-and-forths to turn the Olds around in the street, but she made it and carefully backed up the drive to her former home.

The stench was even worse.

"I happen to know, from personal experience, that most clothes can be deodorized," Charlie offered. "Invest in a boatload of baking soda and follow the directions on the box. Might take a few washes. Hey, Pop."

The other firefighter turned to meet them, and Sugar would have known he had to be Charlie's father from the striking resemblance the two shared. It wasn't just the identical navy windcheaters, white KCFD tees and blue jeans. Her father was darker skinned, suggesting that Charlie's mother had been fair, but the light brown eyes, high cheekbones and chiseled nose were a match.

"Do I want to know what that was all about?" He indicated the departing sheriff with his chin.

"No. Just a typical asshole trying to get away with typical asshole stuff. This is Sugar Sorenson, who used to live here."

"You were lucky." His gaze was matter-of-fact. "The fire began in an electrical short that had nothing to do with the oven operation. Could have happened in the middle of the night. Given the proximity of the sleeping area to the source, and the lack of kitchen facility ventilation, it's likely you'd have never woken. The smoke alarm—" He pointed. "It's not between the bed and the cooking area. So it would have gone off only after smoke had reached the bed."

"Oh." Sugar didn't know what else to say.

"This, by the way, is the site arson investigator," Charlie said. "My father, Chuck Bronson."

Sugar held out her hand. "How do you do."

His handshake was firm and brief. Charlie got her muscles from him as well. To Charlie, he said, "Do you want to step through this with me? It's textbook. Something like it'll be on the exam. Plenty of code violations."

"Yeah, thanks." To Sugar she said, "That's why I tagged along. I'm hoping to move over to the arson unit. Pop and I'll finish up then I'll bag clothes for you."

"You mean you didn't come here this morning to rescue me one more time?"

Charlie gave her a lopsided smile. "That was all icing on the cake."

"Speaking of . . . I'll start looking for stuff I can take with me now." Sugar smiled at Chuck, not knowing quite how to thank an arson investigator.

"Oh, hey, here." Charlie thrust a business card at Sugar. "Could you call me early next week?" She rolled her eyes meaningfully at her father, who had turned back to his clipboard and diagrams. "About, um, your business?"

"You mean . . . ?" Sugar raised her eyebrows.

"Yeah." Charlie nodded enthusiastically after glancing once again at her father. Maybe it was his birthday, Sugar speculated.

"Sure." She glanced at the card. "At the mobile number?"

"That would be perfect."

After an exchange of conspiratorial smiles, Sugar turned to the soot-smeared cupboards. The cheap faux wood veneer had peeled and cracked. The first cupboard of cookware was full of heat-ruptured nonstick pans, including the ones she used to boil the sugar solution that became fondant. The second one she checked was her bakeware. Some of the Pyrex pieces had shattered, attesting to the high heat near the source of the sudden blaze, but the anodized metal pans and baking sheets looked like they might have survived.

It was a while before she could bring herself to look at the recipe files. The metal drawers full of five-by-seven cards were still wet. She was amazed to find the cards inside mostly dry, but the moment she touched the card in front it crumbled like a dead leaf. "Oh, no!"

Charlie was at her side in an instant. "It does that. Paper rarely survives any kind of high heat."

"I was saving up to buy a scanner." Sugar blinked back tears. Her carefully constructed business plan had not included *Complete Catastrophe* as a line item.

"What a shame. I know it's not any help right now, but Pop is right, you could have lost more than that."

Sugar nodded, trying to be comforted. "I know." She murmured thanks when Charlie handed her a tissue. "Sorry to be a baby about pieces of paper."

"Hey, I've seen grown men bawl at the sight of a singed teddy bear." Charlie all at once had the gaze of a direct, no-nonsense professional. "If you're thinking you got away with no damage, you're wrong. A fire is *always* traumatic. Talk to somebody if the nightmares don't stop after a week or so."

Sugar flushed, unwilling to admit that she had had a restless night. Somehow she didn't like Charlie knowing that much about her, or seeing her as predictable. "I'll consider it."

"It might speed up the process of moving on." Charlie shrugged. "Sometimes it helps to know that what you're feeling is normal. Like it was normal to be so angry you wanted to slice that guy's balls into wafers."

"Charlie, what *are* you talking about?"

"Sorry, Pop. Where were we?"

Their voices faded to the back of Sugar's awareness as she buckled down to sorting through bath and kitchen towels. Her printer, answering machine and other electronics she stacked in grocery store boxes she'd picked up on the way over. She had little hope for the printer—water had been standing inside it.

Charlie was still occupied when she started on the clothes. If they'd lose the smell, most were okay. A lucky discovery was the apparent survival of her CDs, which had been in an old iron foot-locker in the corner of the room farthest from the fire.

Charlie helped her carry the footlocker to the car, then beepers sounded and with a distracted good-bye, Charlie and her father bolted for the sedan, leaving her barely enough time to say thank you.

She didn't depart for several more hours. The glass guy came and went, and her car looked odd to be so filthy and yet have spot-less windows. He even vacuumed up all the glass, so the interior looked better than it had in years. She locked it up and left it at the curb until she could get a lift to pick it up.

She looked at the tiny space as she left. She'd arrived almost eighteen months earlier, dreams built up and belongings pared down. The exhaustion of restaurant work had been behind her and only her ambition of a cake empire had occupied her mind. Even then she'd needed a small moving van for her belongings. Now they all fit in a car, with some room to spare.

She badly wanted to stop somewhere for a drink. She was hungry, depressed and still feeling numb. Right, alcohol would help all that.

As she drove toward Grannie Fulton's again, she realized that, for the moment, she was going to have to call it home. Wasn't that a kick in the head? Thirty-four years old and sponging off her grandmother. Reality sucked.

The sight of a King County sedan in front of Gran's house tem-porarily sent her heart rate through the roof. She was worried, a bit, that since she'd known the rental "cottage" was illegal, and rented it anyway, that she'd owe fines or something. She was afraid to ask Patricia, her eldest sister and the attorney of the family, for her advice. She'd been against Sugar's giving up a "real job for a stack of bills" from the get-go. Quinn, sister number two, had worried it was too small—and she'd been right. Sister number three, Rose, had said cheap, illegal rentals were everywhere, so why shouldn't she save a lot of money in the early stages of her enterprise? There you have it, she thought to herself, you should have known when you were thinking like Rose that it wasn't going to work out.

She supposed she ought to call one of them. As the official baby of the family, Sugar was used to receiving their unsolicited advice, and the situation had persisted into adulthood after their parents' death in an automobile accident. Her sisters were also good for sympathy and practical advice, even though the lectures were oftentimes infuriating. She wondered if Gran had already called.

Finally, dithering about things that didn't matter, she got out of the car. A glance into the county sedan as she passed made her feel much better. She'd know that emerald bag anywhere.

Tree looked entirely at home at Gran's kitchen table, a jelly-smeared English muffin in one hand. "Hi, I was hoping I wouldn't miss you. And then, well"—she toasted Sugar with the muffin—"I was tempted to loiter."

Gran started to rise. "You look done in, Sugar."

"I can get my own snack, Gran, you sit," Sugar said quickly. "Yeah, I'm pretty beat. It was worse than I thought, and . . ." She peered into the refrigerator. "And better than I thought, too. Stuff I didn't expect to be okay was. I don't think the CDs even got warm."

"I'm glad to hear that," Tree said. "I stopped by to do a follow-up and give you this pamphlet about posttraumatic stress and symptoms you should expect."

Sugar started to protest but remembered her panicked awakening. She took the proffered pamphlet, saying, "Thank you. I have to admit it was a shock. Oh! And that's not all." She quickly recounted the ugly scene with Robert.

"That Charlie sounds quite the fellow," Gran observed.

"Charlie is short for Charline," Tree said. Her smile was not quite reaching her eyes. "We go way back. Charline is in honor of Barbara Jordan, and Charlie can be quite the impassioned orator."

There was obviously history there that Sugar wasn't sure she wanted to know about. Not that she had any reason to be thinking about it, but she liked them both. She spread tuna salad on thick brown bread and gratefully sat down at the table. "I was very fortunate she was there and cared. I suppose I should ask Patty what I'm liable for now."

Gran looked over her bifocals at Sugar. "I'd think Patricia would help you get money from that man's insurance company. The fire was his fault."

"I wish it was coming out of his own pocket," Sugar said. She bit vengefully into her sandwich and instantly felt better.

"Your blood sugar was low." Tree's dark gaze swept over Sugar's face, leaving Sugar feeling breathless. What a ridiculous reaction, she thought.

"Perhaps you can manage a shower in a bit," Gran suggested.

"I will. I know I reek. But I couldn't go another step. After a shower I'll unload the car and head for a laundry." She was finding it hard to sit still. She wanted to be doing something. She wasn't used to being able to talk easily to her grandmother, so a coin laundry was a good excuse to get out of the house for a few hours.

"You do it all here, Sugar. Don't waste your money on those machines."

"It's best if done quickly," Tree advised. "The unwashed clothes will transfer the smell to everything. Much better just to get it all finished."

To Sugar's surprise, Gran didn't argue. She actually seemed mild in manner around Tree. It must have been Tree's air of authority, tempered with an all-encompassing calm. She'd have to practice that aura herself.

Tree licked her fingers free of apple jelly. "I feel like a kid, I swear. And I really hate to gobble and run, but I've got another follow-up call to make."

"I'll see you out," Sugar said, forestalling another attempt from Gran to get up from the table.

Tree hesitated a moment, then said to Gran, "You really should make the necessary arrangements about what we discussed. Trouble now, but freedom later."

"What was that about?" Sugar closed the front door behind her before asking Tree the question.

"Your grandmother is putting off surgery she needs."

"She's worried about being laid up for a while."

"She'll be laid up permanently if it's not done while she's healthy. Will you be living here a while?"

"Yes, I think so."

"Then you can be her support system. That's all the hospital is waiting on, that there's someone else living with her, capable of some basic lifting and household chores, shopping, cooking, that sort of thing."

"Oh." Sugar blinked. "I didn't realize." She wouldn't feel so bad for encroaching on Gran's long-established routines.

"I'm a big buttinsky," Tree admitted. "It's sometimes part of my job. Like, um, yesterday."

Puzzled, Sugar arched her eyebrows.

"When I said my partner liked peach jam."

"She doesn't?"

"She does, but she's not my partner anymore. I'm back in the dating pool."

"Oh." Sugar wondered why Tree had even mentioned it, then, especially after it was plain that Sugar hadn't ever come out to Gran. An excuse to accept the gift? "I'm sorry, about your partner."

"I hate fibbing, and I felt guilty about it. So I'm glad my conscience is clear now."

There was an awkward silence that Sugar couldn't define. "Thank you for everything you've done," she said abruptly.

"Comes with the territory. If you don't mind, I'd like to check back with you in a week."

Sugar suddenly knew what she was feeling. It was that tickling, uneasy, itchy feeling that came with asking or being asked out. The dating vibe—holy moley, she hadn't felt it this strongly in *years*.

She felt like a nervous teenager. "Does that come with the territory?"

"No." Tree flashed Sugar a broad, easy grin. "This job has few perks, but one is usually having a valid reason to ask an interesting woman her phone number."

"Oh. Well. Um . . ."

"I'm sorry," Tree said quickly. "Really. I'm being inappropriate. I'll call you in about a week. And if you'd like to have coffee or something that would be very nice. If not, just tell me you're allergic to coffee and I'll close the, uh, file."

Sugar laughed. "Okay. That's a deal." She watched Tree drive away, feeling more than a little bemused. Even with days of preparation she barely merited the fallback compliment of "cute," so Tree's interest was confusing. Add that she stank of burnt house, her hair was wild and her breath smelled of tuna salad. What on earth could Tree see in her at the moment?

Tree wasn't going to call for a week, she recalled. She had plenty of time to think about it later. She wanted time to go on hold for a few days so she could catch her breath. Then she caught sight of Gran's car, loaded with the remnants of her life. She had a project to finish, a business she'd worked too hard to keep afloat to let it founder now. She took a deep breath and told herself those weren't tears stinging her eyes.

Chapter 3

Fortified with two oatmeal raisin cookies, Sugar decided her most urgent task was a prolonged visit to the nearest coin laundry. The longer she waited, the more the car would stink when she was done, so there was nothing for it but to tackle the job. She unloaded the flotsam and jetsam of her cookware and other belongings—most of which would have to be scrubbed or deodorized—into Gran's garage, told Gran she wouldn't be back in time for dinner, grabbed a can of soda and headed for the nearest strip mall, hoping she wouldn't have to wait for machines.

To her relief, the laundry was nearly deserted. Thursday nights at the laundry near her old house had been busy, so it was just as well that most people hadn't quite left work yet. She quickly had nine loads sorted, coins in, baking soda measured and detergent poured.

The only other people there had laptops to amuse themselves while they waited for their clothes, which made her miss hers all the more. On the way over she'd stopped at an Internet café to check her mail and send out the news of the fire. She took the chicken's way out with her sisters and sent them all the same note en masse. They'd descend in their own time to demand details.

She'd been immensely cheered by an order from JaeLynn, a party planner she'd worked with twice before, requesting a cake replica of a '55 Chevy that would serve sixty and wasn't due for four weeks. JaeLynn had even sent the deposit to Sugar's online money-transfer account. She'd left the café feeling that maybe her business was going to be okay.

She was just starting to feel sorry for herself when a honk outside the storefront heralded Noor's arrival. Sugar had called her after leaving the café, deciding that Noor of all people deserved a phone call. She'd said little more than, "The house burned down" before Noor had insisted on meeting her to hear all about it.

Even better, Noor had white fast-food bags in hand, and the grease spots forming on the sides of each foretold of French fries. In the other hand she had what Sugar hoped were milkshakes.

"You are a godsend!" Sugar peered into the bag Noor gave her after they exchanged a friendly smooch. "This smells divinely bad for me. Oh, and the vanilla's for me? You remembered my favorite. Thank you."

"Of course I remembered." Noor perched in the chair next to Sugar's and unfolded a napkin carefully over the lap of her chic pink shorts. "I'm so glad it's my day off, girlfriend. What happened?"

Around a mouthful of meat, lettuce and special sauce, Sugar said, "Bad wiring. Not my fault." While they ate she described the flames, firefighters, her poor Honda's windows, Tree, Emily, Charlie and nearly everything she could think of to share.

"What all did you lose?"

"The worst is my recipe cards. They were all toast. Laptop unknown—it's drying out. On my way here I looked up on the Internet how to possibly save it, but I'm not holding out much hope."

Noor delicately dipped a French fry into her strawberry shake. "Your recipes? That is so terrible. Are you going to sue?"

"It wasn't my house."

"Yeah, but houses aren't supposed to burn down when you're renting them. You've lost business—"

"Not really, but some maybe. My car got new glass for free."

Noor, who had always known how to work an angle, sighed. "Pain and suffering? Don't people get tons of money for that? And the recipes can be replaced with the time and money to hire someone to do it for you. Oh, hey, you could say your laptop was in the car and got ruined. Your auto insurance would cover that."

"Maybe, but it wasn't in the car."

"They don't have to know that."

Sugar shrugged. "I'm not that desperate that I'd lie about it. I'm a terrible liar. Every time I lie I get caught."

"That's just your Goody-Two-Shoes upbringing."

"No," Sugar insisted. "Every time I lie I get caught. Not ever getting away with anything is a deterrent to even trying."

"Well, you should talk to Patty about suing."

"Oh, I'm sure it'll come up. I think she'll have to threaten Robert to get my deposits back."

Noor giggled. "Wouldn't I love to read *that* letter."

Sugar had to agree. "When Patty's on a roll it can be pretty impressive. God, I have so much to do. Phone calls and restocking and looking for something permanent and dealing with my sisters. And that's just Monday. I'm not doing anything about anything until then. I've got a cake to finish and that's about all my brain can handle."

"How are you going to stand being at your grandmother's for any length of time?" Noor tore open another salt packet and tapped it over her fries. At Sugar's nod, she sprinkled the last of it over Sugar's fries as well.

"It's the strangest thing, but I think she's changed. I came out to her and she didn't do more than sigh. I'm still blown away." She explained about Tree's nudge toward coming out and Gran's possible surgery ahead. "Gran had no trouble with Tree at all today, either. I don't know what to think."

"I'd have thought the planet would crack in two before she'd change her mind about gays." Noor chewed thoughtfully for a moment. "I'd say that was a sort of silver lining. Your family thing was one of our problems."

Sugar shrugged. "Yeah. It's been a problem all along. I mean, I never felt so much for anybody that . . . Sorry."

Noor was smiling wistfully. "Yeah, I know. It's okay. I wasn't willing to give up certain things for you either."

It was true. Sugar hadn't been enough in love to give up her family for Noor. Noor had always been honest about her once-every-blue-moon itch for Deenie. Sugar had been mostly okay with that until they moved in together. Then she had wanted a commitment. Noor had thought she could end her just-sex relationship with Deenie. Instead, it had only made the itch more pronounced. Now Noor and Deenie lived together and so far both seemed happy.

"Wow, so you're out to your grandmother. That's really good."

"I sort of got asked out, too. Life is strange, huh? House burns down and I get noticed for the first time since, well, you."

"You'd get noticed more if you ever did a thing for yourself." Noor dabbed her fingertips on the napkin. Sugar had always liked that pale pink tint on her nails. Certainly Noor was looking the picture of health. Her dark eyes and long, glossy black hair were both shining. Sugar had no trouble remembering their many good times. Even bad times hadn't been painful so much as . . . sad. Intimacy had been grand. They'd both worked the typical chef's long hours, but time together had mostly been fun. Still, something had been missing and they both had somehow known it.

"We can't all try to be as glam as you, sweetie."

"But you could *try*. When was the last time you had your hair cut? And hey, who asked you out?"

"Tree. Well, she said she'd be calling to ask me if I'd like to have coffee. Sort of a pre-date warning."

Noor continued to look at her expectantly.

"Okay, it's been probably a year since I had my hair trimmed. But no way am I spending a dime on that until I know if my laptop works."

"And you wonder why you don't get asked out. Do your cakes look any old way you feel like?"

"Yeah, yeah, presentation is everything, but I'm not a pastry and I'm not for sale."

"Of course you are. We've all got our hearts on the auction block."

"I don't. I don't have time, especially now."

"Don't use a disaster as an excuse." Noor frowned at her. Sugar thought it best not to point out that the expression on Noor's face bore a striking resemblance to Noor's mother. "Working too many hours was the excuse for years. I finally got you to get out regularly and you admitted there was more to life than work. But ever since you went into business for yourself—which I think was a great idea, you know that—you've not had any money to spare. No time. No energy. Now it'll be that your house burned down. You're going to shrivel up."

"That's not really fair," Sugar protested.

"What have I said that's wrong? When was the last time you had a nice time in bed?"

Sugar wasn't going to admit it had been with Noor so she finished the last of her burger without answering.

"Gone to a movie? Gone dancing? You haven't been out to a club since my birthday party, have you?"

Sugar seized the red herring. "Want to know something really weird? A woman I danced with—she's the producer from *Best of Seattle* who showed up."

"Hunted you down?"

"Oh, I hardly think so. As you pointed out, I'm not exactly a well-plated entrée here."

Noor's eyes flashed. "Cut that out! Geez, I just hate that about you! Okay, your hair's a mess and you could use a facial and a manicure. But you've got a body that women are paying thousands of dollars to have sculpted by exercise or surgery. Plus when you *want* to be, you can be funny and interesting."

"Maybe I don't want to be. Maybe . . . Oh, I don't know. Maybe I'd like to make a name for myself before I see if there's anybody who wants to share it. Bring something to the table in a relationship."

Noor rolled her eyes. "Conquer the world and then go looking for Ms. Right? That just seems so . . . lonely."

Stung, Sugar crumpled up her empty bag. "Maybe loneliness is better than heartbreak. Better than respecting someone and finding out they're lying to you."

"I never lied to you!" Noor stomped to the trash can.

"I wasn't talking about you. Damn it, Noor. I'm sorry."

"Then what did you mean by that?"

"I'm talking about Rose—marriage number three. I'm talking about how the only real love you ever see is in a movie where nobody's fat, everybody's got a cushy job with assistants, and all the possible dating material has not only a fabulous sense of humor but a Lear jet. Sometimes I think it's not real. None of it's real. My parents would have gotten divorced if they hadn't gotten hit by that truck first. It's not real."

Noor stood staring at her, hands on hips. Sugar had always envied her the high metabolism that kept her almost too thin, but she realized that Noor's shorts were a little tighter than she normally wore, and her face was slightly rounder, fuller. She was about to tell Noor that the few extra pounds suited her when Noor said, "You want to know what's real?"

"Sure. Enlighten me."

"This is real," Noor said, as she moved within reach of Sugar. She lifted Sugar's hand and put it on her belly. "This is about as real as it gets."

Puzzled, Sugar tried to pull her hand away. "So you're happy with Deenie and you've put on a few pounds. They look good. It suits you."

Noor grinned. "Hopefully I'll lose it all again in seven months."

Sugar's mouth hung open as she stared at Noor. Finally, she managed, "You're kidding."

"Nope. Baby. I wanted a family. Deenie wants a family. She's through being a kid and so am I. We're not sharing space—we're making a life."

"Wow. That's . . . wow." Sugar didn't know what else to say.

"I'm not saying a baby is the only way to do that, Sugar. The thing is that we both wanted something, the same thing. And we're trying to get there together. Doing it alone is too hard. Doing it with someone you love is still hard, but at least there's someone to cry and laugh with along the way."

"I'm glad," Sugar said belatedly. She personally thought Deenie a case of arrested development, but Noor had never been blind to Deenie's faults. She thought Deenie had changed and, well, maybe Deenie had. Truthfully, she added, "I think you'll make a wonderful mother."

Noor dropped into the chair next to Sugar with an anxious look. "Do you really think so? I get scared."

"I think being scared means there's a good chance you'll do it right."

Noor's face crumpled and Sugar pulled her into a heartening embrace. "I hope so. I'm scared to tell my parents. Muslims aren't all that keen on anonymous sperm donors. This could be the final straw."

Sugar patted Noor's back. "I hope that's not the case, sweetie. They should be proud of you."

Noor sniffed. "I'll let you know. Deenie's folks were actually okay. They like me."

Sugar brushed tears from Noor's cheeks with her thumbs. "They ought to. You're kind and generous and sweet, and a hard worker. Not to mention a good-looking femme."

The compliment had its usual result. Noor grinned and batted her eyelashes. "Thank you. When I blow up to the size of a house you are bound by Robert's Rules of Lesbian Life to continue saying that."

Sugar agreed. It was almost like old times, folding clothes together while Noor vented about work catastrophes and Sugar mused over what she ought to try to tackle next. Unfortunately, a long talk with Patricia about money and legal obligations was looking inevitable. Monday, Sugar thought. She wouldn't think about that until Monday. Clean clothes, a perfect cake for a very important client—that was all she could handle. Family matters and legal issues could just wait.

Her resolve to avoid family discussion was immediately put to the test when she finished stacking her piles of fresh-smelling and neatly folded clothes on the bed. She was, after all, living in a family member's home and there were matters they ought to resolve. On the drive back to Gran's, Sugar hadn't been able to avoid giving her living arrangement with Gran some thought.

Gran eased herself down onto the antique bench inside the doorway of the spare bedroom just as Sugar patted the last stack. "I've cleared out that bureau for you, and since the jumble sale was last month, there's nothing in that closet right now."

"Thank you, Gran. I don't know what I'd do without you, really."

"One of your sisters would have offered."

Not likely, Sugar thought. Not for more than a day or two. And it would always have strings. Live here, live the life we pick out for you. Patty would say, "Get a real job." Quinn would say, "Find a good partner like I did." Rose would say, "Let's go get drunk." Right now Sugar wanted none of any of it.

After a sigh, she said to Gran, "Perhaps. But I think I'll be best here if that's okay with you." She sank down onto the bed, suddenly exhausted. But she had given what she wanted to say a lot of thought while watching the dryers spin round and round and chatting with Noor. "So we should discuss things in a businesslike way. I'm averaging two or three cakes a week so far. Today's e-mail brought a repeat customer who's spending quite a lot. I can pay for my keep, certainly the extra utilities and things like that. Groceries

43

and gas and that sort of thing. And I'll be able to save for a deposit on a new place."

Gran nodded. "I won't pretend it would have been hard to make ends meet, but we'd have done it. But you're very sensible, Sugar. You always have been."

It was an assessment with which her siblings would have never agreed. "Good, I'm glad that's settled. That's leaves the matter of me disrupting your life, and I know there is no way I can make up for that."

"It's no bother, child."

"Yes, it is," Sugar insisted. "I hogged the oven this morning, and your favorite bowls were dirty, and little things like that can really annoy. It's one of the reasons I didn't want a roommate sharing an already small kitchen in some apartment. But we're roommates sharing a big kitchen and we ought to be able to work it out."

"Well, we'll just speak our mind when we need to and everything will be fine."

"Okay, I promise not to bottle things up, too."

It was a *shocking* agreement to have reached so easily. Gran was the in-house champion of speaking her mind about what other people ought to do to get right with family and the Lord, but she never admitted that anything actually bothered her. Her leg could be cut off and she'd say it was nothing. If she asked how you were and you said anything less than "great" her reply would be, "I'm sorry to hear that."

The talk was going so well that Sugar went for broke. "I've given it some thought, and one way we can make a fair trade is if I help you out while you get that surgery."

Gran's eyes narrowed. "Gantry's been talking, hasn't she?"

Sugar shrugged.

"Well, I can't say it was her business. I was just speaking politely. She's a good listener." Gran frowned as she fussed at a thread on her sweater.

"So what do you say? If I'd known you needed someone to live

44

in I would have suggested it. The place where I was living—it worked. But just barely. The refrigerator was a joke."

It was a safe distraction. They moved to the kitchen to put together a light evening snack and talked about the importance of movable shelves and controls a person could see and reach. Only when Sugar had dabbed up the last crumbs of the best peach crisp she'd had in years did Gran return to the subject of her surgery.

"I suppose, if you'll be here, you're right. I'd be a fool to pass up your help."

Sugar stole a glance at her grandmother, pleased. But her smile faded quickly to concern. "Gran, it'll be okay."

Gran frowned at her tea. "I don't like hospitals. People go there to die."

"And to get well. They got one hundred percent of Quinn's husband's cancer, remember? I'll be with you the whole time. And anyone else from church you might like."

"No!" Gran looked momentarily shocked at her own vehemence. "I'd rather not have any of them near, except maybe Bridget. I'll think on that. Not when I'm feeling sick."

"I understand," Sugar soothed. "Tomorrow is Friday and we'll call the doctor and get the ball rolling, okay? And I'll finish the order for Saturday. Oh, that reminds me, I've got to work the icing." She quickly moved their dishes to the sink, then got out the plastic-wrapped ball of fondant. She divided it into thirds, and set about the process of kneading the softball-sized lumps one more time to make sure the sugar didn't recrystalize. It was a matter of minutes until she put the rewrapped balls back in the refrigerator.

"You're going to have to show me how you make that again. I can't believe icing for a cake can be treated that way."

Sugar turned off the kitchen light as she followed Gran down the narrow hallway to the bedrooms. "Wait until you see the finished product."

"Oh, I know what you can do, Sugar. Those layers I took out of the oven looked perfect. And I'll never forget that wonderful cake you made for your grandfather's memorial service, complete with his golf clubs leaning against the car."

"That was a flat cake, Gran. Wait until you see a three-dimensional one."

"I'm looking forward to it. You get a good rest, child. It's been a long, stressful day for you."

Sugar watched Gran lumber slowly to the hallway, one hand supporting her weight wherever support could be found. "You too, Gran. Don't let the bedbugs bite, now."

It was early yet, but Sugar was barely able to stay awake long enough to make some order out of her clothing. She finally put the last two piles on the floor and crawled under the covers. She was nearly asleep when she realized that Tree *had* been being a buttinsky mentioning a partner—she'd probably wanted Sugar to out herself. Annoyed, she turned over. She'd be glad to tell Tree she'd had no right when Tree called.

Noor was having a baby—still a shocking thought. Noor had found something real. It all still seemed like an illusion to Sugar.

The prospect of a cup of coffee with Tree wasn't unpleasant though. Just as she nodded off, Sugar remembered she needed to call Charlie about the order she'd alluded to. The prospect of seeing Charlie again wasn't unpleasant either. And Emily she'd see again on Saturday, but that was work, wasn't it?

There's no room in your head for women and dating and babies and things like that, she told herself drowsily. No room for it at all.

Fondant wasn't a very forgiving material, but so far the new premises and slight variation in humidity wasn't making a ruin of her project. Once again, Sugar found her jittery morning nerves settled by the focus of work. A trip to the restaurant supply store had provided new bottles of run-resistant food dyes and other things she needed for the difficult—but highly rewarding—task of tinting her European recipe.

If she'd had her tints last night she would have worked some of the colors in then. The extra kneading would make the fondant a little tougher than her best results. But it would taste just as good and hold up through an evening just fine. She'd forgo a protective layer of marzipan because the cake would have achieved the perfect texture and moistness by the time she assembled the finished work.

The smell of Gran's Friday-morning baking washed over her as she returned from the garage with another item removed from Gran's car. A bubbling apricot cobbler sat on the counter, cooling, while Gran was occupied with a tea towel, rubbing the skins off of still warm boiled potatoes. "That looks heavy, dear."

Sugar gratefully set the heavy marble slab next to the sink. "That's because it is." She saturated the surface with deodorizing non-abrasive cleanser, then set about rinsing it thoroughly in the sink. Some people might use bleach but she always thought she tasted the chemical thereafter.

Finally, she rubbed it down with some ice and dried it carefully. She snipped off a walnut-sized ball of fondant, which had been out of the refrigerator since she'd sluggishly crawled out of bed, and flattened it on the slab.

"Do you think if I cover it with wrap and leave it for thirty minutes that would do it? That if there was going to be a smoke taste, that would pick it up?"

Gran looked up from the bowl of potatoes. "Seems like long enough. Surely enough to tell if anything's going to transfer."

Sugar nodded. "Let me help you slice those while I wait." She had just found a paring knife when her cell phone rang.

"I just thought I'd check on how you were doing," Emily said.

Sugar fought back a blush. She'd had a dream about a red-haired angel who had been deliciously unangelic. That was before she'd been awakened by the certainty that she'd heard a fire engine's wail. "Great. In fact, I'm going to tint the icing today and carve the cat. Where and when would you like it delivered?"

"My place. Would it be ready by tomorrow afternoon, say, four? If you need another hour or two that will work, it's just that I'll be setting up—"

"Four is fine."

"Wow, you're fantastic. I sent a deposit this morning, by the way. I checked your site and wanted to make everything's on the up and up. Don't want to worry your accountant."

Sugar chortled. "My accountant, whose name is Sugar Sorenson, worries about other things at the moment. But thank you for taking care of that."

"I can imagine." Emily said her address slowly and clearly, then gave precise directions for finding the house. Sugar knew Mercer Island only slightly. Not like anybody she had ever known could afford to live there. "There's a stand of five old paper birch trees in the front. They're hard to miss."

"Got it," Sugar assured her. "And I've got your number if anything should go amiss. The cake will need to be kept in a very cool location before it goes on the buffet table. Otherwise the icing can bead up and it doesn't look as nice."

"Understood. Look, about Seattle Eats, if we're going to feature you we'd need to settle that quickly."

"Oh, I'm game to do that if you can work it out logistically. I'm afraid I don't know what that all entails."

"For you it means a camera underfoot, I'm afraid. The category for event desserts, which is going to be the most exciting filming, has only five competitors."

That was welcome news. She'd been worried that as an unknown she wouldn't be taken seriously. "That gives me a fighting chance, doesn't it?"

"It certainly does. I may be able to find out who the judges are and give you some tips on their favorite things. I know for sure one is Chastity McLain."

"Wow. Seattle's own dyke diva." Abruptly, Sugar was aware of Grannie Fulton's listening ears. She doubted anyone had said *dyke* in Gran's house before.

"She likes leather and pierced navels." Emily laughed. "But I'm not sure the other judges would go for a dog-collar cake."

"I could do one. But I don't think I will." She started to tell

Emily her idea, then stopped. She wasn't sure Emily was all that interested, and since it was a good idea for a contest theme of "the diversity of Seattle's culinary communities," she didn't know if Emily wouldn't tell someone else. It would be horrid if two people presented the same thing.

"I look forward to talking over your plans," Emily said easily. "And we do need to get together again to discuss the *Best of Seattle* segment, which I still very much want to do, now more than ever after meeting you. Maybe we could get together next week for coffee or dinner?"

"That sounds great," Sugar answered. Her dating vibe was jangling again, and it was disconcerting to say the least. A dream was just a dream, but actually going out with Emily? Goodness, two women had asked her out in twenty-four hours. Well, not quite asked out. Besides, she reminded herself sternly, Emily wanted to talk business, not romance.

"Well, how about dinner, then? Next Thursday is the first time I'm free. What a week. Do you know where Malvio's is, in Redmond?"

"No, but I can find it."

"Let's say eight, and I'll call the day before just to make sure you haven't forgotten. Oh—what?"

It took Sugar a moment to realize Emily was speaking to someone else. The phone was temporarily muffled, then Emily's voice came back loud and clear. "I'm sorry, Sugar, I have another call I have to take. See you tomorrow, okay?"

"No problem. Until tomorrow."

She hung up the phone slowly, then picked up the paring knife. Joining Gran at the table she said nonchalantly, "That was my client for tomorrow."

"Oh?"

Sugar didn't know quite how to interpret that. "She's a producer at King Five."

"Now that sounds like an interesting job."

"They're going to do a feature about my cakes in an upcoming

Best of Seattle episode. I was supposed to meet with her to discuss it, but the house burned down instead."

"What a wonderful opportunity, though. All that free advertising."

"It is." Sugar finished her first potato and started her second. "She's one of those gay women, too."

"So I gathered. Do you think you might go out with her?"

"Maybe. I don't know. I don't date very much, Gran. I really don't have time."

Gran's knife made short work of the potato in her hands. "I had fifty-three wonderful years with your grandfather, may he rest in peace. I might be alone now but I've got the memories of companionship and affection and that's all that matters at my age. You are not getting any younger. You need to make time."

Sugar diced another potato, glad to have her hands occupied. Had Gran actually just encouraged her to date women? Was the sun going to rise in the west tomorrow, or what? "I know, but life just dealt me a setback."

"All the more reason to find someone to help. That's what it's all about. Why, thank you, Sugar, that was quick work. The salad is for a potluck this evening at Bible Study. You're welcome to join us."

"I'll probably be decorating most of the day." Sugar steeled herself for Gran's attempt to change her mind. "I've never done a cat before."

"I know it's a lot of hard work. I thought you might want to meet Judy's daughter, the one who lent you the clothing yesterday. She's a lesbian, too."

The potato she was cutting bobbled out of Sugar's hands. "Oh, is she?"

"Yes, and she's a dentist."

"I've never worn a dentist's clothes before." Lesbian—Grannie Fulton had actually said *lesbian*. Good lord, Sugar thought. The house burns down and I'm in some sort of alternative reality. "I've never dated a dentist, either." She sighed. "I've really dated very little. Slaving in a restaurant didn't leave much time, and it's very true that you'll work harder for yourself than anyone else."

Gran's phone rang and Sugar hopped up to answer it.

Patricia never wasted time on preliminaries. "How did you burn the place down?"

"It wasn't my fault," Sugar told her eldest sister indignantly. "The oven wiring was installed wrong and the fire could have started at any time, even with the oven off. I was lucky I was awake!"

"But you're okay?"

"Yes, I'm just fine." She turned to face Grannie Fulton and added mischievously, "Gran's just now trying to set me up with a woman at Bible Study tonight."

"You are such a liar—"

"She's says I'm lying, Gran."

"Her name's Denise and she's a dentist," Gran said loudly enough for Patty to hear.

"See?" Sugar was pleased for once to have left Patty speechless. "But I've got a long, complicated project to finish so I'll have to take a rain check. What's new with you?"

"I was just calling to find out how you are, but you seem to be quite cozy with Gran all of a sudden."

"I'll be here a while. The place where I lived was totaled. I've got enough cash to keep going, but not for a new place until I get my deposits out of the landlord. I need to talk to you about needling him."

"Can you fax over the rental agreement?"

"Oh, I don't know if I have it." Sugar closed her eyes to visualize its whereabouts. She kept stuff like that in the footlocker with her CDs, and everything in the footlocker had seemed to survive. "Yes, I do have it. I'll fax it."

"Then we'll fire off a letter demanding the deposits back."

"Ouch. Do you think you could use another metaphor?"

Patty's tone was borderline exasperated, but then it nearly

51

always was. "We'll also find out who the claims adjuster is for the premises."

"He did try to steal my stuff, too." Sugar quickly explained about the garage, the sheriff and the photographs she'd taken.

"Now we're getting somewhere." Patty actually sounded as if she might be smiling. "This could be fun. I can virtually guarantee you that you'll get your deposits back. Maybe we'll enclose a photo of your warped Tupperware."

"Sometimes I like the twisted way you think, Patty."

"Thank you." Patty's voice fell back into a more businesslike cadence. "Until then I could loan you first and last, if that's what you need for your own place."

Sugar wanted to shake Patty. They'd tried that the last time, and Patty had wanted approval on every place that Sugar looked at. Most apartments didn't have a properly sized oven, and Patty had never appreciated that a small oven was an absolute deal-breaker. "I don't think that's going to work. I'll be here and save my pennies." She started to mention Gran's surgery but thought it was up to Gran to talk about it.

Patty seemed uncommonly flustered. "I'd have thought you'd be miserable. I mean, Bible Study? You?"

"That's turning out okay. Not sure why."

"You seem settled, then."

Sugar had the distinct impression that Patty was disturbed by that. "I am, for now. A couple of months, I think."

"For as long as you like," Gran said firmly.

They agreed on an appointment next Wednesday, and Patty was still proposing alternative arrangements when she hung up.

"I don't care what time it is, it's too early for my sisters," Sugar said. "Quinn'll be next. Rose will weigh in at some point. They'll all know what's best."

"They love you and want to help."

Sugar shrugged. "Funny way of showing it."

"Love is no guarantee you'll know how to go about helping the best way. I told Quinn so just a few weeks ago."

Sugar was still blinking in surprise at that revelation when she went to answer a knock at the door. And there stood Quinn, who had sworn publicly that she'd never darken Grannie Fulton's door again.

"Hey, you don't look singed," Quinn said. She gave Gran a hug on her way to the coffee maker.

"I was lucky." Okay, so, she'd had her head down for quite a while trying to drum up business and pay her bills, discover new, faster ways to do everything in her craft, and so as a result her entire family had changed personalities.

"Do you need a warmup?" Quinn hefted the pot in Gran's direction.

"No, dear, I've had my one and that's all I get these days."

Quinn settled at the table as Sugar resumed dicing the peeled potatoes.

Any other day of any time in the past, Sugar would have pretended there was nothing wrong with the picture of the three of them sitting harmoniously at the same table. Any other day in the past, she'd do what they did in their family, which is ignore the dissension until somebody couldn't take it anymore and started yelling.

It's a new era, Sugar thought. Gran knows I'm gay and she and Quinn are speaking again. "So, I have to say I'm surprised to see you here, Quinn. I think I've missed a few things."

"I finally had the courage to tell Quinn I was sorry I'd been such a fool." Gran assessed the potatoes in the bowl. "Jacob has been a wonderful husband and father. He's a good man and I behaved badly."

Any minute now the earth would start to spin backward. Grannie Fulton had admitted she was *wrong*? That her hunger strike, and case of the faints before, during and after Quinn's wedding had been bad behavior? Jacob's grandmother had been much the same, but that didn't make it easier on anybody. The rabbi at their wedding had said that just getting to the wedding day sometimes was proof a couple could go the distance, sentiments echoed shortly thereafter by the minister representing Quinn's faith. It had been one of the most fun weddings Sugar had ever been to, aside from the fainting grandmothers, that is.

She mused that the cake hadn't been very good. Maybe that was the day she'd decided she would try to outdo that baker someday. Considering how much wedding cakes cost it seemed to her they ought to be the best cakes anyone had ever tasted.

Quinn shrugged in Sugar's direction. "Gran called me out of the blue and apologized, and it was one of the happiest days of my life. The kids hardly knew her and Richie's going to high school next year."

"Sugar is going to stay for a couple of months while I have surgery on my hip," Gran was saying. "Though a fire isn't the way I'd say God chooses to work, it's still allowed both of us to get something we needed. A mutually satisfactory arrangement."

"Oh, I'm glad," Quinn said sincerely. "I was actually going to talk to you on my way home from my class this afternoon, but then I got Sugar's e-mail this morning and hurried on over. But it's all settled now and a much better solution than I could have ever offered."

"Patricia seemed bothered that I was staying," Sugar shared. "Not quite sure why."

The look in Quinn's eye said she had a guess but wasn't going to say in front of Gran. "Don't worry about Patty. Heard from Rose?"

"No. What's new?" At forty, Rose was six years older and the closest in age to her, but Sugar had always felt they were strangers, possibly because Rose was relentlessly, aggressively, openly in-your-face heterosexual.

"Divorce court. Again." Quinn shrugged. "It's not as if any of us, including her, expected it to last."

"I hoped," Grannie Fulton said. "I did hope. But . . ."

"Did he ever find any kind of job?" This would be Rose's third trip to Oops, I Did It Again.

"Nothing legal." Quinn rolled her eyes. "And when they raided that so-called club of his it was sheer luck Rose wasn't there."

54

"I am so behind the times." How could so much happen in five months?

"You missed Easter," Gran said mildly.

"True," Sugar admitted. "I was quite busy with bunnies and lambs. I thought of you and Jacob, Quinn, because I baked and decorated one cake under rabbinical supervision for Passover. Well, without the leavening it was more of a torte. I learned a *lot*."

"Sounds like some seder," Quinn observed.

"It was at a restaurant with people who'd met in Europe at the end of World War Two. I wish I could have stayed. I left just as the very first guest arrived and the tears were flowing."

"Food-service people are the ones who miss holidays with their families." Gran sighed.

Sugar dumped the last of the potatoes into the mixing bowl. "I hope someday to be successful enough to be able to finish everything two days early so I don't get into the habit. I'm sorry I missed the gathering," Sugar added. "That must have been some Easter."

"It was a beautiful meal," Gran said, though the expression on Quinn's face said it had been quite a day. "Patricia outdid herself."

Quinn stayed a little longer, helping with dicing celery and peeling hard-boiled eggs. When Sugar scraped the test fondant off the marble slab, Quinn agreed with Gran—there was no taste of smoke at all.

"And that's delicious—pure sugar, huh?"

"Sure," Sugar admitted. "But fat free and all natural."

"Everything's a trade-off," Quinn observed. "I should be going. I'm teaching in Issaquah this afternoon."

"Oh!" Sugar looked at her sister hopefully. "I don't suppose I could hitch a ride, could I? My car is still at my old place, parked on the street."

"Sure," Quinn said easily. "We'll catch up."

Sugar quickly rewrapped the fondant, then grabbed a sweater and keys. The day had turned brisk with an inland-blowing breeze.

As she walked out with Quinn to her car, Quinn said, "You're handling this very well."

"I would be a lot worse off if it wasn't for Gran. She's been great."

"I guess when she fainted at Easter she got religion." Quinn cracked a smile.

"She *fainted*?"

"Nobody told you?"

"No!" Sugar was incensed. It was one thing to treat her like a baby, but quite another to keep her in the dark about Gran's health. Her seat belt clicked with an angry *snick*.

"Well. That'll be something to convince Patty of. She's sure you heard about it and promptly made your way here."

"Why? Okay, I know Patty thinks I'm a do-nothing sponger now, but my business is steadily improving." Honestly, you'd think she hadn't spent eight years of her life working ten hours a day, six days a week in that five-star hellhole in downtown Seattle. "I was hoping to hire help starting at Thanksgiving."

"Patty always has her two cents. It's about the two cents." Quinn backed out of Gran's driveway and turned in the direction of East Lake Sammamish Parkway. "Gran fainted and I guess Patty and Rose had her in her grave by the end of the year. So Patty updated Gran's estate papers. Remember? She did them after Grandpa died."

Sugar nodded. "What was so strange about that?"

"Well, that was eight years ago, and the last appraisal of the house at that time was already ten years old. So her estate was valued on the price of this house, eighteen years ago."

Sugar blinked. "Oh. It'll have gone up?"

"To put it mildly. Gran may be on a fixed income but she's living in a millionaire's mansion in the dot-com real estate economy. Patty and Rose are *concerned* that Gran's affairs be handled *equitably*."

"I couldn't give a crap. I mean—"

"I know." Quinn sighed as she negotiated traffic. "I lived seeing Gran only at holidays for fifteen years. I'm thanking God every night now that Gran and I are okay again. She says she saw Jesus when she fainted, and he scolded her. I don't care what happened. She's happier than I ever remember. I hope she outlives all of us."

"So Patty thinks I'm going to try to edge everybody out on a piece of this house? That's . . . that stinks." Sugar cleared the quaver from her voice. "I work damn hard and I'm pretty proud of what I'm trying to do. I may not have anything to show for it, but someday I will. And even if Gran was the way she used to be I'd still want to help her out. I didn't know she was putting off surgery. And doesn't anybody care why she fainted?"

Quinn put her hand briefly on Sugar's. "She told me her doctor said it was probably low blood sugar, though I'm not convinced. But she accepted that explanation. And I believe you're not here to slip a new will in Gran's hands to sign. They won't. Want a piece of advice from your bossy older sister?"

Sugar laughed. Of her three sisters, Quinn was the one she'd always gotten along with best, even if she was nine years older. "Okay, lay it on me."

"Don't let Patty and Rose get to you. Ignore them. It makes them absolutely bonkers, which is part of the fun. My goodness, look at the lake. Isn't it a lovely day?"

Sugar had to agree. Lake Sammamish sparkled with glittering wind-sculpted waves. "The paper said there's a chance of rain tomorrow afternoon."

"So? What else is new?"

They chatted companionably for the remainder of the drive. Quinn's worries included her eldest's study habits and if her contract as a part-time arts teacher would be renewed. Sugar was relieved to see her Honda undamaged as Quinn pulled alongside. She didn't look toward the ruin of her house, but Quinn did.

"Holy ma-joley! I'm so glad you weren't hurt."

"Oh, me too," Sugar said fervently. "Hang on and let me make sure the old girl starts up, okay?"

Quinn idled as Sugar slid gingerly into the driver's seat. Having been closed up, the car now smelled like wet carpet. It had seen a lot of abuse in its two hundred thousand miles. Being overrun by firefighters was the capper. She turned the key with trepidation, but with the second attempt the engine grumbled to life. She and Quinn shared cheery waves, then Sugar turned back in the direction of Gran's. The little car valiantly chugged all the way there and smelled much better by the time they reached home. She left the windows down and headed back inside. She was very glad to have been able to fetch the car, but she had a tickle of concern that she'd not yet accomplished enough on Emily's cake.

Gran's potato salad had progressed. The large bowl held cooked, cooled potato dices, crunchy celery and onion and chopped egg. Gran was stirring up a dressing of Miracle Whip and mustard. After Sugar had settled into her own work, Gran said seriously, "So, now tell me. What exactly is rabbinical supervision?"

Sugar grinned. "First off, you have to get a rabbi who's approved to do it, and the restaurant had one, of course. I had to do everything there. Rabbi Weinstein knew incredible stuff about food. I mean—I wish I'd had him at culinary academy. So then everything is cleaned like you have never seen." She set out the yellow and black tints and cut a baseball-sized lump of fondant away from the rest. The cat had patches of tan fur all up and down—she glanced at the picture—her sides. "Cookpots filled to the brim with water to a rolling boil, and then you throw a rock in to be sure the lip gets boiled, too."

Sugar measured tint colors while Gran measured turmeric and celery seed. Soon the quality and properties of peppers were discussed and they moved on after that to kosher versus sea salt. I *was* lonely, Sugar thought with a flash of clarity. After the bedlam of restaurant work, having no one to please but herself had seemed heavenly. But solitude had been a kind of invisible trap. Chatting while she worked felt wonderful, and very . . . homelike.

Driving with Quinn had felt fine, and the sunshine and fresh air had made the fire seem long ago. She'd been inside too much. A drive to Mercer Island tomorrow was suddenly an exciting prospect. Thoughts of a get-together with Tree and a businesslike meal with Emily weren't far from her mind either. There wasn't time in her life for romance and heavy dating and certainly not settling down or anything like that. But maybe there was time enough for coffee or dinner.

By early evening, Sugar had the colored and textured icing ready to apply to the finished cake, and the ganache filling was made. One of the reasons she'd suggested a pose of the cat on its back was while the cake itself would be harder to sculpt, the belly and inner legs were a single color, saving her an enormous amount of time. She'd stack and secure the layers in a little while and begin sculpting, but she was in serious need of a break first.

She didn't understand why she was so tired. She'd worked that long on a single project before, many times. Her vision was fuzzy at the edges, yet she'd had plenty of water.

Bridget, Gran's closest friend from church, had stopped by at the appointed hour to take their various goods to the shelters. Gran wouldn't be back until after Bible Study. Sugar realized guiltily that no call had been made to Gran's doctor. Another thing to take care of on Monday, she thought tiredly.

Thinking her weariness was from leaning over her work, Sugar decided it was time to determine the damage to her computer and printer. Both were gently resting upside down on towels in the garage. If the laptop didn't boot up, she'd head out to the Internet café again for a real break.

Following the guidelines she'd found on the Internet, she used the blow dryer on cool to force air into the CD slot and every other opening she could. She wasn't sure she didn't hear water sloshing inside it, but that could easily be her imagination. She stood with the power cord in her hand for a long time, trying to make herself plug it into the wall outlet. What if it exploded? What if she burned down Gran's house?

She wasn't willing to examine closely why she thought of Charlie. Well, she *had* promised she'd call about that order. Given what Charlie had done for her already, she'd do just about any project for free. Charlie might know how to safely plug the laptop in—that's why she was calling. Of course.

She had long enough while the phone rang to get a frog in her throat. The ringing was answered just as she coughed into the receiver. "Oh, hi. It's Sugar Sorenson."

"Hi. Hey, I'm glad you called." Charlie's voice was as warm over the phone line as it had been in person. "How are you doing?"

"Well, thank you. My grandmother has been great."

"Good. I really am glad you called."

Sugar broke an awkward silence by saying, "I wanted to follow up. And I have to admit, I need some professional advice."

"Which would you like first?"

Oh, my goodness, Sugar thought. Why on earth did that question make her breathless? Was it that near-purr in Charlie's voice? "Well, you did ask me to call and I presume it's because you need a cake. Is now a good time to talk about it?" The trouble with mobile phones, Sugar had always thought, was that you never knew where the person on the other end of the line actually was.

"You guessed right." It sounded as if Charlie was grinning. "I need a cake. Now's good because I'm on days off. My dad is retiring at the end of this month and I've been looking around. I want something more than letters on frosting."

"I can do more than letters on frosting. How many people are you feeding?"

"Just us guys, so twelve. This is for the small party on his last official workday. There's a district-wide bash, for about two hundred rank and file, brass, the works, but that didn't get scheduled until the end of June. I want to do something on his last day."

"What's the date?"

"A week from Monday. Is that too soon for you?"

Visualizing her calendar, Sugar knew it was awfully close to when she'd want one hundred percent of her focus on the Seattle Eats contest. Entries in her category had to be delivered, completed and presented for judging at noon on Thursday of that week. But it wasn't impossible and she owed Charlie a lot. "No, that's fine. Any thoughts about what you'd like it to resemble?"

"He loves to fish, so . . . something . . . about that?" Charlie rushed on. "Except not a fish, because I'm not sure I could eat a cake in sockeye salmon colors."

Sugar laughed. "How about a tackle box or a creel? In fact, I'd suggest a creel, because a design with lures and things like that would be interesting."

"Okay, that sounds really fun. In fact, I could probably smuggle you his favorite lure. He's got one that he's had since he was a boy." There was a little sigh in Charlie's voice and Sugar pictured her stretching her legs out in front of her as she settled in to talk.

Banishing the vision of just how long Charlie's legs were, Sugar said, "I'd love to copy something like that. I really like my cakes to have meaning to the people I create them for."

"I could drop it by anytime this weekend. My next seventy-two-hour stint begins Monday at one p.m."

"Okay." Sugar gave Charlie the address and Gran's phone number. "If I'm not home you could leave it in the mailbox, and I'll get it back to you."

"Oh, well, I was hoping you'd be there. I was thinking we could go for coffee or . . . something."

"Okay," Sugar squeaked. That made *three!* Three dates in three days—it had never happened to her before. Charlie was so . . . attractive. And so was Emily. And so was Tree. What did they see in her?

Charlie wasn't laughing but she sounded very close. "Good. I was hoping you'd say that."

Smug, Sugar thought. Way too smug and poised and smooth at asking women out. She was probably dating a dozen women.

Before Sugar could recapture any aura of aloofness, Charlie added, "And what was it you wanted professional advice about?"

"My laptop. This will sound silly, but I've tried to dry it out and now I'm afraid to plug it in. Sparks, explosions, you know?"

"It's not silly at all. You should be okay if you stick with a GFIC outlet and of course don't be holding it or anything like that."

"Oh, of course." The special wiring for outlets outdoor or near water was required in restaurant kitchens. "One problem, though, my grandmother's house is about forty years old and I doubt the outlets are wired that way."

"Do you have a surge strip? It's not as safe, but a good one will help insulate the appliance from the rest of the household electrical load." Charlie was in full firefighter mode as she added, "And you could take it outside. Keep some cat litter or flour handy."

"Okay. Thank you," Sugar said sincerely. "I think I'm making way too much of it—"

"Better safe than sorry. Most people don't even think about it."

"Most people didn't have their house just burn out from under them."

"Oh, hey, the report on the cause of the fire will be filed by end of next week. Be sure to request a copy from the main district office." Charlie's voice grew warm again. "Are you sure you're doing okay?"

"Yeah. I'm surprised tonight at how tired I am."

"You had quite a shock to the system. Have you eaten?"

"I suppose I should. Not since lunch."

"How fortunate, because neither have I. Do you like Vietnamese food?"

"Yes," Sugar said. *She just asked me out*, a little voice inside marveled. "But I—"

"You're busy, I understand."

"Well, yes. I need to get the cake that's due tomorrow set up tonight so I can assemble the icing in time."

"You do need to eat, though." It sounded as if Charlie had gotten to her feet. "Why don't I bring Pop's lure and some noodles over? We'll talk, you'll work and we'll both get fed."

Marveling that such a flirtatious tone could come out of her own mouth, Sugar said, "Do you always have such efficient, well-thought-out plans?"

"Not always, but I do try when it matters."

"Okay." That's what you get, Sugar told herself. You flirt, she flirts back and now you have no idea what to say. "I'll be here."

Charlie laughed. "Now that I've said I can find that lure, I'm not sure. I think I know where his tackle box is. Thing is, his side of the garage is so tidy that it'll be obvious if I move things around. But I'll give it a shot. See you in probably about an hour."

Several minutes later Sugar shook herself out of a stunned reverie, her hand still on the phone. Was this a date? It seemed like a date. There had been flirting and suggestion of getting together. Now they were. Holy heaven, it *was* a date.

She dashed to the bathroom, thinking to shower or something, but settled instead on a change of clothes. Charlie had seen her looking worse, and given how, well, how cocky she seemed in asking women out, she could just learn right now that Sugar was a busy woman who wouldn't primp and perfume herself at the slightest sign of interest.

Good God in heaven, how long had that enormous black hair been growing out of her chin?

Chapter 4

Sugar peeked from behind the kitchen shades for the fiftieth time at the sound of an idling vehicle. This one was a truck, one of those shiny silver double-cab kinds of trucks. The kind that sat up so high off the ground that it required skilled gymnastics to get in and out of with any sense of grace. Unless, of course, a person was tall.

Charlie was tall. She exited the truck so nimbly Sugar would have awarded her a 10.0 for the dismount.

Tall wasn't a requirement for her. Noor was shorter than she was. Things had worked out just fine for important activities.

I'm unhinged, she thought as she went toward the door. *The fire has smoked my brains*. This wasn't a date, this wasn't anything. They'd just met. Charlie felt sorry for her. You're a stray puppy she's helping out, she told herself. It's not a date.

She waited for the doorbell, counted to ten, then opened the door, hoping she was smiling.

Charlie's jeans had razor-sharp creases, and the collar and cuffs of the denim shirt she'd pulled on over a close-fitting white tank were pristinely starched.

It was a date.

"Come in," Sugar finally managed. Without the layers of safety gear, Charlie's slenderness was even more apparent. Her short black hair, no longer showing the effects of the heavy protective helmet, was wavy with curls.

"Thanks."

"My grandmother is at Bible study. I was just getting ready to assemble the cake, that's why it's such a mess." Charlie's off-duty attire also included a plain gold earring clipped to each ear.

"It smells heavenly in here." Charlie set the bag of to-go containers on the counter. "Can we talk and eat? I'm sorry, I'm starving all of a sudden."

"Me, too." Sugar got out plates and cutlery. "My grandmother doesn't keep beer and wine, I'm sorry to say, and I haven't yet been to the grocery store for myself."

'That's okay. I'm on call until midnight."

"Tea?"

"Sure, sounds great." Charlie set out the cartons and the kitchen was redolent with the aroma of savory, tantalizing herbs and spices. Sugar's stomach growled loudly.

"I'm really hungry," she repeated unnecessarily. She started to blush but wasn't sure why.

"I'm making you nervous."

"A little. I'm out of practice at entertaining."

"The women in this town are nuts."

Sugar didn't quite know what to say to that, so she busied herself with mugs and tea bags.

"I got to the restaurant and realized I had no idea if you ate meat. So I went with tofu in some, and one has shrimp. I hope that's okay."

"That's wonderful. I do eat seafood and a lot of soy. It comes from working in a restaurant. Trust me, if you like dining out, don't ever go in a restaurant kitchen."

"That bad?"

"Sometimes, but actually it's the repetition. After the first thousand you grill, a filet mignon is just another piece of meat. Is that *tom nuong*?" Sugar loved Vietnamese rice vermicelli dishes. Without thinking she made appreciative yum-yum noises and Charlie laughed.

"Thank you," she said. "I was afraid I'd have to eat slow and be dainty. Which I can do, don't get me wrong. But I'm used to eating with big burly guys who pick rib bones cleaner than piranha."

Sugar handed over serving spoons. "Dish up and don't be dainty." Feeling much more comfortable herself, she gestured at the table and they both sat down.

For several minutes, they said little other than "Could you pass this" and "What's that?" and "Wow, that one's spicy."

When the clink of forks against plates slowed a little, Sugar let out a satisfied sigh. "I didn't realize I was that hungry. Thank you so much."

"It's my pleasure. Hey, on the way over I realized we didn't talk about the price of the cake."

Firmly, Sugar said, "That's because there isn't one, not on this one. You saved my knives, let alone everything else, and you simply did not have to do that. So please let me say thank you this way."

Charlie stared down at her food for a moment, and Sugar held her breath, hoping her rehearsed little speech would settle the matter. "Well, I, uh . . . When you put it that way, I guess."

Pleased, Sugar wondered if Charlie's head was down to hide a blush. Not that one would easily show through that lovely light mocha skin. "Good, I'm glad you're a reasonable woman."

Charlie glanced up through her lashes with a look of pure mischief in her light, almost golden eyes. "Reasonable? Depends on who's asking. But I'm not cheap and never free."

Feeling better by the minute—*gee, Sugar, think you ought to have eaten more than a handful of almonds and dried fruit today?*—Sugar threw an unopened packet of soy sauce at her. "Flirt!"

Charlie ducked it, looking shocked and pleased at the same time. "Be careful what you start. I finish everything."

Sugar gaped, blushed and laughed. "I can't tell if everything you say is really about sex."

"Good," Charlie answered. She dabbed at the corner of her mouth with her napkin. "I do like to keep a girl guessing."

"Well, my grandmother will likely be home in the next hour."

"Oh, then we should get to it, huh?"

Something in Sugar stilled. "You're not serious, are you?"

Charlie looked startled. "Of course not. We just met. I'm having a helluva good time flirting with you, though."

Struggling to gain her composure, Sugar said, "Me too. I just . . . I haven't dated in a while. And even when I did I felt like I was a Studebaker in a Ferrari world."

Her gaze narrowed, Charlie asked, "What did Gantry tell you about me?"

"Nothing. I get the idea there's some history there, though."

Charlie's expression was frozen. "Yeah. Someday I'll tell you my side."

"She didn't say a thing. Really."

"Okay, I believe you. We're on opposite sides of a couple of issues, that's all. We have friends in common, but we've always rubbed each other the wrong way."

After she swallowed a last mouthful of rice, Sugar said, "The plot of nearly every romantic comedy ever made says that's a guarantee of happy-ever-after."

Charlie rolled her eyes. "Life is rarely like the movies. Did you really think I was going to try to seduce you tonight?"

"No." Shoot, she always blushed when she lied, and it wasn't fair.

"All I can say is that if I want to do you, you won't have any question about it."

How arrogant, Sugar thought. Stung, she fired back, "If I want you to do me, you won't be guessing about that either."

"Good." Charlie's seriousness abruptly melted into a smile. "Well, I'm glad we're clear about that. Usually that doesn't get settled until date three or four."

Sugar didn't know quite what to say. She'd made it sound like all she was after was getting done, but she enjoyed doing, too. What if Charlie didn't like that? Why on earth was she thinking about sexual politics? "Isn't that when the U-Haul is already in the driveway?"

"I don't do that U-Haul thing. Tried it. Hated it."

"Tried it once. It was okay, but we weren't the proverbial soul mates." She rolled her eyes. The concept of soul mates had always seemed hokey to her. "I've been working since I was sixteen, plus six years of college and culinary academy. I worked in restaurants for nine years, including two at Prime Cassis, and had little to show for it. So I decided to work for myself. And I still have nearly nothing to show for it," she added ruefully.

"But it's *your* nothing. You made it all by yourself."

Uncertain if Charlie was making fun of her, Sugar shrugged. "Whatever happens, yeah, I own it."

The cartons were empty, the tea all consumed. Charlie abruptly seemed at a loss for words.

Sugar busied herself with carrying their plates to the sink. Charlie leapt into action, nesting empty containers into the bag she'd brought them in.

"I should get to work on this cake," Sugar said, feeling unaccountably nervous once her hands were dried. "That was part of the plan, right? I would work while we talked?"

"Do you want to try plugging in your laptop first?"

"Oh." She hadn't thought of the laptop since the moment she'd watched Charlie vault from her truck. "Yes, I would."

Charlie followed her to the garage, where she'd set the laptop and power cord next to an available outlet on Grandpa Fulton's old workbench.

Charlie lifted the slender case to her ear and shook gently. She closed her eyes and shook again.

"Oh, it's all a façade. As I have long suspected."

"Darn, I told you the club secret. I'm going to have to turn in my butch membership card now."

Sugar laughed and felt the tension in her body easing. "Can't have that, can we? I won't tell on you."

"Thanks."

All at once Sugar was aware of the slow, easy night sounds of crickets and the breeze moving leaves in the apricot trees. She was aware that everything she thought tended to show in her face and so she tried very hard not to think about Charlie kissing her, but with Charlie's lustrous eyes studying her face she felt naked.

She swore that neither of them moved, but somehow they were even closer together. She could feel the heat from Charlie's arms.

"Cake," Charlie said abruptly.

"Yes."

"You were going to work on the cake."

Sugar nodded. "I really have to."

Charlie opened the sliding glass door and stepped back to allow Sugar to precede her. "You do that and I'll go to the truck to get the lure. And I found a photo album that's got some good shots of his gear. I didn't know if you could freehand a creel."

Sugar tried to find a light, easy tone. "I'd have gone to the Internet, but I'd much rather shape it like one he's used."

"Shape?" Charlie looked confused. "I thought you'd draw it, like on top or something."

"Oh. I don't do that kind of cake." Sugar wished she had photographs she could show Charlie. Ridiculous tears stung her eyes for a moment. "I used to and I still can if that's really what you want. But my specialty is three-dimensional. It'll look like a fishing creel, as real as I can make it."

"I don't think I get it, but I'm willing to give it a try. Be right back."

Sugar took advantage of Charlie's brief absence to dab her flushed cheeks with cool water. This was absurd. She didn't respond to animal magnetism. She wasn't impressed by brawn. But her brain

71

wouldn't stop wondering what it would be like to be conscious the next time Charlie picked her up and carried her somewhere. Her imagination was running rampant, picturing Charlie sweeping her off her feet, carrying her up a staircase to their sumptuous, sensuous bedroom and spreading her on the bed while the pounding sea outside the window urged them to equally wild heights.

She didn't like that he-man stuff. She didn't need some Princess Charming or cocky Charlie Bronson treating her like Scarlett O'Hara. To be fair, Charlie had not suggested anything of the kind. But her eyes had that look, and her voice was so incredibly sexy—

"This is it."

Sugar nearly jumped out of her skin. She knew she was blushing again when she turned around.

Charlie looked chagrinned. "Did I startle you? Sorry, I thought you heard the door."

No, she'd only heard the waves and her own moaning but there was no way in hell she was admitting to that. The fire had completely melted her reason and the fried laptop had made her jittery all over again. That's all it was. She had been frightened and Charlie was a safe authority figure.

Safe.

Right.

"I was lost in thought, sorry. Oh—how pretty." She took the long lure, which shimmered with green and blue iridescence. It was nearly as long as her little finger. "I've seen jewelry not nearly so colorful."

"I didn't want to tell my dad that I've often thought it was an earring. Somewhere there's a high femme missing the perfect accessory to her favorite party dress."

Sugar grinned, still fighting her blush. Charlie's cologne was still hitting Sugar's brain like a drug. "Well, I can duplicate the colors. It'll be a challenge, but that's fine. I'm practicing different effects in the hopes of winning the Seattle Eats contest week after next."

"Sounds interesting." Charlie hefted a photo album into view. "Sorry, I had to bring the whole thing. These photos have been in here so long they've bonded with the page. I was afraid they'd tear if I tried to take them out."

Sugar had to lean in to see clearly as Charlie turned the pages and the closer she got the more cologne she inhaled. She had fit perfectly in Charlie's arms. And Charlie's waist had been the perfect height for wrapping her own arms around.

She tried to shake off the memory by studying the photographs. She saw Charlie's father standing with his arm around a strikingly beautiful Caucasian woman with the same effortless, elegant carriage that Charlie had. Obviously, this was Charlie's mother, and in a few photos it was clear she'd been a model of some sort. There was a baby girl, all in pink, on the following pages. Sugar wanted to linger over them, but Charlie kept flipping.

"It's right along in here. There—last fishing trip he and my mother went on together. That was right before she'd had enough of motherhood, married life and bucolic pursuits like fishing."

There was a hint of bitterness in Charlie's voice, and Sugar could understand why. Little Charlie, embraced on each side by her parents, couldn't have been more than seven. "So that's the creel?"

"Yes, he still has it. Still uses it when we go out." Charlie touched the photo lovingly while Sugar took a good long look.

"I know," Sugar said. "I'm so glad to see this. I had been envisioning one of leather or cloth, not this nice curved basket. Let me get my camera and take a picture of the picture. I've done it before—digital technology is a wonderful thing."

She was back from her bedroom in moments, catching Charlie gazing again at the earlier pages in the book. She wondered if Charlie and her mother had any contact. She knew she had often felt abandoned, and her parents had died when she was seventeen. That young, Charlie must have really felt the loss of one parent.

She quickly took the picture, glad she had invested in a camera with a good optical lens. Without questioning why, she zoomed out and took another photo of the entire page. Curiosity, that was all. She wanted to look more closely at little Charline. "That'll do it. Thank you, that helps a lot."

"I can't wait to see what you do."

How, she wondered, did Charlie do that? How did she make a simple statement sound like a proposal for activities that would leave them exhausted? "I hope you like it."

Charlie's grin was lopsided. "I'm certain that I will."

Sugar was suddenly annoyed with her sweating palms and thumping heart. Whether Charlie meant any of her flirtatious remarks, Sugar was not some breathless schoolgirl waiting to be seduced by Tall, Dark and Handsome, no matter how charming, or how attractive, and no matter how slender yet powerful her fingers appeared to be.

Turning to the counter, she picked up her spreading knife. "I was about to start stacking this cake if you want an idea of what I'll do. Tell me your father's favorite flavors."

"Well, he loves coffee, chocolate—vanilla ice cream is his favorite dessert, though. Pistachio, not crazy about almonds. Loves spice cakes, too. Banana bread. My grandfather was a baker and I think that's why he likes such a variety of things."

Sugar plopped a half-cup of the ganache onto the thin bottom layer of Emily's cake, working quickly while Charlie talked. A few minutes later she stacked the second layer on that, spread on more ganache, and topped it with the last delicate layer. The familiar motions and concentration steadied her nerves and she felt almost normal.

Glancing at the picture of the cat she'd taped to the cupboard door above her work area, she commented, "I usually don't make the layers so thin, but the cat isn't that tall. I probably should have just done two layers. But people think three is somehow more elegant. You do get more filling that way."

"How do you build that into a cat?"

"Well . . ." Sugar slid her slicing knife out of its pouch. "It's not what you add, it's what you take away." She lopped off the four corners, and carefully set them aside, intact. "Four legs." Trimming away at what she already thought of as the cat's ribs, she added, "And a tail."

Charlie was smiling as she watched. "So you use those parts?"

Sugar set the extra pieces roughly in position. "I get the shape done the way I like—see how the kitty is twisting slightly? I think I carved that just right. And the tail coils like this. The legs I'll secure with thin wooden skewers, but the tail will stay put with the icing in place. I might need a scrap or two when I shape the face."

"That is amazing," Charlie said. "I can see the cat now. And you'll frost it in different colors?"

"Something like that. The collar with the little jewels will be fun to imitate."

"I am in awe. I've always thought baking was an art form, but this is *really* an art form."

Sugar glanced up, pleased. "Thank you."

For just a moment Charlie wasn't smiling. There was no light flirtation in her eyes, no easy, sensuous suggestion to her lips. The gold-brown eyes blinked, then their penetrating gaze swept over Sugar's face. Charlie's mouth opened slightly and later Sugar was not really certain that Charlie had begun to lean forward to kiss her. What she knew was that Charlie jumped as much as she did at the sound of the front door closing with a slam.

If Grannie Fulton was surprised to find Sugar had a guest, it didn't show. Introductions were performed and Sugar scolded for not having yet offered Charlie dessert and coffee.

Charlie defended Sugar with, "We've only just finished eating dinner, Mrs. Fulton."

"Alma, please."

"Alma," Charlie echoed. "I was very interested in seeing exactly how Sugar creates a cake."

"Charlie's father is retiring from the fire department. I'm going to duplicate his fishing creel." Sugar prayed the whole-body flush she felt didn't show in her face. The staircase and pounding surf were parading through her mind again. Did Charlie have to have such compact, sleek muscles? Since when had she responded to muscles, anyway? "We were just deciding flavor."

Gran settled into a chair at the kitchen table. "You go right on. I need to rest just a bit."

"Can I get you something, ma'am? I've been off work all day and if I don't do something useful I won't have earned my keep."

"Oh, didn't your mother teach you nice manners," Gran answered. "I would love a glass of water with a few cubes of ice. The punch tonight was far too sweet."

"My father was my mentor in all things," Charlie said nonchalantly. She followed Gran's directions to the glasses and figured out the in-the-door ice and water dispenser. "Given your kitchen, I am guessing you mentored your granddaughter in a few things, too."

"I'd like to think so. The most important skill in cooking is patience, and that is something that is hard to teach."

"Really," Sugar commented. "Go right ahead and talk about me like I'm not here."

"Okay." Charlie had that far-too-smug look on her face as she turned back to Grannie Fulton. "Was she an impatient girl?"

"At times. Baby of the family, sitting around waiting for her share wasn't always the best strategy."

"If I wanted a biscuit at dinner I had to fight for it." Sugar turned her filet knife in her hands, having long preferred it for fine shaping. The cat had a very pettable tummy. She found herself wondering if Charlie's tummy was pettable, and was glad neither of them could see her face.

"With three older sisters, Sugar had to learn to be . . . aggressive."

Charlie had no right to sound so amused. "Did she now? That's not necessarily a bad thing."

Honestly, Charlie could do phone sex or read pornography on tape, Sugar thought. Oh great, thinking about phone sex was good for her composure, right. "Gran, please," Sugar said tightly.

Gran sighed. "I suppose I shouldn't tell tales."

"Oh, please do," Charlie urged.

"Coffee ganache," Sugar said firmly. "I'll make a chocolate-coffee ganache with vanilla bean cake."

"Sounds good to me. Ganache is that stuff you were spreading earlier, right?"

Sugar was unable to help a slightly waspish edge to her tone. "And it requires patience to make, too."

"I don't doubt that at all," Charlie replied.

"So, tell me about yourself," Gran said. "How does a young woman like you become a firefighter? How does your family feel about it?"

"Since it's just my father and me, and has been since his mother died, I don't have to take much of an opinion poll. Pop is proud of me, I guess. We get on well enough to share a house. I'm hoping to move to the arson squad, like he did."

"Does that make your hours more regular?"

Really, Gran was asking such personal questions, Sugar thought. She listened avidly.

"A little bit. It's intriguing detective work, and Pop is really good at it. I've followed in his footsteps all my life."

"Including getting married? Having kids?"

Sugar realized that Gran had absolutely no gaydar, but then why would she?

"That hasn't been in the cards for me so far. But I am like him in that I appreciate and respect women."

Sugar coughed into her sleeve. Was every woman who stopped at the house to see her going to out herself to Grannie Fulton?

"Do you need water, dear?"

"No, I'm fine," Sugar choked out. "Would you guys like some cake bits? I've got what I need."

"I thought you'd never ask," Charlie said. "Let me get yours, too, ma'am."

"Why, thank you. Your father did a lovely job with you. Manners are so overlooked in this modern world of ours." Gran's judgmental tone was softened with a self-deprecating chuckle. "Last week at the grocery I thanked the young man who carried out my bags and he said 'A-oh' in response. I don't even know what that means."

Charlie laughed as she set down the plates with cake. "It's an all-purpose phrase. Means anything from 'thank you' to 'dude, where's my car?' "

Gran's chuckle was cut short when she announced, "Oh, Sugar, this is divine." She paused with her fork in the air. "Just divine. Party cakes are so often sawdust."

Sugar blushed with pleasure. Her cakes did taste good, she thought, and Gran's opinion mattered a great deal.

"Wow. Oh, that is wonderful chocolate." Charlie spoke around her second large bite. "Why there isn't a line of suitors a mile long outside this door I'll never know."

"I'm beginning to think there could be a whole fleet of women knocking on the door and she'd never open it. My granddaughter doesn't date very much," Gran said blithely. "She works too hard."

"What a pity," Charlie said with a sigh.

Sugar spun round to face the counter again but was spared making any kind of rejoinder by the sudden chirp of a beeper.

"Ah, dang, never fails. I gotta go," Charlie said. She examined the display. "Structure fire in a commercial district. I was *this* close to being off call, too. Thank you for the cake," she added briskly.

"You're welcome," Sugar said bemusedly. "Thank you for dinner and the handyman duties."

"The pleasure was all mine." Even in a rush, the bedroom voice was there. "Talk to you soon, I hope."

Sugar could only nod as she watched Charlie take leave of Grannie Fulton.

"It was a pleasure to meet you, ma'am. Thank you for the hospitality of your kitchen."

"Don't let us keep you," Gran said worriedly. "You have important things to do."

The front door closed, then the quiet of the kitchen was broken by the roar of the truck heading for the parkway.

When the engine rumble faded into the distance, Gran said, "Such a nice girl."

"Woman, Gran. Definitely a woman." Sugar returned to her work, annoyed to find that her hands were again shaking.

Given how tired she was, tossing and turning for ten minutes seemed like hours. Tree had warned her she'd find sleep difficult, but Sugar had thought she'd have flashbacks of the fire, or wake from nightmares or something. But no, she was tossing and turning because of the danged staircase and the idea of Charlie Bronson's physique. And humor. And warmth. And bedroom eyes.

She liked sex as much as the next girl, she supposed. There were times when she wondered what all the fuss was about, true, but it was usually a pleasant way to pass the time. She'd read a romantic book and thought maybe someday life would be like that, but it never seemed like women in books had jobs and families and worries—things that made it hard to look around for somebody who might be fun, might want to see if where they were headed in life was the same destination. As fun as living with Noor had been at times, not once had she thought Happy Ever After was their destiny. She didn't really believe in it, and why should she?

She rolled over, vastly annoyed that she should be fantasizing about Charlie. She'd never been attracted to a woman solely because of how she looked. Supermodels and pop stars never even raised her pulse. She liked women with brains, women who liked to laugh. Charlie had both qualities, she reminded herself. Brains and humor all wrapped in a six-foot-two, agile, graceful, elegant package.

Shut up, already, Sugar scolded herself. You've had a nasty shock and your brain doesn't want to focus on reality. Instead, it wants to have some hot fantasy where you're the damsel and she's the hero, and no self-respecting lesbian would buy that whole "swept off my feet" situation, would she?

Okay, maybe for an hour or two. Or a night. A weekend, even. But it wasn't the basis for a lifetime and why the heck was she wide awake thinking about whether Charlie Bronson was interested in lifetimes? Or weekends? Or nights. Even an hour or two had possibilities.

She made herself think about baking after that, about fishing lures and Bible study and if there was life in other galaxies. Anything to get the scent of Charlie Bronson's cologne, and staircases and sumptuous bedrooms out of her mind.

Chapter 5

It wasn't cologne she smelled the moment she woke, but the all-too-familiar stench of something charred. Sitting bolt upright in near total darkness, Sugar was momentarily puzzled by where she was. Another whiff of burning sent her scurrying into Gran's hallway, following the smell.

She found Gran dropping a piece of blackened toast into the garbage disposal. "Oh, you startled me, child. What is it? You're white as a ghost!"

Sugar tried to calm her racing heart. Sure, she thought, you're just fine. Obsessing about some woman's cologne and now trying not to run screaming from the house over burnt toast? "Nothing, Gran. I . . . just . . ."

"Sit down at the table, quick," Gran ordered firmly. She ground up the toast, then more firmly wrapped her housecoat around her. "That toaster has got to go. I don't blame you thinking the house was on fire. Let me get you a glass of milk."

As much as Sugar wanted to spare her grandmother steps, she was grateful to rest her head on her arms and just breathe. The milk did settle her stomach and nerves right away, and within minutes she offered to make eggs before they both started their busy day. A cup of coffee made her feel almost human.

"Now listen, Sugar," Gran said seriously, after dishes were stacked in the sink. "All my life I haven't been in favor of people running to psychiatrists and analysts every time they get a hangnail. That's what family is for, that's why Jesus lives in our hearts."

Sugar was familiar with the gist of Gran's comments. Just when everything was going so well, she was about to get pressured to talk to Reverend Whoozits, who might be, for all she knew, a wonderful, empathetic person who understood trauma. It was the inherent sales pitch that came with the sympathy, that's what put her off. Lots of lovely words and hugs and "we love you, Jesus loves you, God loves you," but she always heard a condition—we'd love you more if you thought the way we do. That fact that you're not one of us hurts us, Sugar, so stop hurting us. Right.

Gran moved slowly back to the table. Once settled, she went on, "But I do find that I'm not as right about many things as I used to be. I was raised in simpler times."

Sugar blinked back her surprise at the turn Gran's words had taken. If Gran thought she'd seen Jesus and it had turned her into a more tolerant person, then perhaps everybody should see that Jesus once in a while. "I don't know if the times were simpler, Gran. It's just that we thought so."

"I'm ashamed to say it made life easy, thinking the world was made up of one culture, one color and one right way to do any one thing." She untied the wrap that covered her curlers and set about unrolling them. "I didn't know what matzoh or bhujia was, and I thought not knowing made me a better Christian, and a better American. I tell you," she added, her voice raising in the hellfire cadence Sugar knew so well, "ignorance is a sin."

"I think I can agree wholeheartedly with that, Gran." Sugar took a last look at the slowly lightening sky visible from the kitchen window. It was clear this morning, but a storm had been forecasted by afternoon. She moved behind her grandmother and helped with the curlers. Saturday was a day for making calls, delivering treats to anyone who felt under the weather and dropping off extra portions of desserts for the shelter. By noon, after six hours of kitchen work, Gran would be off with Bridget, looking the picture of leisure down to the last gray curl. White gloves would hide the burn from the oven rack and a hearty "God bless you" would mask any weariness Gran might feel.

Sugar had thought her grandmother the most tireless person she'd ever met, but, as she brushed the thinning hair in her hands she realized that Gran had likely always been tired. She simply refused to stop because of it.

"What I'm trying to say is that you should seriously think about calling one of those people Gantry left on that list. A specialist, you might say. I can tell already you're not sleeping."

"You can?" Goodness, how bad did she look? Perhaps she ought to consult a mirror herself before she went out in public.

"I don't think I've ever seen you with such circles under your eyes."

"It'll get better, Gran. It's not like I lost anything truly important to me." She thought of her recipe files. "It can all be replaced. Even though I'm sorry to have to start over with some things, I can see that a fresh start might have advantages."

"Do as you think best, of course." Sugar knew that phrase from countless utterances during family disputes, but Gran didn't say it with the same deep you're-going-directly-to-hell sigh.

"I'll keep an open mind."

Gran laughed. "So should we all. They told you what happened at Easter, didn't they?"

Sugar set the hairbrush in the basket with the curlers. "Quinn did. I didn't know until yesterday."

Gran patted Sugar's hand. "All I'm saying now is I need to get right with Jesus. The rest of you are on your own with Him."

"I'll keep an open mind on that, too," Sugar said lightly. "After all, the fire happened when I was able to escape it. Either I'm lucky that random chance fell in my favor, or somebody was watching out for me. There," she continued briskly. "You look like a million bucks."

"Thank you, my dear. It's so much easier when someone else does it."

"You're welcome. Goodness, it's nearly seven. So what's on the baking plan for today?"

They went over ingredients and timing. Sugar realized she would have to remember that Saturday morning was Gran's heaviest baking day and plan accordingly. It was a good thing her morning was solely occupied with decorating and would take up only one small area on the kitchen table. The dining room had poor lighting and she was glad not to have to move.

"Gran, I'm thinking I may need to rent another refrigerator and put it in the garage. This project is taking an entire shelf, and it was a tight fit at that. Good thing it's not for sixty. I've got a project that size coming up."

"That makes a lot of sense." Gran looked up from dicing dates. "I'm sure there's things you'd like to have chilled, too—pop and beer and that sort of thing. Do you think most of what I make doesn't need refrigeration because I learned to bake when a refrigerator was a luxury? We had an icebox in Tupelo when I was a girl, but it was for milk and butter."

"Maybe you're right." Sugar thought about it. "I couldn't do what I'm doing without it." She lifted the tenting of foil from the half-decorated cat.

Gran gasped. "My goodness gracious, that's amazing!"

Sugar felt a pleased blush steal over her face. "I told you to wait and see what I could really do. I did most of the texturing and painting last night after you went to bed."

Gran was putting on her glasses. "Now let me look close."

Sugar stepped back to give Gran lots of room. She was pleased with her work. A fully-formed three-dimensional cat coiled on its back, with patches of calico fur in beige, gold, brown and black.

"In here. I'm using the lounge. It's much warmer and we can watch the storm on the lake while we booze it up all night." Emily led Sugar through a vaulted foyer.

Sugar had only a moment to take note of the curved, ornate staircase before following Emily into a large, comfortable room with multiple seating groups, an oversized fireplace, tall picture windows and—best of all for her needs—a more-than-adequate sideboard reserved for the cake and gifts. The caterer had set up protective liners, electrical cords and party lights on a nearby table that might otherwise be used for cards or to feed a family of eight, if the need should arise.

"This is perfect," Sugar said. "I have some plain white cloths to protect the table, unless you have linens you'd prefer to use."

"Julie—she's in the kitchen—has the party decorations, and there's something to go on this table. Let me find that while you bring in your artwork." Emily whisked away again, her heels making a rapid tattoo on the Mediterranean tile of the foyer.

By the time Sugar was back with the cake, there was an insulated cloth in place. She was glad she'd fussed getting the cardboard platter wrapped in a subtly patterned wax paper over a lining of aluminum foil. There was no way anyone would call the caterer's dishware and preparations casual. There was also some foliage and glitter to add to the display.

Her worry now was that the lounge *was* warm, and the icing would begin to run before the partygoers had a chance to admire the cake.

"I think you're going to need this," a voice said behind her.

Turning, she saw the caterer holding an aluminum platter with an ice-filled core. "Oh, yes, that would be a big help if you can spare it."

"Emily asked me to bring something along, just in case. Said you'd had an emergency and might not have all the supplies you're used to." The older woman's tone wasn't exactly full of sympathy. Everybody in food service had emergencies.

Sugar held her head up, though she wanted to blush at the

implied criticism of her foresight. "'Emergency' about covers it. A fire. And yeah, I had one of those until Wednesday. You must be Julie."

A nod accompanied a firm handshake. "I cater all the time for the station, so I'm used to Emily's last-minute requests for miracles." She spread a towel on the insulated cloth and set the already sweating platter on top of that. "I confess, given how Emily has raved, I can't wait to see what you've done."

Sugar caught the competitive hint in Julie's voice, but now whatever Julie thought didn't bother her. She knew her work was unique. "I'll have it all set up in about a half-hour. Some assembly still required," she quipped.

Julie didn't take the hint and was obviously lingering to see the cake uncovered. Fine then, Sugar thought. She didn't need to antagonize the woman. For all she knew, Julie had contacts with other people like Emily.

She carefully squared the cake on top of the cold platter and peeled back the foil tent without fanfare. Everything looked exactly as it had when she'd covered it up. "The tail still needs to be attached, but I've all the equipment for that," she added unnecessarily.

"Wow." Julie's tone was laden with grudging admiration. "Emily wasn't exaggerating."

"Thank you."

"How did you get the legs to stay up with all the weight of the icing?"

"Wood skewers. I try to use as few as possible, but it's also the reason why I use cardboard underneath. Something to push the skewer into. The tip of the tail will stand up with the same support."

"How would you recommend cutting that? So I'll know later when we're serving."

"I start with the main body first, leaving the most elaborate parts for last. I've found that the honoree usually claims the fanciest portions."

"I'll offer it that way then." Julie glanced from the cake to Sugar and back again. "You did that since . . . ?"

Sugar nodded. "I got the pictures and order on Wednesday and began work Thursday. I usually prefer to have four working days for any project, regardless of size, but circumstances didn't allow it this time."

"Do you have a business card?"

"A few survived the fire." Gratified, Sugar fished one out of her pocket and handed it to Julie, who passed back one of her own. "There are photographs and pricing outlines on my Web site."

"I've got a graduation celebration in the middle of June for a family just up the island a bit. So far they haven't cared for any of the dessert ideas. I'll bounce something like this off them. They're big U of W alumni, but they don't want just the school colors on a flat cake thing."

Sugar shrugged. "I could . . . do a campus structure, a mascot, a letterman's jacket, anything along those lines. And as a subcontractor on your contract I knock off ten percent if I don't have to do delivery and setup."

Julie nodded. "Okay, then. I'll be in touch if they like the idea."

Shutting the activity in the rest of the room out of her mind, Sugar carefully laid out the pieces of the tail in the curve she thought most elegant, then applied the base layer of white icing. Referring to the photograph, she added patches of color, then worked quickly with a lightly tinted pastry brush to complete the fur effect. Her last effect was the delicate addition of the whiskers.

"That's really beautiful," Emily said from behind her.

"Thank you." Sugar turned to face her client. Emily was just a client, she told herself, taking a deep breath as she noted that Emily had changed for the party. No doubt the clinging raw silk outfit was called loungewear, but one woman's loungewear was another woman's fantasy pajamas. The deep green was a wonderful foil for Emily's red hair, which was now unbraided and loose around her shoulders.

"Oh, thank you," Emily replied. "I'll take the look in your eyes as a compliment, if that's not too forward."

Goodness gracious, Sugar scolded herself. First you get high on Charlie's cologne and now you're drooling over Emily. Give it a rest! "I'm sorry—that color does look really wonderful on you."

"Like I said, thank you." Emily tucked one hand under Sugar's arm. "You haven't forgotten our dinner engagement on Thursday, have you?"

"Not at all," Sugar assured her. They walked together to the foyer.

"Good. I will confess I hoped we'd talk about more than business."

"The thought had crossed my mind," Sugar admitted before thinking better of it.

Emily started to reply but turned quickly as the front door burst open. The new arrival announced, "It's raining cats and dogs out there!"

Emily let go of Sugar with a laugh. "Annette, you look drowned. Speaking of cats, take off your coat and come look in the lounge. Nan's cat is visiting."

Annette slung her coat over the nearest chair and followed Emily. "I thought that creature couldn't travel."

"It's a surprise. Look, right there on the table, naughty thing."

Sugar poked her head into the lounge to get the full effect of Annette's reaction.

"Nan's forever having to drug it. Get it off the table—oh! It's a fake!" Annette's laugh was infectious and genuine.

"It's an edible fake," Emily said, as she drew Sugar fully into the lounge. "Chocolate cake, in fact, and this is the artist who created it."

"At first glance I thought it was She-Devil. That's really amazing."

"*Best of Seattle* is going to do a segment on Sugar's work." Emily tucked her hand under Sugar's arm again.

"Found yourself another new discovery?" Smiling at Sugar,

Annette added, "Emily's the one who originally promoted Chastity McLain."

"Wow." Sugar was impressed. Chastity's latest single was, according to the gay news she'd read online, getting heavy "push" from her label and rising on the charts.

"Thursday we'll go into our mutual histories." Giving Annette an arch look, Emily added, "Don't believe a word this one says. She's a notorious con artist."

"Shut up, Emily. Did you move the vodka?"

"Would I do that to you?" Turning her attention again to Sugar, Emily opened her mouth to say something, but when the lights flickered out, came back on, then went out again, she said simply, "Oh, damn."

I'm cursed, Sugar thought. I am obviously cursed. What petty god of electricity had she offended?

The lights stayed out. In the abrupt stillness of the house, Sugar realized how hard it was raining now. I-90 was not known for good driving conditions in heavy rain. "I'd better head for home."

"It's too late," Annette advised from the dark recesses of the room. There was the clink of ice, then the sound of the mini-refrigerator closing. Sounding casually sure of her facts, she went on, "Traffic was crawling when I came through. With the power out, every idiot on the island will want to go somewhere else. It's gridlocked out there."

"Stay and join the party," Emily said. In the dim light, she looked very sincere.

"I'm not dressed for it, really. Under this smock is a T-shirt that says 'Bad Hair Day,' which, I might add, is true." If you asked Noor, she'd say Sugar was having a bad hair year.

"Hogwash. You look wonderful. And I'm betting that even though you've got, well, more shape than I do, one of my sweaters would get you through. I was going to see if I could persuade you anyway, as I'd really like you to meet some of the people who'll be here. Though," she added in a distracted tone, "the off-islanders likely won't show now."

From the doorway, Julie said, "Well, I've always said there's no substitute for Sterno in a caterer's life. If you've got candles, though, that would be a help."

"I'll do better than that," Emily said. "We lose power twice a year at least, so I've got oil lamps aplenty. It'll be romantic and the light will flatter all of us."

Sugar helped set up and light the charming lamps that cast, as Emily had predicted, a very flattering light on everyone, including Emily. The soft contours of her clothes molded to a body that had—how had Emily put it? A body that had "less shape" than Sugar's? Less breast perhaps, but definitely more toned muscles. Very different from Charlie's, she mused. They were softer in spite of the tone. Then she realized she was thinking about muscles again.

"Let's go find you a sweater," Emily suggested, drawing Sugar out of the room. They crossed the foyer and Sugar realized they were going to climb the curving staircase together. She was glad Emily could not see her blush as she wondered what the heck it was about staircases and her libido lately. Weren't they phallic or something? Did fire and power failures instill a desire for, um, bedroom activities?

"Here." Emily held out her hand. "I know the way and where all the things that go bump are."

Sugar didn't know what to say and the tingle that shot up her arm was quite unlike anything she'd ever felt before. What on earth was wrong with her? Maybe, a little voice whispered, something was finally right. Emily had what Gran had always described as "oomph."

"This is the heavy toe-breaking armoire," Emily narrated, pulling Sugar gently to the right. There was a metallic clatter. "And that, I kid you not—I inherited it—is a suit of armor."

The hallway was dark and Sugar didn't interrupt. She had no wish to walk into anything and, darn it all, she was not thinking that the streaming rain on the windows sounded anything like passionate surf.

Emily was moving more confidently as dim watery daylight

seeped through a stained-glass window at the end of the long hallway. The light cast her red hair to the shade Sugar could only
think of as dried blood. Even with her eyes adjusting to the light,
Sugar couldn't see the top of the stairs from where they were. It
was as if they'd left the rest of the house far behind.

She disguised a shiver. She wasn't a fanciful person, and Emily
was no succubus luring her to her doom. She was an attractive,
charming woman who was only being flirtatious and kind to someone she found interesting—interesting as a project she could pro-
mote.

"Here we are. I think if I open the shades all the way we'll have
enough light. There is an oil lamp in here, though. It's not just
being on the island that's the problem—the house is old and so are
the wires. I've often thought of having it all updated sometime
when I'll be away for a month."

Sugar was very glad of the poor light. Emily's bedroom was
right out of her sumptuous bedroom fantasy, the fantasy she'd only
started having when Charlie had showed up on her doorstep. A
large four-poster bed with draperies dominated the room, with a
mirror over the headboard. Both the bed and mirror frame were of
dark, carved wood that made Sugar think of Henry the VIII's era.
It was a little heavy for Sugar's tastes, and she would have thought
for Emily's as well, except that the sheer size, and that of the
matching dressing tables, fit the room. The large picture window,
were it not sheeted over with rain, would have encompassed a glo-
rious view of Seattle. In front of it was a fainting couch, the kind a
damsel swooned upon as she yielded her virginity to the dashing
scoundrel who had climbed in through the window.

The fantasy in her head had her doing the swooning on the
chaise, and Charlie cast as the scoundrel. But it was Emily's bedroom. This, she concluded, was getting a little too weird for an
ordinary girl from suburbia. She could make no sense of her emotions or her libido.

"How about this," Emily called from the walk-in closet. "I
think purple would bring out your beautiful eyes."

"Now, really," Sugar said, trying to keep things light. "Flattery is nice, but my eyes are not beautiful."

Emily froze, a lush eggplant-hued sweater in one hand. "Nobody has ever said that to you before? I would think it would be every Tina, Dickie and Harriet's pickup line since the day you were born."

"No, you're the first to use it."

"It wasn't a pickup line. You have Elizabeth Taylor's eyes."

Sugar really didn't know what to say. The idea that anything about her was beautiful flew in the face of thirty-four years of being complimented for a great personality. "You're the one with amazing eyes."

"Thank you," Emily said with a smile as she crossed the room toward her. "See how that works? Someone gives you a compliment, you're not supposed to argue."

"I'll try to remember," Sugar replied drily. She wasn't sure she appreciated the lesson in deportment.

Emily handed her the sweater. "This will look great, and you're welcome to wear it."

"Thank you," Sugar finally managed. She started to unwrap the ties of her smock, then realized part of her wanted Emily to turn her back while part of her very much wanted Emily to watch. To watch, and to think about . . .

Think about what, Sugar. Think about exactly what? Taking you to bed? Right here? You danced with her months ago, which she doesn't even remember, and have talked for perhaps forty minutes.

First Charlie's bedroom eyes and seductive voice, now Emily's playful touch to the ties Sugar was fumbling with. "Can I help with that?"

"I, uh, I can manage."

"Pity." Emily moved a little closer, her hand slowly moving onto Sugar's waist. "I'm a very helpful person."

"Emily, I . . . I don't know you."

94

"I don't know you either. What I know," Emily went on she drew Sugar closer to her, "is that a spark is there. Tell me you don't feel it."

"I'm not saying I don't." She felt it plenty. She'd never felt anything quite like it in her life. She'd never felt anything like the rush of attraction she'd felt for Charlie last night either. "But I don't . . . There are things I don't do casually."

"Oh, honey, there isn't anything I do casually."

"Oh, my goodness," Sugar breathed just before Emily kissed her.

She needed the fainting couch but knew if she got anything like horizontal there was no telling what would happen. Emily's mouth was sweet but purposeful, and yes, absolutely yes, Sugar felt the spark.

She felt it up and down her arms, in her spine and definitely tingling its way up her thighs. The spark was why she didn't draw back right away, why she leaned into Emily's kiss and thoroughly, completely, yielded to it. It was a delicious kiss, full of promise for more pleasurable things. Sugar found herself wanting to surrender to wherever it might lead. Then an icy shiver ran down her spine and she pulled away, gasping for breath.

"That was some spark," Emily murmured.

I'm not in control here, Sugar thought wildly. *This isn't me and I don't know why.* It was as if she'd stepped out of reality. "It was," she agreed, "but . . ."

"I know, you don't do casual." Emily gave a light laugh as she let go of Sugar and stepped back. "I'll see what I can do about changing your mind at dinner."

Sugar busied her shaking hands with undoing the ties on her smock. She didn't realize Emily had moved closer again until Emily's fingertips tipped up her chin. "It's so dark in here—but I'm sorry. I think I've freaked you out."

"It's not you," Sugar admitted. "I'm acting out of character, that's all."

"So am I." Emily's smile grew slightly brittle as her fingers left Sugar's face. "I don't often play the vamp. I thought you were responding to that."

Her heart rate settling to something closer to normal, Sugar said shyly, "I'd rather you played you, and we got to know each other."

"Dinner on Thursday, then?"

"Yes, I would like that. Very much." She wouldn't think of what would happen if Emily went on kissing her that way. Sugar could have gone on kissing Emily for hours.

"I'll just use the little girls' room while you change."

Sugar let out a gusty sigh when Emily closed the door to the bathroom, and she quickly stripped off her smock and T-shirt. The sweater was a little snug across the bust, the area where their physiques were most noticeably different. She rarely wore anything that revealed her own attributes so . . . prominently. It was perhaps a little more feminine than she would have otherwise chosen, with scallops of lace around the neckline. It was more Noor's style, and yet it didn't look bad. But in the poor light she couldn't see what Emily was talking about—Elizabeth Taylor's eyes? Maybe with a sweater that felt like pure cashmere someone might be fooled into thinking so, but she just didn't think the comparison was valid.

Emily chattered about the Seattle Eats contest as they made their way downstairs. The lounge was cozy with a fire that nevertheless made Sugar feel a little uneasy. She wondered how long it would be until she felt good about warming her feet next to a cozy fire. Maybe it would depend on cuddling with the right woman.

She excused herself to the quiet of an anteroom near the front door to leave a message for Gran, not wanting her grandmother to worry about her in the storm. When she returned to the lounge there were more arrivals, and even though it was early, the party seemed well underway.

"You weren't upstairs long," Annette observed as she handed

Sugar a glass of something orange on the rocks. "I thought for sure you might be delayed."

"What makes you say that?"

"I know Emily."

"But you don't know me." Did Emily have a reputation for quickies or something? Sugar thought Annette was already showing signs of the first drink. She peered into the glass Annette had given her. "What's this?"

"You're right, I don't know you, which is a damned shame, but Emily saw you first. She's got quite the eye for artists." Annette pointed at the drink in Sugar's hand. "A screwdriver."

"I'm a baker, not an artist," Sugar said.

"Nonsense." Emily slipped an arm around Sugar's waist as she joined them. "You are a culinary artist. I can tell that you need a marketing makeover."

"And you're just the person to give it to her." Annette added, in a Groucho Marx voice, "In more ways than one."

"Did you have a party before this one or something?" Emily took the drink out of Annette's hand. "You're already potted."

"Wedding reception." Annette rubbed her forehead. "I need to drink. All that het superiority. And a darling, intelligent, witty woman dumbing herself down so the ape she's marrying doesn't look as stupid as rocks—it's pure tragedy. I intend to get shitfaced and pass out in one of your six spare bedrooms."

"June's wedding was *today*?" Emily seemed quite alarmed as she put her hand on Annette's arm. "Oh, sweetie, I'm so sorry I forgot."

"I smiled my way through it somehow." Tears glittered in Annette's eyes now.

"Here." Emily handed back the drink. "Just don't forget to eat something." As Annette obediently headed for the buffet, Emily said to Sugar, "I was too distracted. Annette's had a thing with June—her second cousin—since forever. June's way of breaking it off with Annette was to send her a wedding invitation. Bitch."

Wow, Sugar thought, and here she'd thought her house burning down was high drama. She sipped the screwdriver for something to do with her hands. "I'll try to make sure she eats some protein if you'd like. It'll slow down the alcohol."

"That's sweet. You don't even know her."

"Trying to make myself useful." Sugar shrugged.

"You don't have to do that." Emily ran a hand down Sugar's arm. "You're my guest, and the feature of my party is your work of art. I was serious—you should call your work culinary artistry."

"My grandmother would say that was putting on airs."

Emily grinned. "You forget I'm in television. Modesty isn't a virtue in my world."

"I'm getting that impression." Emily's world was completely unfamiliar to Sugar. She didn't know the rules. Emily's hand was still on her arm and the tingling she'd felt earlier came back. She could learn the rules, maybe.

"Oh, there's Elaine. That's who I wanted you to meet. She's an investor in Top of the City."

"Oh." Sugar let Emily tow her across the room. "Would it be a bad idea to mention that I applied there six times and didn't ever get a job?"

"No, we'll leave that out. Besides, you don't want to work there. Elaine says the top chef is an abusive lunatic."

Sugar filed that information away to share with Noor, who continued to apply to one of the few restaurants in Seattle where sous chefs could work their way up into six-figure careers.

There were kisses on cheeks and gossip about people they knew, then Emily introduced Sugar with a blithe, "After Sugar's Cake Dreams is unveiled on *Best of Seattle*, she'll be the hottest culinary artist in the Pacific Northwest."

"So this is who you were raving about last time I saw you?" Elaine shook hands firmly. Her smile seemed genuine. "Emily has been singing your praises ever since she ran across your Web site."

Emily looked abruptly embarrassed. "As well I might. Sugar is one of Seattle's best-kept secrets. And a good dancer."

Sugar hid her surprise behind another swallow of her drink. "I wasn't sure you remembered."

"Of course I do." For just a second it was as if Emily's sophisticated exterior became transparent, and Sugar glimpsed a vulnerable interior. "How could I forget a spark like that?"

Elaine turned to pick up a finger sandwich from the buffet, then briefly engaged Julie in a discussion of the ingredients.

Emily leaned closer and added, "I was sure I'd made an idiot of myself in front of Tree and Charlie, panting the way I did the moment I saw you."

"No, you were fine," Sugar said. "I didn't realize . . . I wasn't in the best shape myself."

"I know." She smiled broadly as Elaine turned back to them. "Sugar's in the Seattle Eats competition. I'm hoping to persuade her to use that as an opportunity to attract investors."

The shock must have showed in Sugar's face, because Elaine laughed. "Let the poor woman in on your plans for her, Emily."

Emily laughed. "No, no, that's not my style at all." She squeezed Sugar's arm. "With a diamond in the rough I just start polishing any part that will hold still."

The feeling of being nothing more than a project to Emily returned full force, but then Emily's hand grasped hers with an intimate squeeze that took the sting out of her words. Still, the idea of being considered some sort of protégée rankled. She wasn't . . . unfinished, was she? She remember Noor riding her about her hair and a manicure, but she was pretty sure that wasn't what Emily meant. She was a very good baker and a fine artist. What was it that needed polishing?

Her annoyance faded as she chatted glibly with Elaine about the ins and outs of running a small business. Emily outlined the components of an investor's package and Elaine expressed interest in seeing it. Feeling somewhat confused, Sugar finished her drink, began another, then followed her own advice about eating some protein from the buffet. The Emmenthaler quiche was delicious; Julie was no slouch in the pastry department. She sampled a sharp, exciting tapenade spread on crisp rye toast rounds and several dollops of brie baked in honey and almonds. Emily circulated throughout the room but always returned after a few minutes to chat with Sugar and introduce her to someone else.

The birthday girl, Nan, was the last to arrive. The storm was cursed for causing a huge traffic snarl, but the rain was pronounced to be easing. A raucous version of "Happy Birthday" was sung, the buffet completely demolished, and then someone began a chant for presents, cake and ice cream. Lanterns were brought to the sideboard where, Sugar realized, her cake had been carefully covered with a light sheet of Mylar.

Emily had her hands over Nan's eyes, and they were both flustered and giggling. If Sugar hadn't known otherwise, she'd have taken them for lovers. "You haven't met the last guest of honor! It's She-Devil herself!"

Nan blinked after Emily removed her hands. "What are you talking about? What have you done with my kitty?"

Emily whisked the Mylar away, and after a stunned moment, Nan let out a squeal that a fifteen-year-old couldn't have matched. "It's *perfect*!"

Sugar grinned to herself, taking note of the tears in Nan's eyes. It really didn't matter to her what her work resembled, it was the reaction of the person she'd created it for that really mattered. Most of the time she wasn't around to see it.

"Time to have some," Annette pronounced. Considering how much Sugar had seen her drink so far, she was remarkably poised. "Who's got a knife?"

"No way!" Nan moved protectively over the cake. "You can't cut it up."

"Not yet, anyway," Emily said. "We need lots of pictures."

"The light's terrible," someone observed.

With a preliminary burst, the lights came on, and everybody laughed and clapped. "Just in time!" Emily picked up a camera tucked under the presents stacked on the sideboard. "Say cheese!"

Within a few minutes bluesy jazz was wafting from the stereo and Nan settled down to open her gifts. Emily took Sugar by the arm, pulling her to the sideboard. "If we're quick, we can cut the cake now before Nan realizes it. I didn't think she might want to leave it intact. Let's make her slice something unrecognizable."

"I should have warned you—it's happened before." Considering that she was mildly tipsy, Sugar nevertheless made short work of slicing up the cake that had taken her so many hours to create.

"Does it bother you to destroy your own work?" Emily handed her another plate for the next piece.

"No, not at all. It's meant to be eaten. It's food, the best I can make. This is the part I like best."

Maybe it was the alcohol that gave her the lack of inhibition required to pick up a bite's worth of cake and offer it to Emily. "Open wide."

Emily's laugh was sultry as she leaned forward to take the proffered morsel. "I don't think I'll have any trouble at all doing that for you." Her intense blue gaze didn't leave Sugar's face until after the cake was in her mouth. Then it was Sugar's fingers that had her attention. With a small sound only Sugar heard, she caught them between her lips.

The light, teasing sensation of Emily's tongue on her fingertips brought a searing heat to other parts of Sugar. She'd had too much to drink. It had been too long since she'd been so obviously desired.

"Oh . . . my." Emily breathed out as Sugar gently pulled her hand back. She closed her eyes for a moment as she savored the cake. "That is incredibly good."

"Thank you."

"So is the cake," Emily added.

Blushing, Sugar went back to plating pieces. When Nan got to Emily's gift, Sugar watched from a distance as Emily helped pull the paper off the large box.

"I'm so glad the power came back on," Emily said as a large, elaborate karaoke machine was revealed.

The two women embraced as Nan exclaimed excitedly. Sugar grinned as the gathering divided into two camps. One perused the playlists and chose songs to perform. The other reviewed the connection instructions and organized a work detail. She sighed. She loved lesbians. No one waited around for permission to do anything. Work got done. Fun was had.

Nan looked a little sad when handed a piece of cake, then shrugged and joined everyone else in enjoying it. Sugar found herself on the receiving end of many compliments and, even better, four business cards.

"I really do want to see an investor's prospectus," Elaine said in a low voice. "Emily is never wrong about trends. She knows a winner when she sees one."

For what felt like the hundredth time that night, Sugar blushed. "I have to admit I hadn't thought of seeking outside investment."

Elaine nodded. "I guessed. I admire someone trying to build something out of nothing but their own wits and talent. With Emily's ideas and drive, though, you could see results in months instead of years. Besides, for someone in TV, Emily is remarkably genuine. It's not hard to be her friend."

Sugar didn't know quite what to make of that or the look in Elaine's eyes. She felt as if she'd been encouraged but warned, too.

The lights were dimmed after a while and Sugar found herself dancing with Emily.

"Just like the night we met," Emily whispered in Sugar's ear.

"But quieter," Sugar noted. "I couldn't hear myself think."

"I was really sorry not to have gotten your name that night. Maybe it was fate that brought up your Web site on an Internet search. I recognized you right away, was blown away by your work, so I set up that appointment."

"I was there with a friend and left when she did." She had looked around for the gorgeous redhead who had liked to dance face-to-face, back-to-back or with thighs and arms tangled, but she hadn't been able to spot her in the crowd.

"I'm not a big club-scene gal. But every once in a while it's nice to polish the floor with someone who excites me."

At the time, Sugar had attached little importance to the time spent dancing with an unknown woman. It had felt good, but she'd had too much to drink, too. The next day it hadn't been at all difficult to imagine that the attractive redhead who had danced with her had been drunk as well. Now she was dancing with that woman again, neither of them was more than slightly inebriated, and circumstances were very different.

There was no space between them and Sugar found herself not the least bit surprised. Emily was a woman of ambition and drive, who knew how to work a crowd and discuss big dreams with ease. They were skills Sugar hadn't ever possessed, but getting to know Emily would no doubt provide opportunities to learn. Maybe she was some kind of project to Emily, but the warmth in Emily's hands on her waist said it was more than that.

She'd felt like a nervous schoolgirl with Charlie, and maybe that was because Charlie was a kind of hero. Tall, dark and handsome, Sugar mused. Emily was dynamic, vivacious. She'd seen Sugar at her very worst and yet was still attracted. To be fair, Charlie had seemed attracted as well, maybe, but Charlie was a girlish fantasy. Sugar didn't feel like a schoolgirl right now, she felt very much a grownup. And it was grown-up things she was thinking about as their bodies pressed closer and closer.

They swayed together more and more slowly and Sugar found herself recalling Emily's bedroom. She dreaded the idea of Emily asking her to stay the night, but she wanted Emily to ask, too. She didn't know what her answer would be. It wasn't like her to get intimate with someone she'd just met, but Emily was like no one she'd ever met before.

The party began to break up. Annette precipitously retired to a distant bedroom, predicting a miserable morning. The rain had let up. A light drizzle fell as Nan's gifts were taken out her car. Several women, Elaine included, made a point of saying how glad they were to have met her. One even reminded her, in a low voice, that her home number was on the back of her business card.

It had to be the sweater, she thought, the tight sweater—and that she was a novelty. The house burns down and she's suddenly sexy? She didn't think that was the way it worked.

Julie and crew had long since packed up and headed out. Emily closed the door behind the last guest and leaned against it, gazing across the foyer at Sugar. With the exception of Annette, no doubt passed out somewhere else in the house, they were alone. Sugar's heart was pounding.

"I left my smock and shirt upstairs."

"I know. I could go up and get them." Emily pushed off from the door. She was naturally graceful and Sugar found it impossible to look away. "Or you could come with me."

"I think," Sugar said unsteadily, "it might be best if you got them." If they went upstairs they'd go to bed, she was sure of it. It was hard to think. She really wanted to experience where this heat and excitement boiling throughout her body would lead. She'd wanted a woman before, but it hadn't felt like this.

Emily looked disappointed, but she went up the stairs in a whisper of silk. Sugar returned to the lounge, where the fire was nearly embers.

Her mind turned over the glitter and laughter of the evening, trying to sort it all out. She'd liked the attention, liked the appreciation of her work, but how much of that was party and fluff, and how much of it had been real? How much of what she was feeling for Emily was based on fleeting attraction, and how much was something more? What was "something more" anyway?

"Here they are," Emily said as she entered the lounge. "When was the last time you had a drink?"

"An hour, maybe two. Before we were dancing."

"I don't want you to drive out there if you're not sober." Emily had taken off her shoes, and her feet made no sound as she padded across the soft carpet to join Sugar in front of the fire.

"Alcohol isn't why I'm feeling dizzy."

"Why, then?" Emily's hand cupped the back of Sugar's neck. "Is it because of this?"

The brush of Emily's lips over her own drew a small moan out of Sugar. "Yes," she breathed, and then Emily's lips were on hers with increasing pressure.

They stayed like that for a long while, the brush of lips mixing with smaller nips and longer kisses. Their bodies were a slow, yielding melt of hips and thighs finding the way that fit best. When Sugar filled her hands with Emily's silky hair, it was Emily who moaned.

"Do you ever think," Emily said between kisses, "that there are moments you could die a perfectly happy being?"

"Yes," Sugar murmured back. "Like right now. This is perfect."

"What about this?" Emily's hands finally left Sugar's waist, gliding upward to caress Sugar's back.

Sugar involuntarily arched, it felt that good, and she realized her breasts were straining against Emily's. "Also perfect."

"Good." Emily's hands moved back to Sugar's waist, then once again journeyed up the length of Sugar's back. But this time her hands were under the sweater and Sugar gasped into their next kiss.

She wanted to feel Emily's skin, too. The waist of Emily's top was too close-fitting to get her hands underneath, so Sugar instead hesitantly slipped open the bottom button, unfastening it slowly enough for Emily to pull away if that wasn't okay. Emily didn't pull away, and Sugar undid the next button so she could smooth her hands over Emily's stomach.

She tasted Emily's responsive moan in their kiss. The last of her restraint evaporated, then, and more buttons opened as Emily began to draw the sweater over Sugar's head.

She gasped as she realized Emily wore no bra. Emily pulled hard on the sweater and Sugar had to raise her hands over her head, letting go of Emily in the process. With a hammering thrill, she felt her own bra being pulled up with the sweater. The sound of her clothes lightly dropping to the floor sent a thrill up her legs.

Emily murmured, "My heavens, so lovely," then simply, "Yes," as Sugar in turn pushed the unbuttoned shirt from her shoulders.

Nipples met as kisses became wild. Hands grazed shoulder blades and ribs, then she and Emily both half laughed as fingers found their way to breasts.

"This feels extraordinarily good," Emily said, smiling. "Delightful."

"De-lovely." Sugar's nerves were no longer jangling with warnings. They were ringing with abandon.

"I think I'm not going to be able to stand up much longer." Emily drew Sugar to the long sofa that faced the fire. She sank onto her back, inviting Sugar to stretch out on top of her.

The kisses seemed endless but always new. The sound of their taut breathing and the press of skin on skin sent tingles the length of Sugar's spine. Emily was arching under her in a rhythm that matched her own, as if they had never stopped dancing.

Sugar had no idea how long they had been moving against each other, but her hips were between Emily's legs now and their rhythm was taking on a new urgency. Emily was nodding into their kisses and with each breath a soft sighing "yes" escaped her.

"Are you sure?" Sugar kissed her way down Emily's stomach. She had to listen for Emily's answer over the roar of her own blood in her ears.

"I think if you don't touch me soon I'll explode."

"I'm feeling that way myself." Sugar raised up a little to unbutton, then unzip Emily's soft pants. Moving up again, she stretched the length of Emily's body and their kisses grew longer, deeper. Sugar tasted the depths of Emily's mouth and offered her own in return. She shook off a sensation of falling, but it was a struggle to remember where she was. The world was contracting around them until there was nothing but the sound of their rising passion.

Her hands slid across the small of Emily's back, then downward to push the pants lower. Emily shuddered under her.

"I want to feel you," she said with a gasp. She struggled to sit up. "Please, Sugar."

Sugar's knees were still spread when Emily slid out from under her. Emily's pants slithered off her in the process and Sugar shivered as Emily's scent reached her sensitive nose and her mouth watered in response. She barely had time to register how much she wanted to taste Emily when Emily's hand pressed hard into the crotch of her jeans.

"I want you," Emily said, her blue eyes dark with passion. "I want this."

Sugar thrust herself down on Emily's hand as she frantically unbuttoned her jeans and pushed them down. Emily just as quickly moved her hand from fabric to Sugar's exposed flesh, cupping it with a sound like a growl.

"Oh, please, yes," Sugar said, and a moment later Emily was inside her and they both froze, only their eyes in motion as they sought each other's gaze.

Emily slowly nodded, then her fingers moved slightly and Sugar couldn't stand the tension anymore. "Don't tease me—"

Emily pushed Sugar onto her back and yanked down her jeans. She was inside Sugar again a moment later and the kisses this time were hot, needy, quick and hard, the same way Emily's fingers were moving inside her.

Red hair fell around Sugar's face and she gave a disbelieving gasp as an early shudder of climax rippled through her. After all the kissing, this was going to be fast, incredibly fast. "Yes, like that!"

"You feel so good, so hot."

Their voices twined like their bodies, sometimes in unison, sometimes in give-and-take. The spiral was sharply upward until Sugar felt something in her give way, something guarded and secret that was now of no importance next to the throbbing contractions of her body. She cried out and Emily strained against her in matching energy. Sugar felt washed in the blue of Emily's eyes as she arched one last time and Emily went deeply inside her again.

She was sobbing when her body began to feel real again. Emily was on top of her, breathing hard as she made loving, quiet shushing noises in Sugar's ear.

"That was amazing. I loved that," Emily murmured after a few minutes, while Sugar could only nod.

A hundred heartbeats later, more or less, she realized Emily's hand on her stomach was wet. She lifted it to her own mouth and was pleased to feel Emily's body tighten at the touch of her tongue. She traced the length of Emily's palm with just the tip and felt another shudder. "Do you like that?"

"Yes," Emily breathed.

"Mmm, good." Sugar turned to press Emily into the back of the sofa and wriggled downward until her mouth was level with Emily's breasts. "How about this?"

"God, yes." Emily moaned as Sugar's tongue flicked one reddened tip. "That feels fantastic."

Sugar took her time, enjoying the hardening texture of Emily's nipples and the responsive thrusts of Emily's hips when she bit down ever so gently. Gradually she moved Emily onto her back and teased both breasts, watching with increasing arousal as Emily's nipples grew more red and distended in the ruddy glow of the last of the fire.

"Sugar, please," Emily finally said.

"Please what?" Sugar looked up, feeling that here, at least, she was not the protégée. She knew perfectly well what Emily wanted.

Emily took Sugar's face in her hands, pulling her up for a hard kiss, then pushing her down, down past her breasts, her hips. Sugar took hold of Emily's hands then, gripping them in her own as she lowered her mouth to Emily's open, soaked center. It was hard to say what was intoxicating her most. Was it the utter abandon with which Emily arched her hips, inviting Sugar to taste her? Was it the heady aroma of a sexy woman's desire? Was it her own responsive clenching at the thought of immersing herself in the purest of a woman's passion?

It didn't matter after her tongue slipped inward to circle and tease. Pleasuring Emily and enjoying every second of it was all there was in Sugar's mind as her tongue reveled, tasted and danced. Emily's legs were tight around her shoulders and her long, fevered moans were the only sound that mattered.

They reached a peak where Emily's cries were increasingly hoarse and Sugar wanted to hear them break free. Without raising her head she slipped her fingers inside Emily, curling them to find the places that yielded and those that pushed back. Emily's hands were in her hair, pulling her up, and Sugar went into Emily hard, her hips behind her cupped hand.

"Oh, yes, like that," Emily cooed. Her legs wrapped around Sugar's waist as they kissed frantically. "Like that!"

Sugar didn't stop moving inside Emily even when Emily went rigid. She felt flutters against her fingers and then her palm was wet, her hips were wet. Emily cried out as she went limp under Sugar. Sugar coiled around her as best she could in the limited space, and for several minutes there was only the sound of their breathing, in matching rhythm.

Sugar startled awake, then caught herself before she moaned from the crick in her neck.

Emily stirred under her. "Sorry, I dozed off."

"So did I," Sugar admitted. "That was . . . you were . . ."

"So were you."

There was a faraway noise of a toilet flushing, followed by a groan of pain and the extremely unromantic sound of vomiting.

"Oh, Christ," Emily said. "Annette. She'll need a blanket if she's going to camp in the bathroom."

"I should go anyway—"

"Please, don't," Emily said softly. "Stay the night."

"I'd love to," Sugar said honestly. "I've just remembered that if I'm not home when my grandmother gets up she's going to panic." *And she'll know what you were doing when you walk in the door, you know she will.* "She rises very early."

"She wouldn't approve of your being out all night?"

"That's part of it," Sugar admitted. "And part of it is she's been very kind and understanding and I don't want to repay her right off the bat by frightening her."

Emily sighed. "I understand. Oh, lord," she muttered as sounds of Annette's misery reached them again. "The whole thing with June is *so* dysfunctional."

"I look forward to hearing the history." Sugar sat up, looking for her clothes. She felt drained but wonderful.

"Dinner, Thursday night?"

"Yes." She found her bra and T-shirt and slipped into them. "I am really looking forward to it," she added.

"Maybe we could have dinner here? And you could stay the night?"

"I'd like that," Sugar said softly. She watched Emily rise from the sofa, her lovely body rousing feelings that ought to have been sated for longer than thirty minutes. She could do everything they'd already done all over again. "I'll return your sweater then."

"Keep it," Emily said easily. "It looks so much better on you than on me. I loved the feel of it, but it never looked right with my hair. You look like a movie star in it. I'd be happy knowing it went to a good home."

"Oh, well, in that case . . . okay." She shyly folded the sweater up with the smock.

"You'll drive safely?" Emily was dressed again, but Sugar had no trouble recalling exactly how that beautiful, soft lounging outfit came undone.

"I promise."

They walked together to the back door, and Sugar stepped into the chilly night air. The drizzle had stopped. There were even stars out. "What a night."

"Indeed," Emily agreed. "It was a great deal more than I bargained for."

Suddenly anxious, Sugar turned back to search Emily's expression for reassurance. "But that's good, right?"

"Very good." She drew Sugar to her for a long, lingering kiss. "More than I had dreamed, and everything I had fantasized."

"Oh. You are such a sweet talker."

"I speak only truth." Emily touched Sugar's face for a moment, then jumped at a clatter from inside the house. "Oh, dear, Annette is going to hurt herself."

"Go be Florence Nightingale, then."

"More like Big Nurse." Emily frowned. "This is the last time she acts this way over June or I'm kicking her butt to the nearest therapist."

They shared another kiss, then Sugar hurried to the car before she got thoroughly chilled. Emily waited at the door until the engine started, then kissed her fingers in a parting wave.

The highway was quiet. Her heart was no longer pounding. The world seemed peacefully asleep. It was just her and the moon and the scent of Emily on her fingertips.

Chapter 6

Though it arrived far too early, Sunday morning found Sugar doing something she had not thought she could actually enjoy. She rose an hour later than Grannie Fulton, showered, had a small breakfast, then went with her to church.

Whereas she had once hated and resented having to go—her parents had required it at least twice a month—she found herself able to spend the sermon reviewing her To Do list. She'd always liked the music, and today she found she actually enjoyed the sense of community. News of other parishioners, which she'd previously thought mere gossip, was actually part of a sophisticated information net. It was the same net that had brought her clothing when she needed it. She couldn't argue with that—she wasn't even a member of the church, but she'd been in need, Gran had asked, and help had arrived.

She met the dentist and returned the clothing with her thanks. A nice enough woman, Denise, and some other time Sugar might have acceded to the pressure they were both getting to "get together" soon. Denise, however, was equally polite and as non-committal as Sugar was, so perhaps Denise was seeing someone, too. At the moment Sugar could only think of what the future might hold with Emily. The previous night was starting to fade in clarity, but there was no doubt in her mind about the high it had been to make love with Emily. Doing so again on Thursday night was an altogether exciting prospect.

The next several days flew by. She and Gran went to a presurgery meeting at the hospital where they were shown the pieces of artificial hip that would be inserted, and the procedure itself was explained. They left with a packet of pre- and postoperative instructions. Gran didn't complain about the pain, but the entire journey was obviously draining. Sugar could only imagine what Gran's church meetings and baked-good deliveries cost her. How had she kept going when every movement caused her such discomfort and stress? The doctor was hopeful that an opening would come available in three to four weeks, and Sugar was crossing her fingers, too. Otherwise the wait would be ten long, painful weeks.

The remainder of Monday and Tuesday Sugar worked on her next project, a replica of a rare bird found in the marshes of Puget Sound. It was so rare she worked from drawings in Audubon Society books provided by the client. Wednesday evening the cake would be consumed by the local ornithological society.

She delivered the cake, complete with a brown-sugar straw nest and tiny speckled eggs, on time, Wednesday at noon, seeing it safely into the party host's refrigerator. From there she went to her appointment with Patricia. She dreaded meetings with her sister. It wasn't that she begrudged Patty her success. Patty had worked hard for it, and the leather and cherrywood office was a testament to where she ranked in one of the oldest law firms in Seattle. It was the feeling Sugar always got that the only reason she needed her sister's legal advice was because she was a screwup.

Patty's brusque greeting brought the feelings out in full force.

Spread out in front of her was the fax Sugar had sent on Monday and printouts of the photos she'd e-mailed.

"We'll start with the bad news. Yes, you may have to pay a fine for knowingly having rented premises that were not licensed by Fair Housing. However, that will not preclude you from being a claimant against the landlord because he used a standard rental agreement. In it, there is a clause stating that to the best of his knowledge, the premises met state and local building codes in force at the time of construction. With me so far?"

Sugar nodded. She knew better than to speak when Patty was on a roll.

"He may not know, but you certainly do, that your address on your business license was out of date."

Sugar blushed. "I know, I know. As soon as I got commercial premises again I was going to get it all fixed."

"If he calls the health department you could be up the proverbial creek."

"Which is why I don't want to screw the guy over. He's a jerk, but I'm not exactly an innocent here either. But I did *not* cause the fire. I had the oven on at the most for fifteen to twenty hours a week, no more than someone who preferred home-cooked meals would have."

"Nothing is cut-and-dried," Patty said officiously. "As long as we're clear about your goal in this matter. What you have in your favor is two things. First, his unsuccessful attempt to help himself to your belongings, and those pictures you took are an excellent block to any legal action he might try to start. You were nice enough not to file charges, but you still have the upper hand in a civil action. Of more immediate benefit is the desire on the part of his insurance company to make this go away for as little as possible. So tell me exactly what it is you lost."

"My laptop fried and the printer never came back on either. I lost some cookware, cooking supplies, books and worst of all, my recipe collection."

"Jewelry? Art?" Patty looked up from her notepad. "Sorry, that's a no to both."

"I invested in my business," Sugar said slowly, trying not to lose her temper. "You can't bake a cake with diamond studs."

"So what about lost business?"

"I've been able to meet every contract, and will be, since I'm staying at Gran's. And I can pay my way there. I'm short on capital. I really need my deposit back from Robert. I could get together first and last, but given the size of kitchen I realize now that I really need, the rent will be steep. I'm not in a position to rent separate baking premises yet. I *had* hoped to have a good nest egg by the holidays so I could rent commercial premises short-term and hire a couple of helpers to get through the busiest season." She didn't tell Patty her hopes had also included two or three wedding-season cakes, representing thousands in income, but those hadn't happened. Other orders were more than she had planned on, though. It was stressful, keeping track of where she was financially, but it came with the territory.

"I think I can get you a good nest egg and you'll be able to move out on your own," Patty said.

Well, Sugar reasoned, if getting her out of Gran's house was what was motivating Patty, more power to her. "Okay," was all she said aloud.

"It'll all hinge on the report on what caused the fire. A copy has been ordered."

Sugar abruptly recalled Charlie's eyes and easy, open laugh. You're with Emily now, she reminded herself, at least, you will be. Might be. Your stomach ought not be flipping over at the thought of Charlie. "The arson investigator was very clear about it."

"Then he or insurance will pay. We'll push the value of your life's work of master chef's recipes. I wish your car had been totaled. We might have got you a replacement there."

"I don't want to bankrupt the guy's family. I didn't lose that much. I was very lucky."

"But that's no reason why he should get lucky. He endangered your life." Patty snapped the cap back on her pen. "That's money in the bank."

"I just want my deposit back and the money to replace my laptop," Sugar insisted.

"We'll do better than that."

"Okay, then some of it goes to Gran for rent."

Patty sighed. "So you'll be staying a while?"

"Yes," Sugar said firmly. "We're finding a mutually beneficial arrangement. I don't care how much money her house is worth after she's dead. She and I are quite content for the moment, both very much alive and well."

"Quinn told me Gran's going to have surgery."

Sugar nodded. "I'll be there to help her through. We're both getting something out of it. Heck, I didn't even mind going to church."

Patty's eyebrows shot up. "You?"

Sugar shrugged.

"You've changed."

"I don't think so. But Gran certainly has."

"You're not as militant as you were."

Sugar gaped at her sister. "Militant about what?"

"About being different. The rest of us went to universities, but you had to go to an 'academy.' Even Rose got a business degree."

"Look at the good it's done her."

Patty's sigh was sharp and quick. "Point acknowledged. Still, you seem much more laid-back than you were last time I saw you. Are you seeing someone?"

Thankfully, Sugar did not blush. The fact that she'd had some very good sex last weekend was not the reason they weren't yelling at each other right now. "Yes, but it's not serious yet. I just had my feet kicked out from under me, and I don't know . . ." She shrugged. "I do feel like I'm seeing the world in a slightly different frame of mind. Coming out to Gran was the best thing I've ever done."

"You what?" Patty's mouth hung open for a moment, leaving Sugar quite pleased to have stunned her sister for once.

"I came out to her. I could have died in that stupid fire and I didn't see the point of lying. Gran has really changed."

"Or she's desperate for home healthcare."

Sugar flushed with anger. "I don't think the thought crossed her mind when she told me I could stay as long as I needed to." *You'd have never opened your door for me that long*, she wanted to add. *Not unless I was willing to sign on some dotted line.*

Patty's intercom beeped. She lifted the handset, listened, then disconnected. "I have to go. Settlements with insurance go pretty quickly, though the cash doesn't flow quite that fast. I should have news for you by next week."

"Okay." Sugar pushed the notes she'd made about Robert's address and phone and the King County Fire District contacts toward Patty. "Thank you, Patty. I hope for once you'll be able to show some billable hours from a family member."

Patty's smile relaxed slightly. "If I collect from him, you can bet the firm will too."

On the way back to Gran's she stopped again at the Internet café. So far it was proving a necessary daily trip, but useful in that it got her out of the house, giving Gran some alone time. She found another order from a previous client, an e-mail from Julie, Emily's caterer, asking her to confirm a subcontracted price for a graduation cake, and several more notes from friends expressing best wishes in her recovery from the fire.

There was also an e-mail from CBRONSON. Sugar was temporarily stunned at the way her stomach went to knots. It was just hero worship, she told herself. A beautiful woman in uniform—obviously she had a previously unknown fetish for that sort of thing. Charlie hadn't been in uniform at Gran's house, she reminded herself, but she pushed away the disquieting thought. She was with Emily. Sort of. Emily hadn't called and Sugar had felt awkward making contact when their date was already confirmed.

She shouldn't be thinking about talking to Charlie again for anything but business, should she?

The note from Charlie read, "Sorry I had to rush out just when the conversation was getting so interesting. Did you decide what you needed for the cake? Let me know if there's anything else I can tell you."

An unbidden imp inside her wanted to write back, "Tell me how you like to kiss, tell me if you like to flirt and touch for hours, tell me everything about yourself." She controlled the urge, but the effort was so unsettling she decided she wouldn't answer until tomorrow.

Gran was at the kitchen table drinking tea when Sugar got home. Spread out in front of her were the papers from the doctor and hospital. After greetings, Gran observed, "It says here that side effects of this surgery could include infection and heterotopic bone formation, whatever that is. And there's the other one, right there."

Sugar followed Gran's pointing finger. She felt a little chill at the black letters on the cold white paper: *Death*. "They have to say that. It's for insurance, I suppose." She squeezed her grandmother's shoulder. "Your doctor said you're healthy as a horse, and one of the best candidates your age he's seen for the surgery. I think you're going to do really well."

"I'm praying that if it's my time I go without a lot of bother and expense and pain."

Sugar didn't quite know what to say, since she certainly understood where Gran was coming from, so she squeezed her shoulder again before going to make her own tea. "I remember when I had my wisdom teeth out, you brought me flower-drop soup." The memory dated to shortly before her parents' deaths in a freeway pileup. That entire summer had been an unhappy one, to say the least.

"You always liked it. Thought it was the fanciest thing you'd ever had. I didn't have the heart to tell you I was sneaking some eggs into you."

Sugar laughed. Growing up she'd been convinced eggs would make her fat, even though she liked them. "It worked, I have to admit it. I thought I'd make you some when you get home and feel like having a little bit of something. What else would you like to have on hand? If they get an opening in the next few weeks we should be prepared, don't you think?"

They chatted companionably throughout the afternoon, and Sugar was interrupted several times by calls on her cell phone. They were all for business, until one just after dinner proved to be Tree.

She'd forgotten Tree was going to call, but the moment she heard Tree's voice she recalled the kind, serious and gentle look in Tree's eyes when she'd forewarned Sugar of her intention to ask to get together for coffee.

After inquiring how Sugar was doing, and her grandmother, the car, her belongings and ongoing business affairs, Tree asked quietly, "And how is the allergy to coffee?"

Sugar realized if she turned Tree down, it would be a rude brush-off. Tree was too nice for that. "I'm not allergic. I'd certainly like to talk."

Tree's voice warmed further. "Good. Yes I'd like that, too. I was trying to wait until the weekend—give you some time to settle in. But I have to admit that when I was looking at this long evening ahead, I thought of you and hoped you hadn't developed that allergy."

Sugar laughed. "Not at all. It's hard to believe that it happened a week ago."

"I don't suppose you'd like coffee and dessert tonight? You probably have plans."

"You know, that does sound good." And it did, Sugar thought. She'd forgotten how calming it was just to talk to Tree. It wasn't the least bit like being around Charlie, or even Emily. Tree would certainly make a good friend.

They agreed on a popular coffee-and-pastry bar near Redmond Town Center. It wouldn't be too congested on a weeknight, Sugar thought. She changed into her favorite black slacks but hesitated over a choice of shirts. Usually she'd grab the cleanest tee and bolt, but Noor's nagging about her hair and Emily's "Elizabeth Taylor's eyes" remark of last Saturday had had Sugar gazing into the mirror more than usual.

Her hair was an unruly mess, most of the time. Naturally curly, its undistinguished color was hardly the inspiration of poets. She was too busy to keep it highlighted, but trimmed was probably not a bad idea. She had to finish this week's order tomorrow, but maybe a quick visit to a haircutter first thing in the morning might work. She'd look that much better for her date with Emily. In the meantime, a purple hair scrunchie tidied her appearance. But it also meant whatever shirt she wore would be more noticeable.

She hated dithering over her appearance. Nothing she did made much difference anyway, and most days there wasn't time to primp. Still, she was meeting an exceedingly beautiful woman in a public place, and even if anyone with a brain would smartly spend her time looking at Tree, she oughtn't embarrass Tree with a scruffy T-shirt. Digging into the pile, she found a polo shirt in soft, clinging jersey and ribbon trim on the collar and sleeves. She'd bought it at Noor's urging but had never thought it looked as good as Noor said.

Hair tied back, and shirt tucked into the slacks, she wasn't displeased, however, with the way the buttery yellow worked with her eyes. She found dangling earrings of mottled purples and the color of her eyes seemed even more pronounced. But they were *not* Elizabeth Taylor's eyes, no matter what anyone said.

"My, don't you look nice," Gran said. "That color is perfect for you."

They're all in a conspiracy, Sugar thought. Noor, Gran, Emily—even Charlie. Yeah, but a conspiracy to do what, another part of her asked. A conspiracy to make you feel better about how you look? What's wrong with that?

It wasn't true, she thought stubbornly. That's what was wrong with it. "I need to lose some weight."

Gran peered at her over her reading glasses. "That's got nothing to do with how nice you look. I personally think you're just right. So many girls are skin and bones these days."

"Thank you, then."

"That's better."

"I'm trying for a positive attitude." Emily had certainly found her attractive enough on Saturday, she recalled. It was the low light, the sweater, the party glow. Couldn't be her, or anything like that.

"Will you be late?"

"I don't think so," Sugar said. "Tomorrow night I will be, I think. I might not get home until the next morning." Sugar gulped, not meaning to have announced that quite so baldly.

"As long as you respect yourself," Gran said seriously, "you'll hear naught from me. Like I said, I can't get right with Jesus through other people. It's me I need to worry about, especially going under the knife."

Sugar kissed her grandmother on the cheek as she said goodbye. "I promise you I'll take a page from your book and worry about myself a little more, too."

The Electric Bean was hopping, but not as crowded as it would be on a Friday or Saturday night. Sugar found a parking space easily. She slipped the strap of the denim bag she was using as a purse these days over her shoulder and got out of the car. She smoothed her shirt into her slacks again. For some reason she was finding it hard to breathe. This wasn't a date, and yet she was quite nervous, as if some new part of her was exposed. She was dressed up, for her. It felt good, but strange.

She tried to look cool and collected as she calmly walked to the entrance, but as she stepped back to allow the people exiting some room she found herself face-to-face with Charlie.

Well, given Charlie's height, it was more face-to-shoulder. Then she vividly remembered what Charlie's strong shoulder had felt like. "Oh," was all Sugar could find to say.

"Hi." Charlie seemed likewise at a loss for words. "How are you?"

They moved out of the doorway, and Sugar realized the cute, tall blonde standing next to Charlie hadn't moved on. She was with Charlie. Oh, she thought, well of course. Charlie was gorgeous and charming and witty. Of course she had a girlfriend.

"I'm good," she finally managed. "I got your e-mail, but didn't have a chance to answer."

"That's okay." Charlie was smiling and her eyes were doing that bedroom thing, which was simply not appropriate in front of other people. The light brown eyes suddenly darkened, however, as Charlie said, "Oh—you're meeting up with Tree. She's at a table in the back."

"Yes, I am," Sugar agreed coolly.

Charlie abruptly stepped back, putting one hand on the blonde's waist to escort her forward. "Have fun."

"You, too," Sugar murmured, not sure at all if Charlie had heard her.

Well, she fumed, so much for hero worship. She's out with one woman and trying to flirt with another. What kind of cad was she? Had testosterone ways rubbed off on her from all those macho firefighters? Sugar tossed her head and went inside, thoroughly annoyed.

The dark, heady aroma of roasted coffee helped settle her nerves, and by the time she spotted Tree, in the back as Charlie had described, she was completely over the encounter. Charlie could boff a thousand women and it was nothing to her, she thought.

Tree waved and Sugar found it easy to return her welcoming smile. "This was such a good idea."

"Thank you, I thought so too. I did the asking, so what can I get you?" Tree craned her neck to peer at the dessert case. "I've got my eye on that slice of lemon cheesecake."

Sugar looked over. "Oh, the fruit tarts look really nice. I love kiwi and strawberry."

"One fruit tart it is—and to drink?"

"Plain decaf coffee will be perfect." She watched heads turn to follow Tree's progress. She wore a simple pair of cropped pants and a casual sweater of soft hemp that threatened to slip off one shoulder. Though she was no taller than Sugar was, her body was lithe and slender, giving the impression of height. Sugar caught one guy turning from Tree to look speculatively at her, probably wondering what her relationship to the beautiful blonde was.

She gave him her best "Roll your tongue back into your head, she's with me" look. Reality didn't really matter when it came to letting straight boys know two women could actually pass an evening without their intrusion. She was irked when he continued to stare as Tree returned to the table.

"They'll call our number in a few minutes." Tree lightly touched Sugar's shoulder as she passed her. "So—even though I don't want to talk shop, how are you doing? Personally?"

"Good, really. I did have a few nightmares, but I've been sleeping well the past couple of nights. My grandmother and I have worked things out. I saw my sister—"

"The lawyer?"

Sugar was surprised Tree remembered. "Yeah. It's a relief to let her take care of things and think she might actually get paid for once. So, all in all, I'm doing really well." She thought it best not to mention that she was seeing Emily. Somehow she would lead gently into the topic of seeing someone else.

"I'm really glad," Tree said quietly. "Not everyone is so fortunate."

"I know." There was an awkward silence during which Sugar realized she was staring at Tree's shoulder where her sweater was threatening to once again slip off. She didn't think she'd seen anything so sexy in her entire life. "I ran into our friendly neighborhood firefighter on the way in."

"Yes, I knew she was here with Devin."

"I gather—not that either of you have actually said anything—that you have a rocky history of some kind."

Tree shrugged, and her sweater did slip down, revealing an expanse of evenly tanned, bare shoulder. Sugar had to swallow hard. Honestly, her libido seemed to be in overdrive lately. "Charlie can be very stubborn, and persists in seeing accepting help as a weakness."

Sugar could well imagine that. "And you're not?"

"Stubborn? Oh, I am. Very. That's why we usually end up hissing at each other. But she's a good woman, and goddess knows she's seen some awful things in her work."

"I imagine you've seen your share of both the best and worst in people, too."

Tree's dark eyes were even more shadowed. "I have. Burnout is a hazard of the trade. I may go back to private practice for a while. That case—the man who set fire to his girlfriend and her kids?"

Sugar shuddered. "Yes, I remember. That was horrible."

Tree gazed at her nails for a moment. "I was the social worker on the scene. Not that I could do anything for the kids, of course. I had to work far too hard to do my job where he was concerned, and he was a victim of his own actions and other factors in his history, too."

In cases like that, Sugar always found her reaction bloodthirsty. She hoped the bastard was killed in jail, and she hoped it hurt first. He deserved no mercy. She just wasn't that kind and gentle.

Softly, she said, "I can see how that would take a lot out of you."

Tree nodded, then rose as their number was called. She returned in a few moments with desserts and coffees. Sugar had spent the time wondering how old Tree was. Sometimes she seemed in her forties, other times no older than Sugar was. She'd seen a lot of awful things, of that Sugar was certain, but it didn't show in her face.

They chatted about movies and Sugar's business, but Sugar never got the feeling that Tree was relaxing. She'd seemed almost vivacious when Sugar had arrived but the longer they talked, the quieter Tree became.

As she finished her tart she was resigned to the fact that this would be the first and last time they got together. Okay, she was a little hurt when she ought to be relieved. She didn't have enough room in her life for one woman, let alone two. Charlie no longer counted, she told herself.

Tree leaned toward her and said in a low voice, "I'm sorry, I'm being bad company. But I would really like to leave."

Startled, Sugar nodded. "I understand. Thank you for—"

"That's not what I meant. I'll explain outside, if you're ready to go."

"Of course. Is something wrong?"

Tree nodded, but added a reassuring, "Not yet."

As they left Sugar noticed the same guy as before watching Tree. Jerk, she thought. If he'd even glanced at her she'd have given him her best evil eye.

"Thank you," Tree said immediately. "There was someone in there who was trying to figure out where he knew me from."

"Oh—the guy in the orange shirt? He was staring."

Tree fished for her keys. "Yes, well, last time he saw me I had my hair back in a repressive bun and was wearing a plain black suit, testifying in court about my firm belief that he was unfit to see his kids. Sooner or later he was going to remember and the violent streak that I'm quite certain he still has was going to erupt."

"That must be such a scary feeling." Sugar could hardly imagine what it must be like to bump into people who might well blame you for ruining their lives.

"It is." She paused a moment, car keys in her hand. "I've seen his handiwork."

"I'm sorry you had to run into him."

Tree smiled wanly. "I'm sorry our date had to end this way."

"It doesn't have to end," Sugar said. Tree was obviously so

down, and Sugar didn't want to abandon her. Even though it was her job, Tree had been there for her when she'd needed it. She was gentle and sweet, both a good listener and good talker. "We could walk through the shops."

"Or we could—" Tree looked as if she wanted to call back the words.

"We could what?" Sugar didn't think Tree was about to proposition her, so she was surprised at Tree's next words.

"Go back to my place." Tree grinned. "I realized how that would sound. I was actually thinking that a soak in the hot tub sounded good. We'll likely be chaperoned by somebody or other—it's the communal one at my apartment complex I'm offering."

In spite of the grin, Sugar could sense that Tree needed to talk. She must listen all day to other people's problems. Sugar wondered if there was anyone who listened to hers. "That actually sounds good, but I don't have a swimsuit."

"I've got a couple of spares. One will fit. Why don't you follow me?"

Sugar agreed and a few minutes later followed Tree's taillights out of Redmond toward Bellevue. A relaxing soak in very hot water was sounding better and better.

Tree's apartment was lightly scented with sandalwood, and hardwood floors were covered in woven rugs of brilliant, jungle hues. The dominant living room wall was a rich blue with white tangled lines that she realized were the branches of trees. It was spacious and airy for an apartment and clearly had two bedrooms, one being used as an office.

Tree returned from the other bedroom with a red swimsuit in hand. "This should fit. Would you like a glass of wine or iced tea to take down with you?"

"The tea sounds great, actually. Wine and hot tubs always makes me dizzy, not that I've a history of hot-tubbing."

"I've found that if drunk slowly, a glass of red wine is really therapeutic."

"I'll stick to chocolate." Sugar grinned, but Tree responded seriously.

"That's a sound choice. Dark chocolate has flavonoids. It's heart-healthy, too. It just doesn't work well in a hot tub."

"No, that would be quite a mess," Sugar agreed as she went into the bathroom. As she changed into her swimsuit she recalled Julia Child, her childhood cooking idol, once commenting that food should first be regarded as pleasure, not medicine. She didn't stop, usually, to consider what any given dish contained. Moderation and keeping a general eye on the food pyramid was as much as she worried, usually.

She looked at her butt in the bathroom mirror and sighed. A swimsuit wasn't very flattering at the moment. It wasn't food that had put on those few extra pounds; it was total lack of activity. She'd gone from being on her feet ten hours a day, six days a week, to sitting on her butt. It showed.

She wrapped the towel Tree had left around her waist and found that Tree had changed as well. She wore a black one-piece suit that made her skin all the more pale. Her long, silky hair was twisted on top of her head and held in place by what looked like a pair of chopsticks. Sugar could have tried for days and had help, yet never achieved anything so casually elegant.

The night was growing chilly, so they quickly padded down the stairs to the end of the complex. No one else was in the steaming water, and they slipped in with happy sighs.

"That feels wonderful," Sugar breathed.

"Blessings of the goddess, without a doubt." Tree closed her eyes as she submerged herself up to her neck.

The warmth soaked into Sugar's bones. It felt lazy and was most welcome for that. She did sit on her butt far too much, but her work was still intense and draining. The bird's nest had been an experiment, and the first three attempts had failed. She'd finished shaping and decorating one of the faux eggs then promptly knocked it off the table with her sleeve. The final effect she had very much liked, and her Seattle Eats competition cake would include something similar. She had to get serious about making her shopping list and planning out the baking schedule. Sunday, she thought. She'd have to shop on Saturday to get a good start on

Sunday. She would make this event a success. It would be something to show her sisters, for once.

You're not doing it for them, she reminded herself. Meeting with Patty was always stressful, but today's encounter had gone better than most. Maybe she *had* changed, a little bit. Her home had burned down and yet her life hadn't gone up in flames. Maybe, she mused, she had a better set of priorities. Being safe mattered more than scoring points off any of her sisters. Keeping her dreams alive was far more important than Patty's opinion of her. Feeling natural, sweet, easy human affection and love in its many forms was worth more to her on the inside than any possession.

Tree didn't seem to want to talk, which was okay with Sugar. She was glad to see color in Tree's face again, likely from the heat. Even in repose, Tree was again smiling slightly, as if she and the universe shared an amusing secret. This was the woman who had walked calmly past fire hoses and disaster a week ago, and even without saying, "It's all going to be okay," she had made Sugar feel that it would be. For a relatively small woman, something about her was large.

It was probably ten minutes before Tree stirred. "I think I'm going to live," she said softly. "I had a rotten day. Sorry to take it out on you."

"If this is how you take it out on me, I'm not complaining." Sugar swished her feet in the water. "I am starting to feel parboiled, though."

"Let's sit up for a bit."

"Good idea." The cold air felt bracing and Sugar sipped the herbal raspberry tea Tree had poured for her. "Is Tree really from Gantry? I was noticing the painted wall in your apartment."

"That's a sacred white oak. My Wiccan name is Tree."

"I don't know very much about Wicca, although my ex had an ex who practiced it as well." Noor had said, among other things, that the sex had been sporadic but mind-blowing.

"It's more than a practice," Tree said quietly. "It's a way of life. Gentler, less judgmental, and hurts no one. It's a spiritual belief that doesn't necessarily conflict with other religions. It gives me great renewal." She sipped from her glass of wine.

"Is it ceremonial? I mean, like with services and so forth?" Sugar really didn't know how to ask without being offensive. She knew, of course, that Wicca was routinely equated—wrongly—with Satanworship. She didn't want Tree to think she felt that way.

"It can be. Some people get caught up with doing everything properly. Wiccans aren't the only ones who fall prey to that, though." She smiled. "I have a friend who can't start her day without observing various steps. If she misses one she feels she has a bad day as a result. Still, since she nearly always gets it right, that means she feels she nearly always has a good day."

"I worked with a guy who couldn't start his workday without making a perfect sunny-side-up egg. Egg didn't turn out, the rest of the day was rocky." She shrugged. "Whatever works."

"Exactly."

Two men arrived, talking boisterously about a Mariners game they had just finished watching. Tree scooted closer to Sugar and they soaked in quiet for a little longer. When a couple with obvious romantic intentions arrived, Tree shinnied up to the edge and they shared a nod of agreement. They'd had their peaceful minutes; now it was time to go.

Tree invited her to use the shower to rinse if she liked, and Sugar took her up on the offer. She redressed in her clothes, feeling like a very relaxed million bucks. Tree had changed into a short robe and was curled up in one corner of the soft, inviting sofa.

Sugar carried her tea over and joined her. Sinking into the cushions, she said, "You must fall asleep here all the time."

"I do," Tree admitted. "Tonight isn't exactly going as I had planned, but I hope it wasn't a washout for you."

Sugar turned her head to regard Tree seriously. "I had no expectations beyond talk."

"Neither had I. But I'd forgotten how—when you arrived tonight I did briefly consider other things. You're so alive and I was feeling a bit down. This will sound fanciful, but I thought if I could somehow get you to hold me I'd feel a great deal better."

Sugar regarded Tree for a few seconds, then said, quite honestly, "That's perfectly okay with me." Tree was without a doubt one of the sexiest women she'd ever met, but she wasn't feeling any sexual heat for her at all, which was a bit of a relief. There was nothing wrong with a prolonged hug and cuddle. Weren't those basic human needs?

Tree hesitantly slid across the sofa toward Sugar. "Are you sure? I don't know what's wrong with me tonight."

Tree settled into the crook of Sugar's arms feeling more like a feather than a body. "This is wrong? It feels pretty good to me."

"I'm not usually so needy."

"But there's nothing wrong with it when you are. Everybody has their days."

"I missed Crystal tonight, though it's been months since she left."

"Your ex?"

"She wanted a different space. Seattle didn't feel right to her any longer."

Tree spoke sadly and Sugar felt a pang of pity, though she was confused. If Tree wasn't over Crystal, then why the interest in her? Why the phone calls? "That must have been a difficult decision to reach."

"Oh, that twenty-something sex maniac she left with I'm sure softened the blow." Before Sugar could react, Tree added, "Sorry, that was spiteful. There's no point to being angry. She was just doing what she felt was right for her at the time."

"But she hurt you in the process. Doesn't that matter?"

"If I was hurt, it was that my own expectations were unrealistic."

Sugar frowned. "How so?"

"Crystal made me no promises. That I presumed promises were made anyway was my error."

"How long were you together?"

"Eleven years."

Sugar blinked. "Well, I think I'd be just a little bit pissed if I got left after all that time with no more than 'it doesn't feel right' as an explanation. Especially if there was someone else in the picture."

"It's wasted energy, being angry about what I can't change." Tree sighed and Sugar felt like she'd disappointed Tree by needing to have that explained to her.

"But anger is one of the great forces of change, isn't it? I got angry at being treated like a slave and paid less than the men with less experience than I had. But there were a dozen women who would have gladly taken my job on those terms, so it wasn't like I could change the boss. So I started my own business. I think it was the right thing for me to do. But I'd still be slaving my life away for that pig if I hadn't gotten angry about it."

Tree sat up. "But what would change if I got angry about Crystal? She won't come back."

"You'd feel less like a victim." The words were out before Sugar thought better of them.

To her complete surprise, instead of being upset, Tree laughed. "Oh, perfect! You get a junior therapist merit badge for that. Dear heaven, I *am* being self-indulgent tonight."

Sugar didn't quite know what to say, and wasn't all that sure she'd said anything brilliant, but was happy enough when Tree snuggled cheerfully back into her arms. It was a very comfortable, warm feeling. Sweet, definitely sensual, but not sexual. Tree smelled faintly of chlorine and oranges, a combination that made Sugar think of summer. She closed her eyes and took a deep breath, remembering Emily's comment from last Saturday. Yes, there were times when she was happy enough with the world that if she died right then she'd have no real regrets. This easy, safe contentment wasn't quite as perfect as all that, but it was close.

For the second time in a week, she woke with a crick in her neck. Tree's head rested on Sugar's stomach and the warmth of her body woke a primal urge inside her. It was the darnedest thing, then, that she thought of Charlie and the heat she'd felt standing on Gran's patio in front of the fuse box.

131

You're cuddled on a couch with an incredibly beautiful, warm, insightful, loving woman, and you're thinking about someone else, she scolded herself. Even if you're not going to bed with Tree— and she wasn't—you could at least not be fantasizing about someone else.

Was she fantasizing about Charlie? Why? Emily was dynamic, witty, charming and hotter than Tabasco. She was interested in Sugar's life, her dreams, her plans. Charlie was likely only interested in one thing. She was a big flirt. It was just . . . heat. Big deal. She had plenty of heat with Emily. And, at the moment, plenty of warmth with Tree.

The digital clock said it was now after eleven. She shifted slightly, not meaning to wake Tree yet, but Tree startled awake with a little gasp.

They stared at each other in the low light. Sugar tried to think of something light and amusing to say but before she could, Tree moved upward, and her hand came around the back of Sugar's head.

Uh-oh was the only thought Sugar was conscious of, then Tree's lips met hers and they kissed. Goodness, Tree had a wonderful body, firm and female. It wasn't at all unpleasant to kiss her. But after the high she'd gotten from kissing Emily, it was simply not the same.

Tree broke the kiss after a few moments, then settled into Sugar's arms with a sigh. "I had thought—" She paused to clear her throat. "I had thought we might walk the goddess way, but I don't think it's in the fates for us."

"I'd very much like to be friends, though," Sugar said softly.

Tree slowly sat up. "Sorry, I didn't mean to be quite so mystical about it. I find it very comforting and calming to be with you. But . . ."

"But there's no real spark."

Tree laughed quietly. "Exactly. And I'm realizing that I've still got some wounds to heal before I could consider sharing myself with someone again."

Relieved, Sugar gently disentangled her legs from around Tree. "Not to sleep and run, but I think I should head for home. Why don't we plan on a movie or something?"

"We'll call it respite, not a date. Yes, I'd look forward to that." Tree walked with Sugar to the apartment door. "Thank you."

"For what?"

"For . . . not pretending you felt something that you didn't. For not taking advantage of me, because I think if you had we'd still be over there on the couch. I'm not over Crystal, and I think I'd convinced myself if I went to bed with someone it might help in the process of grieving. But that was hardly fair to you."

"I'm not sure it would work, either."

For just a moment, Tree grinned at her flirtatiously. "Oh, given how gorgeous you are I think it would have worked—for a while, anyway."

Sugar wrinkled her nose. *Gorgeous?* "I'm glad we didn't complicate things."

They kissed one more time at the door, but it was a friendly smooch. Driving home she couldn't help but compare how she felt now to how she had felt leaving Emily's. Holding Tree had been peaceful, as if her heart had been soothed and nourished by their contact. Yet there was no way they'd ever be lovers. So why was she sad about that when Emily offered such passion?

The moon had grown from crescent to half. Not grown, she told herself. The moon was always the same. What changed was light and perspective. Tomorrow she'd be with Emily again. If the power stayed on and they stayed out of bed long enough, light and perspective would erase the nameless confusion she felt.

Chapter 7

Sugar sipped her frothy café mocha and flicked through her e-mail. Even though the expense wasn't welcome, her time at the Internet café was. She had already typed up her shopping list for the competition cake she was planning, and within a few minutes she'd leave for her date with Emily.

She'd packed an overnight bag, which all by itself had felt odd. The first time she'd spent the night with Noor she hadn't expected it. Other trysts had been equally unplanned. She'd been sexually active for seventeen years and today was the first time she'd explicitly prepared for a night of—she hoped—abandoned intimacy during a date. She'd even included her sexiest pajamas, although her desire was of course not to need them. Her only regret was not having had the time to get her hair cut. The purple scrunchie was only capable of so much.

Dinner, she reminded herself. You're having dinner first. Conversation, getting to know each other more. Her palms were slightly damp and her body was starting to feel heavy and swollen. She wanted to skip dinner and proceed directly to a dessert of Emily and Sugar flambé.

The early afternoon drizzle had blown through and the day turned into a promise of summer right around the corner. She drove into the setting sun to get to Mercer Island, her windows down and the radio tuned to classical. Emily was sure to be dressed in her apparently habitual feminine elegance, so Sugar had chosen soft linen slacks and a button-down blouse of peach silk, another of Noor's long-ago choices. She'd even spent time with eyebrow tweezers, a razor and moisturizers.

Not being distracted by rain and the safety of a cake, Sugar noticed more about the island and the homes as she drove. Even with a television producer's salary, Sugar doubted Emily could afford to live on her part of the island without money from some other source. She had said she'd inherited that suit of armor in the hallway. She had a poise that spoke of a very different upbringing than Sugar's. She wasn't draped in conspicuously expensive jewelry, and her home didn't sport the latest in electronic baubles. Still, she didn't know what Emily's hobbies were, or if she lived her work the way Sugar did.

She wished Emily had called after Saturday night. She was feeling stupid that she had not called Emily either. It wasn't embarrassment as much as not being at all sure what the right thing to say was. Neither of them had meant to end up the way they had, but it had been deliciously wonderful. Their dinner was no longer a business meeting, it was a date with a definite yes already in place for further intimacy. Business and pleasure were mixing so very well.

She followed the driveway to the back of the house again, but then didn't know if she should get out of the car with her overnight bag. Wouldn't that be presumptuous? Overeager? What if Emily had changed her mind?

She decided at the last minute to leave the bag. She could come back for it. Maybe they'd stroll down to the lake after dinner and on the way back she'd casually mention that she had it. Yes, that would be better.

She got out of the car and realized that Emily had opened the back door and was watching her.

Breathe, she told herself. *Breathe.*

Emily lounged against the doorjamb, apparently enjoying Sugar's blushing approach. She wore a white ruffled apron and nothing else. Sugar felt her body grow even heavier with desire. Wanting Emily's touch and craving the sensation of Emily's response to her hit her like a fabulous drug. Raw want ran up her spine, down her legs, swirled in her breasts, and her skin felt as if it tightened on her bones.

"I suppose I don't need to ask what's for dinner." Sugar hoped she sounded somehow in control. The sight of the exposed outsides of Emily's breasts and hips made her mouth go dry.

"Dinner is paella."

Sugar slid her arms around Emily's waist. Her heart was hammering against her ribs. She felt positively primal as her hands swooped down to caress Emily's firm, inviting ass. Emily melted into her embrace with an unmistakable shudder. "I hope it can wait a while."

"It's warming in the oven. We have appetizers first." Emily seemed to be having as much trouble breathing as Sugar was.

"Like this?" Sugar found Emily's mouth and they moaned together into a long, deep wet kiss. Her hips ground into Emily's and Emily responded by coiling one leg around Sugar's.

Used to mutual, slower dances, Sugar wasn't prepared for the wave of erotic power she felt as Emily arched against her. Emily's back was pressed into the doorjamb and a pull on the tie at her neck revealed her soft, round breasts. Sugar ran her fingertips lightly over one nipple as they kissed and reveled in the panting "Yes" that Emily whispered into their kiss.

They rocked together in the open doorway. Not at all sure where she got the confidence to try such a thing, Sugar pulled both of Emily's legs around her, supporting Emily's body on her thigh.

They moved slightly and were against the wall next to the door now, Emily moaning feverishly as Sugar thrust her hand between Emily's exposed wetness and Sugar's thigh.

"Please, yes, right now." Emily moaned. "I've been crazy all day, I couldn't think, I wanted this so much—yes, oh, like that."

"Like that," Sugar echoed, as her fingers slid into the hot, wild welcome of tight muscles coated in slippery, copious wetness.

Calmed by the depth of their contact, Sugar pulled her head back to make sure Emily was okay with how deep, hard and fast they were going. Emily's eyes were closed, her teeth bared. With an almost feral groan, she said, "Oh, don't stop now."

"Like this?" Sugar withdrew her fingers, then surged in again, this time her hips behind her hand. "Is this what you want?"

"Yes, baby, don't stop!"

Their pace grew frantic. Sugar had never felt so much in control of what was happening. She could feel every pulse of Emily's body through her fingertips, and Emily's wild cries were intoxicating. She could feel Emily's body coiling for release, and wished they could stay just as they were for a little longer. It was so unbelievably arousing to realize she was responsible for Emily's abandon and the reason Emily's cries of passion were edged with tears.

She smothered Emily's scream with a kiss and held on tight while Emily shook against her. Her thigh was wet and for a moment they were suspended in perfect balance, chests heaving in rhythm. Then Emily's legs slipped back to the floor and she gasped as her knees threatened to buckle.

"Over here," Sugar said, laughing from the high of Emily's climax. She pushed Emily onto the nearest counter, then wrapped both arms around her, pulling Emily's head to her shoulder. "Here, I've got you."

"That was amazing."

"You're amazing. That was some greeting."

"I couldn't decide what to wear." Emily laughed softly into Sugar's ear. "I knew whatever it was I hoped not to wear it for very long."

"You had an unfair advantage." Sugar lightly ran her fingers up and down Emily's naked back. "I didn't exactly want to wear anything myself, but I had to drive."

"Poor thing," Emily murmured. "How can I make it up to you?"

"Will dinner really keep a while?"

Emily grinned. "Yes."

"Let's go to bed, then." Feeling like an acolyte of Venus, Sugar added in what she hoped was a sultry, alluring voice, "Take me to bed."

Emily's mouth opened slightly as she took a deep breath. Her incredible blue eyes seemed to darken and then she was kissing Sugar again, with heat and abandon. Emily's fingers were at the buttons of Sugar's blouse. "All the way to the bedroom? It's a five-minute walk."

"I plan to stay there a while." She pulled Emily to the edge of the counter, her hips moving suggestively between Emily's legs. "I want to do what we just did, all over again."

"I'm not sure I can walk," Emily admitted. "It's been a long time since I . . . responded like that to anybody."

"I'm not sure I ever have, but I liked it." Sugar grinned at Emily, then realized Emily was blushing. It was adorable.

"I can't believe I met you at the door naked."

"You weren't naked." Sugar pulled on the askew apron still clinging to Emily's waist.

"Nearly. On Saturday we were both a little overwhelmed and I wasn't sure if you'd still want to be with me again, and the more I thought about it, the more I realized . . ."

"What?" Sugar nudged Emily slightly, thoroughly enjoying being the one with the poise for a few minutes.

"That I wanted you to walk in the door and fuck the daylights out of me." Emily hid her face in Sugar's neck with a sigh.

"And did I?"

"Yep." Emily sighed again. "My other admission is that I'm

138

starving. I was so keyed up I didn't eat most of the day. If I'm going to do to you all the things I want to, then I have to eat something."

Sugar laughed, even though part of her was disappointed that she'd have to wait for the release her body was clamoring for. "Okay, we'll have dinner."

Emily pushed Sugar away. "That doesn't mean I don't want a snack of you first."

Sugar felt as if the breath had been knocked out of her by the look of hot desire in Emily's eyes. Emily slid down off the counter like a cat, her fingers busy at Sugar's waistband. Sugar felt the kitchen island at the small of her back and her legs shook as Emily pushed her slacks down.

"Oh . . ." Emily's hands caressed Sugar's hips as she draped herself over Sugar's body. Skin met skin as Emily sensuously slid to her knees in front of Sugar. "I've been thinking about this all day."

The sensation of Emily's tongue slipping through Sugar's soaked folds drew a hoarse cry from Sugar. She wanted to spread her legs open more, but her slacks were in the way. With an eager, throaty groan, Emily pressed her face between Sugar's legs, and Sugar cried out again as she felt Emily's tongue, her lips, her teeth, capturing, holding and stroking everything she could reach.

It was more than enough. Sugar's legs were shaking as she arched against Emily's hungry mouth. She'd never been this abandoned with anybody before. Sex finally made sense—it was about this unbearable tightness that ached to explode. About the sharp stab of fear that if she exploded she'd never find herself again, and the undeniable pleasure that pushed her past the fear. For a brief moment Sugar could not remember where she was, and that scared her, too. She was being moved, pushed back so she could lie back. She heard clatters but didn't care. Her slacks were no longer in the way and her legs were being pushed apart. And then Emily's mouth came back, and Emily was inside her, too. Everything was yellow and flashing purple behind her eyelids, then her body finally found a shattering release.

Laughing, they picked up the scattered fruit and bowls that had fallen to the floor when Emily had pushed her up onto the kitchen island. Tidying up ended with long, dancing, straining kisses and Emily the one on the counter while Sugar—with a laughing leer— "snacked."

They ate dinner, though Sugar couldn't tell if it was paella or poi, and she didn't care either. Her body felt unreal. She'd never come like that in her life, and apparently she was entering a greedy phase because she wanted more. It also seemed that the bedroom was not required for her libido, because she found more of the same ecstasy spread out on the stairs, with Emily stretched out on top of her.

They found the bed, eventually, and the soft, crisp linens seemed to cool them a bit. They grew languid and sensual with touches meant to tease. Sugar pulled Emily to her, reflecting that she felt every sexual desire with Emily that had been so absent with Tree.

"We haven't discussed a bit of business," Emily said with a laugh. Her fingertips smoothed along Sugar's shoulder blades as Sugar collapsed limply onto the pillows again. "I'm starting to think if we don't between fucks we never will."

Sugar giggled. "I know what you mean." Her body was getting closer to satisfaction, but every time it seemed like they were both replete, something would set them off again. Emily's fingertips were like magic. "What do we need to discuss?"

"A million things." Emily rose to her knees, giving Sugar a wonderful view of the pleasures she abruptly realized she'd love to taste again. "Because we're filming the competition I've had reason to talk to all the judges and the organizers in the last week. And I have to admit I wasn't above creating a little bit of buzz for the unknown culinary artist who created Cake Dreams. I'm not sure that you'll win, but I can guarantee you'll be seriously considered."

"Wow." Sugar didn't quite know how to respond. She wanted to win the prize based on her talent, but she also knew how such events worked. Only those who were thought to be "in the running" before the competition even began would get serious notice. Based on that reality she had almost not entered. She needed some big names on her client list to be noticed. "Thank you. You really didn't have to do that."

Emily leaned forward and her loose, silky red hair swept over Sugar's back. "I know. As soon as I said you were one of the stories we'd follow with cameras it was pretty much assured you'd be a finalist. You deserve to be. Your work is amazing, easily equal to the established names. I have to admit it kills two birds with one stone. By us creating buzz for you, they're going to work a little harder, making for a better competition and a better story."

Sugar hadn't thought of that. Really, she was just a baker at heart. Machinations on Emily's level weren't beyond her, they were just of little interest to her. "I promise to do my absolute best. Do you know if the guidelines we got are strictly adhered to?" Emily's hair was teasing the backs of her thighs now and she wanted to melt.

"How do you mean?"

"Well, they said that the finished entry had to feed no more than forty."

"They're dead serious about that. Magnitude won't win it. They're looking for a realistic event dessert of high quality, not an eleven-tier monstrosity. What were you thinking of doing?"

Sugar rolled over and caught Emily's hair in her hands. Emily's mouth parted as Sugar pulled her gently down for a kiss. Sugar swore she could see sparks flickering in the air between them as hands slipped between thighs.

It was several minutes before Sugar answered Emily's question. "I was thinking of the base being a vintage placemat, five squares down and eight across, plainly serving forty. Each square would be a different Seattle landmark decorated flat, so hand drawn. I've got a photo of a placemat I want to copy."

"Okay." Emily sounded skeptical. "So it would be retro Sixties?"

"Yes, red borders with black lines. The landmark drawings would be very intricate, like the main façade at Pike's Market. I'd only have to do about twenty of them because of what's sitting on the placemat, waiting to be consumed."

"Oh, that's starting to get interesting. So what is it?"

"Since the big coffee outfit is a sponsor, I thought I'd use their corporate colors to create a cup and saucer—"

"Oh, good, that's brilliant."

"And it would appear to contain a signature cappuccino of theirs. It would be accompanied by a large slice of luscious-looking cake—the scale is about three times normal. So cutlery next to the plates, a napkin with full texture of course, and how could I resist a sugar packet on the saucer decorated with my own corporate logo?"

"Oh, that would be . . . I mean it sounds like exactly something they would order themselves for a high-level corporate party. It's imaginative, detailed, very Seattle with the landmarks." Emily pushed up to one elbow to gaze into Sugar's eyes. "And it kisses up without being explicitly kiss-up."

"I don't think of it as kissing up so much as if they ordered a cake from me, that's what I'd give them."

"Wow." Emily leaned over to kiss her. "When are you going to start work on it?"

"Shopping tomorrow. Boiling up fondant on Saturday. Baking layers will happen on Sunday, but I also have a cake to make for a client due Monday—for the firefighter, Charlie."

"Oh?"

Sugar quickly explained the scene with her landlord and Charlie's intervention. Picturing Charlie's long, tall body and laughing eyes was not the reason she arched under Emily's hand. "So it's a thank-you. I'll have all day Tuesday and Wednesday to sculpt and work on the fondant decorations."

"Mmm," Emily murmured. "Some thank-you. Oh, look at that." Her mouth captured Sugar's hardening nipple.

Sugar closed her eyes, fighting a sudden confusion. She and

Emily were having a fabulous time. Business and pleasure had never mixed so well. They'd make a great team, with Emily's acumen and Sugar's talent. Emily had a reputation for spotting unknowns. Had she bedded any of them along the way? The thought was unworthy because it was none of her business, really. Emily's teeth grazing her stomach was what mattered.

With a sound of disbelief she arched again to Emily's mouth. She wanted more, again, and Emily showed no signs of being the least bit tired. Would Emily want her if she weren't a project needing her help? Then she remembered Emily meeting her at the doorway, and the hard, quick passionate encounter with the door still open, everything forgotten except how much she wanted Sugar. Emily did want her, and had since they'd danced at that club, grinding pelvises in what had then been uncharacteristic abandon for Sugar.

They were grinding together now, Emily's voice urging Sugar on. Legs shivering, her body trembling, Sugar yielded to the pleasure of Emily's tongue dancing over her aching flesh. Emily's fingers found, with increasing expertise, the right places to stroke. It felt so good that Sugar was surprised to experience that earlier flash of fear all over again. She was going to explode and she wasn't sure she'd survive. It was a ridiculous fear, she'd survived the first time, she told herself. *Don't think, feel.*

Emily's coo of response as Sugar rose to meet her thrusting fingers pushed Sugar over the edge. Her legs gave out and Emily melted next to her with a sighing laugh.

Sugar knew Emily was saying something but abruptly there was nothing in the world that could make her open her eyes. Emily's voice got farther and farther away.

The next thing Sugar was aware of was a harsh blaring noise that suddenly ceased, then Emily's voice saying, "God, I don't want to go to work today."

Shaking herself from sleep proved difficult. "I wish you didn't either, because I can think of things I'd like to do more of. That is, after I visit the potty and brush my teeth."

Emily's chuckle sounded drowsy. "I know what you mean. But I've got an early meeting with the station manager. This week has been hellacious, and next week will be even more so."

They did agree it would save time to shower together, and after a delightful, heart-pounding fifteen minutes, they emerged clean, and even more wobbly-legged. Wearing Emily's robe she dashed outside for her overnight bag and got dressed in the downstairs bathroom.

Sugar quickly made them an omelet with spinach and mushrooms while Emily produced delectable fully caffeinated coffee. She chattered about the shooting schedule for the contest and asked numerous questions about when Sugar would do what and if her grandmother's kitchen would work as a studio. "I'll have to come and see it, won't I, but I really don't think I can do that until Sunday at least."

Sugar nodded as she gobbled up her share of the breakfast. She felt absolutely hollow. "That'll give me time to make sure my grandmother is okay with all of this. It's more than she agreed to."

Emily's eyebrows rose as if to say Sugar's grandmother's reactions were the least of her concerns. "I'm sure she'd be happy to put up with a little inconvenience. We'll have her in a shot or two, if she'd like that."

Sugar wasn't sure Gran would. Frowning, she said, "I think she'll be okay with it, but she's a busy woman herself and it will be inconvenient."

"We'll make it worth her while somehow," Emily said blithely.

Sugar supposed Emily would not be as successful as she was if she didn't presume all difficulties could be resolved one way or another.

Emily reached for her hand. "Last night was incredible, Sugar. Absolutely amazing. It's been a really long time since I have felt like that with anybody."

Sugar blushed. "Me, too."

"I'm free Saturday night if you'd like to . . . stay over again?"

"I'd love to."

"You know," Emily said, her eyes growing even brighter, "maybe we could film your segments here? We've filmed here before. Then you'd be out of your grandmother's way."

"That could work," Sugar agreed. "Though if I'm here I'm not going to get much work done."

"When it comes to business, I can keep my hands off you," Emily assured her.

"Like last night?" Sugar grinned as Emily flushed.

"There was no reason to leave you alone last night."

"I'm teasing," Sugar said. She dropped a kiss on Emily's forehead as she carried her dishes to the sink. "Should we take care of these before you leave?"

"No, someone comes in on Fridays, and we can leave them." Emily sighed. "I really have to go or I'll be late."

Sugar picked up her overnight bag. "Saturday night will be nice if we can spend some time together in the morning before I start baking again." Even though they'd managed to talk about their lives somewhat, most of their time together had again been spent making love.

"I promise," Emily said. They went out the back door together, shared another heated, desirous kiss at Sugar's car and parted company with wistful backward glances.

Her shopping list for the coming weeks' extensive baking still on the passenger seat, Sugar decided to detour to the restaurant-supply outlet before heading home. By the time she walked in the door at Gran's, laden with a box of dyes, baking sheets and pans, she could smell the first of Gran's baking day well in progress, but there was no sign of her grandmother.

"Gran?"

"In my bedroom, dear. I think you must be in the knick of time."

Sugar found her grandmother sitting on the little vanity chair in front of the bathroom mirror. She was unusually pale and her hands were shaking. "Are you okay?"

"Well, I think so, but I am having an extra hard time today getting to my feet. It's quite upsetting."

"Let me help, then."

"Yes, please." Leaning heavily on Sugar, her grandmother slowly stood. "I hadn't realized how much I'd already gotten used to your being my legs. Baking this morning seemed to take me forever, and when I got back here I didn't know if I could get up again."

"I hope there's a surgical opening soon, Gran. I really do." Visions of walking into the house to find her that her grandmother had fallen and badly hurt herself danced through Sugar's head.

"Yes, yes, you're right." They made their way slowly to the kitchen. "I shouldn't have been so stubborn about using that walker. I was going to get it this morning but I didn't think I'd manage the steps in the garage."

"Let me get it," Sugar offered. In just the week since she'd arrived, it was obvious Gran's condition had worsened significantly. She'd had no business lollygagging on the way home, dithering over tints and baking molds. "I'll just put it next to the table."

Gran looked less pale when Sugar returned, and Sugar felt a pang for the older woman's fearful morning. How long had she been sitting there, Sugar wondered, afraid to try to get up? Thank goodness there hadn't been anything in the oven. Gran might have tried to get up if she'd heard a timer. Sugar realized she might have to postpone more overnight stays at Emily's, or simply plan on getting home much, much earlier.

"So how was your evening, Sugar?" Gran looked up from peeling peaches.

Sugar knew she was blushing. "Fun. We had paella for dinner."

Gran grinned at her, suddenly looking years younger. "Oh, isn't your face a picture!"

"What?" Sugar knew she was utterly failing to look innocent.

"I remember the morning after I married your grandfather. We were too poor to go away anywhere, so we were at home in the first place we lived, out in North Bend." Her voice softened. "Vernon was out trying to coax life into the car, which had barely gotten us home from the church, and my mother stopped by. She asked me that same question about my evening and I do believe I must have had the same look on my face as you do right now, because I'd had quite a fun evening myself."

"Gran!" Sugar knew she was now a bright, hot red. Her grandmother was talking about *sex*.

"The good Lord gave us our bodies, child, and there's nothing wrong with wedded bliss. Your grandfather and I had that, and we had all the easy times, too, when just laughing about something together was nearly as good as more intimate things. He always said I was too worried about other people's goings-on." She sighed. "When Jesus spoke to me on Easter, I thought that Vernon must have asked Him to help me."

Sugar set out her purchases as she considered how best to organize them in Gran's pantry. "I would like to find someone who was as good for me as Grandpa was for you."

"Your date last night isn't?"

Sugar paused, realizing she wasn't sure of the answer. The sex had been fantastic, addictive. Their career interests overlapped, certainly, and they laughed together. "I'm not sure yet. We've not spent a lot of time getting to know each other aside from work." She blushed again because she'd nearly said, "aside from bed."

Gran laughed in such a way that Sugar was certain she'd known exactly what Sugar had meant. "Give it time then. I rather thought that Charlie girl was sweet on you."

"Maybe so, but I think she likes being single. Has no plans to settle down." Sugar recalled Charlie saying she hadn't liked living with someone.

"A pity. I've used all the sugar—could you get another bag, dear?"

"I bought more this morning. I've a lot to do in the next week. Oh, that reminds me, I need to talk to you about some of the plans." Sugar was about to launch into the gory details of Emily's ambitious shooting schedule when Gran's phone rang.

The slightly officious voice on the other end of the line asked for her grandmother. Thinking it was a marketing call, Sugar said, "This is her granddaughter. Can I help you?"

"I'm calling to inform you that we have a surgical cancellation, opening up an early date for the surgery she discussed with the specialist on Monday."

"Oh, that's wonderful news!" Sugar was vastly relieved and gave her grandmother a big thumbs-up gesture. "When?"

"She'll need to report here at seven a.m. Tuesday for presurgical evaluation and instruction by physical therapists in postoperative exercises. If the tests come back favorably, the surgery will commence around two."

"Oh." Tuesday. A thousand things went through Sugar's mind. Emily's generosity, the filming schedule, the buzz that would get her entry taken seriously. She thought of her hopes for her business, the sudden boom that would result from both participating in the competition and the subsequent coverage aired on local television. But she could not get past the frightened, pale look on her grandmother's face this morning. There was no guarantee that another opening would happen as quickly, and it seemed to Sugar that there was a very real danger that her grandmother might fall and then the surgery would have to be performed under vastly more hazardous circumstances. Maybe, she thought desperately, someone else could actually spend the time with her at the hospital. But, she countered with a sinking heart, who would take on Gran's baking schedule? That promise had been the one that had swayed Gran into accepting the surgery as inevitable.

"If that date is inconvenient in some way, I will contact the next person on the waiting list."

It was the guarded hope in Gran's face that decided Sugar. "No, she'll be there."

"Excellent. It is absolutely essential that she stop taking any aspirin today. She shouldn't eat anything after six a.m. on Tuesday, and no water after ten a.m. You should contact her primary care physician immediately to verify if any prescriptions are required now, as there may be something she should take before surgery."

"I'll do that," Sugar said numbly. She hung up the phone after jotting down a few notes, then turned to face her grandmother. Somehow she found a bright cheerful tone. "Surgery is now scheduled for Tuesday."

Gran paled and put her hand on her heart. "That soon? Dear Lord. Oh, there's so much to do."

"Yes, there is," Sugar said. A million things to do, and the more she thought about it the more Sugar knew she could not finish her contest entry at anything like the level of detail she had planned. The distraction of Charlie's cake was bad enough. A night out with Emily had strained her planned timing even further. But now she faced an afternoon of phone calls, arranging for the rental of a hospital bed for when Gran came home, lists and, most importantly, keeping Gran calm and confident that everything would be fine. Thank goodness she'd not yet told Gran much about the contest, because Gran would likely insist that she wait. But Sugar did not want to come home to find her grandmother alone and frightened again. "We'll make lots of lists and check them twice."

As they sorted through various complications and issues, Sugar resolved that she would have to withdraw from the contest. Maybe Quinn or Patricia could take the time to see Gran through the day of surgery, even visit the following day when Sugar was trying to assemble hundreds of pieces of fondant into a coherent design. But neither of them could do Gran's baking, plus all the things they needed to see to before Tuesday morning arrived. It was beyond what they could be asked to do.

She was the one who had made a pact with Gran about seeing her through this. She was the one who had made Gran see the specialist. Seattle Eats and all its possible free publicity would be there next year. Next year she'd make sure she had a full week with no distractions at all. Of course, she'd planned that this year, but fate had firmly taken a hand with a fire, and now this.

She slipped away halfway through the morning and called Emily. She knew Emily was busy and wasn't surprised to get her voicemail. With the door to her bedroom closed, she said quietly, "I've had a change in plans that I'll explain later. My grandmother's surgery has been moved up and I won't be able to complete my entry for the competition. I wanted to let you know right away. I'm so sorry, you went to a lot of bother. Maybe we can talk tonight? Or when we get together tomorrow night? I'm really sorry about all of this, but there's nothing I can do."

She went back to making lists with Gran.

Emily didn't call until almost nine. "I couldn't believe it when I got your message. Tell me everything."

Sugar explained about the surgery and what it meant for Gran. She closed her bedroom door as she was speaking and added, "I can't tell you how scared she was this morning when I got home. I felt so guilty."

"Can you hire someone to take care of her? This contest is so important to your future. I think you've got a huge shot at winning."

Ruefully, Sugar replied, "I am the person we hired to take care of her. I made her a promise and encouraged her to do this as soon as possible. I can't take that back."

"Of course you can. She'll understand."

"I haven't told her."

"Well, as soon as you do—"

"I'm not going to because you're right. She'd insist on waiting so I could do the entry I really want to do. But she shouldn't wait. She was frightened this morning, and so was I. If she falls and actually breaks a hip because I made her wait, I will never forgive myself. Emergency surgery is far more risky, and in many cases it's not even possible. That means a wheelchair, permanently."

"I don't understand. A hip replacement isn't urgent."

150

Sugar was having a hard enough time keeping her resolve, and it didn't help that Emily wasn't getting the point. "She let it go too long."

"Well, then, that's not your fault. Why should you lose because of it?"

Sugar sighed. "Getting angry about it and deciding it's not fair doesn't get me anything." She abruptly thought of Tree. Tree wouldn't argue. "I am really sorry to be disappointing you. I know this will set back my plans and yours. But there is next year."

Emily was silent for a long time. "I think if we break down what needs to be done we'll find a way for you to finish your entry."

"I'm sorry, Emily," Sugar said slowly. "All my instincts about what I'm capable of doing and what my obligations are tell me I won't do the best that I can. And that's what it'll take. I think entering something inferior, especially after you've given me such a leg up, would reflect badly on both of us, and some people would never forget it."

"Let me be the judge of that."

Sugar fought down a sudden surge of anger. "When it comes to what I create in my kitchen, I'm the judge."

"Well. That puts it pretty plainly. I think you're making a mistake. With those priorities you're not going to get where you want to be."

Anger faded as Sugar realized the truth. The image of investors and fame in her future was certainly appealing, but they didn't fit with her life right now. They were like pretty party decorations that Emily was putting up, but on the wrong day. "No, it means I won't get where you want me to be. But I'll be very happy with where I am if my grandmother comes home safe and healthy because I was there for her as I promised I would be. I know you're upset—"

"I told Elaine you were a pro. I've been raving about you to everybody."

"I understand, and all I can say is I'm sorry. The contest will be there next year, but my grandmother might not be if I screw this up."

"Well, you've made your choice," Emily said, her voice tight with anger. "The contest might be there next year, but I might not be."

The click in her ear was as quiet as the resulting silence was loud.

Hours later, still fuming, Sugar concluded that not only was her date tomorrow with Emily off, so was the relationship. If it ever had been a relationship, that is. The sex was great. They'd been rabbits together. Fine and good, the best sex she'd ever had. But Emily did not respect her. If she did she would have accepted Sugar's judgment about her business instincts. A mediocre entry would be as disastrous as a bad one. Better to withdraw than be labeled forever as just another local talent.

Emily didn't agree and, even worse, she'd seemed to have no sympathy at all about Sugar's plight with her grandmother. It was as if Gran's needs and worries and what they might mean to Sugar were of no interest to Emily. And maybe they weren't. Maybe that was why Emily lived all by herself in a house that could sleep twenty.

She kept thinking that Tree would have instantly understood. She'd have sympathized with Sugar's dilemma, would have agreed that Sugar had made the right, albeit painful, choice. She'd have commiserated, offered a hug and friendly ear. Noor would have done the same.

She'd been so upset by the conversation with Emily that she'd immediately started boiling the sugar-water solution that would become fondant when kneaded. She'd tucked Gran into bed and put her anger into her work. Charlie's cake would be the best damn cake she'd ever made. She didn't care if dyke divas and investors and socialites didn't get to taste it. She'd put a smile on Charlie's father's face, she hoped, and that would be reward enough.

Her hands occupied with rhythmic scrape-fold-pull motion of kneading, she had to wipe her teary eyes on her sleeve.

Chapter 8

Time was no longer short. Sugar woke Saturday morning and devoted her energy to helping Gran get her baking done early. When Gran left with Bridget to deliver the goodies and make calls, she started on the ingredients for Charlie's cake. Charlie's *father's* cake, she reminded herself.

She stripped vanilla beans out of pods and took comfort in their heady fragrance. Grating chocolate for the ganache allowed her to sample a little, just for the flavonoids, she told herself. Gran was back sooner than expected, looking wan and bedraggled from a brief afternoon rain shower.

Sugar had a wonderful idea. Not being pressed for time was a luxury, so why not take advantage of it? "You look like you could use a trip to the hairdresser. If we do it now we can cross it off the list for Monday. Maybe your lady can fit you in."

"Oh, I don't know." Gran brightened a little bit. Sugar remembered long-ago—and little heeded—advice from Gran about all women deserving to have someone else wash their hair once in a while.

"Let's call." Sugar bounced up to take care of it, wheedled just a bit over special circumstances, and they were very shortly thereafter on their way in the palatial comfort of Gran's Olds. "I think it'll be no problem getting you home from the hospital in the backseat. This car couldn't be more comfortable."

"I think you're right." Gran was definitely looking less pinched and worried. "And a nice rinse and set will make me feel so much better. Thank you, Sugar."

"You're welcome. I'll hop over to the market while you're being worked on. I can't believe we're short on salt."

"It's always the little things."

"Salt's only a little thing if you've got plenty." Sugar steered the car into a wide handicapped parking spot. "I love your license plates, Gran. Makes it so easy."

"It does." Gran gathered her purse and opened the door. By the time she had her feet out, Sugar was there with the walker and a strong arm. She saw her grandmother settled into the haircutter's workstation. The stylist promptly put something that looked like a swim cap over her grandmother's head and began pulling bits of hair up through it.

"I'll just go over to the market, Gran. Is there anything else you'd like?"

For a moment, her grandmother, in spite of the silly-looking cap and dwarfing smock, looked like the woman who had once thundered at Sugar "the gates of hell shall not prevail" when she'd missed one too many trips to church. "Yes, there *is* something I would like," she said in her finest brimstone voice. "Honor thy grandmother's wishes!"

Sugar's mouth dropped open. "What?"

"Get thee into the nearest empty chair and have thy hair cut, young woman!"

Sugar laughed. "Oh, Gran, I don't—"

"Yes, you do. This is *my* treat, young lady. You're long overdue."

The stylist working on Gran was laughing. "Pete's available."

Pete practically flew to Sugar's side. He was so swishy that Sugar couldn't believe Gran had tolerated giving her business to a place that employed one of *those* kind. "You," he said repressively, "are a mess."

"But, Gran, the salt—"

"Will still be on the shelf when we leave here."

Sugar found herself in Pete's chair wearing the same cap Gran was. "What are you doing?"

"Highlights. You need highlights. Most people have ten to twenty different shades of hair on their head, but you've been given just the one. We'll rinse after with a nice relaxer, which you are going to buy a bottle of and use regularly, and then we'll see . . ." He sighed. "We'll see what we can do with what you've got."

"I like it long," Sugar said stubbornly.

"So do the rats," he answered tartly, indicating the large snarl he was trying to work a comb through.

The next two hours were frustrating and worrisome. She hated being fussed over and Pete was ruthless. With Gran and the other stylists egging him on, he lopped off *yards* of her hair, leaving her with locks a full inch above her shoulders. The highhanded treatment put her stomach in knots. She wasn't a doll to be dressed up and paraded around. She realized, then, that Emily's "diamond-in-the-rough" comment had truly rankled. She didn't want to be a persona crafted for market share. She did not see why she couldn't be herself *and* be successful—according to her own standards—in her business. The problem was that Sugar was increasingly certain that Emily's definition of success wasn't negotiable. Unless Sugar measured up, Emily would never truly respect her.

Pete finally put down the scissors. Her bangs were combed back into the rest, and the side graduated to frame more of her face.

"I don't like using a blow dryer or a curling iron. It just makes it frizz more."

"You must rinse with the relaxing conditioner. You'll avoid a lot of frizzing if you never use the brush and the hair dryer at the same time. We don't have all day for it to get dry, so I'm being more aggressive than you'd need to be. I think you're going to have a simple wash-and-wear style when I'm done. You be glad to have naturally curly hair. Believe me, there are women who are paying plenty for this kind of wave. You just need to keep your hair thinner and softer than you have."

Sugar watched her hair lighten as it dried. The highlights in the mousy brown were dark gold and she had to admit they looked okay. The short cut would take getting used to, but she'd spend a lot less time coaxing out snarls, she supposed.

Pete stood back when her hair was dry. He tipped her head this way and that, measuring length against his comb and making the occasional adjusting snip until he was satisfied. "There," he said triumphantly. "That's the best I can do."

"Sugar," Gran said with a big smile, "you look wonderful. Without those bangs I can see your eyes."

"Now if you can just peel her out of that awful T-shirt," Pete said.

Gran was positively twinkling. "I think a grandmother can only do so much. I think I'll leave that to one of her girlfriends."

"You have more than one? You go, girl," Pete enthused.

"Oh, please," Sugar said. "Is it time to go?"

Gran finished writing her check. "This was worth every penny. Sugar, you'll look great for that contest. When was that again?"

"Oh, that's not important." Sugar hugged her grandmother before helping her to her feet. "Thank you, you were right. I was long overdue. I have an ex-girlfriend who will be thrilled. You look wonderful, too."

They were in the car and headed for home when Gran asked, "Would that ex-girlfriend be that nice Middle Eastern girl you roomed with there for a while?"

"Yes, Noor and I were . . . together. I'm sorry I lied to you. I wasn't sure you'd love me if I told you the truth." Sugar was amazed she sounded so nonchalant.

Gran's sigh was deep and heartfelt. "I have been very confused since Easter, at times simply not knowing what to believe. My pastor, now, he's not at all sure that Jesus spoke to me, given the way I've been behaving lately, the poor man. I can't say I blame him, because I think he's wrong. I know I was wrong. You can't frighten people into loving God. You can't scare your family into telling you the truth. You can't force love, which means you can't force trust. Your grandfather tried all his life to teach me that. I thought he was wrong. When he died I prayed God would forgive him for being so misguided that he went golfing with Jews and stopped in at that Muslim bakery near his office." She sniffed suddenly.

Alarmed, Sugar fished in her bag for a tissue.

"I'm the one who needs prayers. When your parents died I thought they'd been too lax with all of you. All my raging did was make you lie to me." Her grandmother took the tissue and dried her eyes.

Sugar eased into a left-turn pocket. "I don't know if you saw Jesus either, Gran, but I am so happy to be a family again. It's worth everything." Suddenly, it was. The contest was meaningless. "Let me run in here for some salt. And we're out of creamer, too."

As they rounded the last turn toward home, Sugar was surprised to see a low, sleek Jaguar at the curb in front of Gran's house. She hadn't thought Emily knew where Gran lived. Was she here to apologize or to apply more pressure?

"That's the producer," Sugar said.

"Your girlfriend?"

"Well, that remains to be seen. We're having a difference of opinion about something. A test we might not pass."

"Oh, I see. Well, if you'll help me get into my bedroom, I'll brush hair off myself and read for a while."

157

Emily stayed in the car while Sugar took in the small bag of groceries and returned to help Gran with the walker. Then she took a moment of her own to shake hair off herself by changing out of the T-shirt and into a simple rose-colored top. She wasn't sure it worked with the change in her hair color, but for now it would do.

As she approached the car Emily got out, looking sheepish and welcoming. "I didn't want to disturb your grandmother. I didn't know if she knew about me. I left you a message on your cell."

"Oh—you must have called when I was getting my hair washed."

"It looks great." Emily touched the tidy ends of Sugar's hair with her fingertips. Sugar felt a telltale shiver in her skin. Whatever chemistry it was that they had it sure was powerful. "I like it very much. I was going to suggest you get it done before we started filming. I think I'd have preferred more curls, but I suppose this works."

With a pang, Sugar realized that any future with Emily would have been founded on Emily's plans to change Sugar into some-thing she was not. Not wanting to start a pointless argument, she merely said, "I'm not the feminine creature that you are."

"That's quite okay with me."

Sugar was aware of her body tightening. Emily smelled won-derful, and looked extremely kissable. Those blue eyes were mes-merizing. She said wryly, "At least one thing about me is okay."

Emily seemed to miss Sugar's sarcasm. "I'm sorry I was a bitch. Yes, I was very disappointed that your family needs were going to interfere with such wonderful, fruitful plans. But I wasn't very nice about it."

Sugar shrugged. "I made the right choice, for me."

"I wish we could have talked it over before you decided."

"It wouldn't have changed my mind."

"You don't think so?" Emily laughed, and one hand lazily stroked Sugar's arm. It felt wonderful. "I can be very persuasive."

158

Sugar stilled Emily's hand. "It wouldn't have changed my mind," she repeated. "I've done a lot of thinking about it, and I'm not sure that our visions of my future are heading in the same direction. We moved really quickly in getting to know each other. We skipped over a couple of steps, maybe."

"I don't usually jump on women I've just met." Emily was pouting now. "Even if they have a body wet dreams are made of and eyes I see in my sleep."

We're more than bodies, Sugar wanted to say. Yes, she'd dreamed about Emily's eyes and hands and body, too. They'd done incredibly intimate things together, and yet Emily wasn't even beginning to fill the parts of her that cuddling with Tree had nourished. "Neither do I. Believe me. I was overwhelmed by how turned-on being with you made me."

"It still does," Emily whispered, her gaze sweeping over Sugar's body. "We'd have a really nice time."

"Until we had to talk." Abruptly, Sugar remembered Charlie's saying that the older she got the harder it was to spend time with a woman she couldn't talk to.

"Why is it that I find women I could talk to all day and not want to fuck, and then there's you, where I could literally spend all day in bed and, yeah, we have things in common we could discuss, but . . ."

"I was just thinking along those lines myself," Sugar said.

"I'll make you a deal." Emily pulled her hand away from Sugar's grasp and leaned against the car. "Let's separate business and pleasure. I really do want to do that segment for *Best of Seattle*. Whether you and I are sleeping together has no bearing on that. And next year, if you're in the Seattle Eats contest, I'll be your biggest promoter. And if you're single, and we find we have a night here and there we'd like not to be alone, then maybe we can reach a mutually satisfactory . . . meeting of the minds."

Sugar was laughing by the time Emily finished. "Yes, I would like that, though, as you know, I'm not casual."

"Oh, but please say you'll try." Emily ran one finger under the hem of Sugar's shirt and it took no effort at all to think about Emily's hand running up her stomach to her breasts.

"I can't promise. But I will certainly give it a lot of thought."

"Good," Emily said. She pulled an unresisting Sugar into the shadows of the tree-lined walk. "Something to think about then."

Like all their kisses, it was hot and sent tingles through Sugar of a kind she'd only ever read about in books. It was shockingly good, and for a full minute Sugar didn't think about anything but the sweet promise of Emily's mouth.

Emily released her with a sultry laugh. "Oh, I'm going to be thinking about that for a long, long time."

"Me, too," Sugar admitted, even though at the very end of the kiss it had felt like a kind of good-bye.

"I hope things go well for your grandmother."

"Thanks. Having me to rely on is helping her relax. At her age, her frame of mind plays a big role."

Emily stepped back into the circle of the streetlight, and the soft glow made her look lovelier than ever. "Let me know how it goes."

Sugar opened the Jaguar's door for Emily. "I will. Thank you for coming to see me. I was really troubled by the way it seemed we were parting."

"So was I. This is much better."

Sugar waved and turned to go into the house but paused, frowning. Now that her nerves were settling she recalled that while she was kissing Emily she'd heard a rumbling truck go by on the street. Now a large silver truck was parked just up the block.

They had been standing in the shadows, but it was doubtful Charlie hadn't seen them. Why the thought that Charlie had seen her kissing Emily would fill her with such dismay was a complete mystery. But the driver of the truck couldn't have missed them, and it was Charlie vaulting with such ease from the cab. She walked toward the waiting Sugar with something under her arm.

"Hi." Sugar tried to sound casual. Charlie was wearing black jeans, well-loved and broken-in cowboy boots and a white Western-style button-down shirt. She looked like she'd dropped off a poster for line dancing. Sexy, erotic, hot, downright naughty line dancing. Sugar shook herself. It was just the aftereffects of Emily's presence that had her thinking such thoughts.

"I just have something to drop off, but I didn't want to disturb your . . . romantic good-bye." She handed Sugar the parcel.

"Oh." Inside the bag was a fishing creel. "You found it."

"Yeah, and he won't miss it before the party."

"This is wonderful. I can make a nearly exact replica."

"Good, I'm glad it'll help. See you Monday, then."

Charlie was half turned back toward the truck when Sugar said, "Would you like to come in for tea? My grandmother will be wanting a cup and would be glad to see you."

"No, thanks. I need to get going." Charlie continued walking, leaving Sugar feeling thoroughly snubbed.

What rotten timing, Sugar thought. She couldn't exactly run after Charlie and explain that it had only been fond emotions with Tree and merely hot, endless sex with Emily and not even that anymore. More importantly, why would she tell Charlie that, and why on earth would Charlie care? Why did she care what Charlie thought of her? She could kiss anybody she wanted. And what about that blonde Charlie had been with the other night?

Thoroughly vexed, she stomped back into the house. Charlie hadn't even noticed her hair.

Sunday passed quietly. Bridget took Gran out to lunch after church but Sugar begged off, as she needed to perfect a wicker weave. Losing herself in her work was a welcome distraction from resentful thoughts of Charlie. She'd see Charlie the next day and butter wouldn't melt in her mouth. Why Charlie Bronson thought she had any cause at all to look in on Sugar's love life was beyond Sugar's comprehension.

The vanilla-bean cake layers, six in all, had been halved, layered

161

with the coffee-chocolate ganache and stacked. The creel had been easy to sculpt. It sat, wrapped in plastic, on the lowest shelf of Gran's fridge. She would be glad of the industrial refrigerator she'd ordered to rent when it was delivered tomorrow morning. Even though she no longer needed its capacity for the large contest cake, future orders would need the long shelves.

The icing, however, was proving as difficult as the cake had been easy.

With most projects where a high texture was prominent, it was possible to use a piece of fabric to create traceable contours in the fondant. Linen worked wonderfully. If a fabric was linty enough to leave behind traces, she'd found she could press it through plastic film, even though some of the definition was lost.

Wicker was proving a challenge. Not having any idea how clean the creel was, she immediately opted for plastic film to protect her fondant. But the film blunted too much of the wicker's outline. It was a pretty enough pattern, but it wouldn't look like wicker.

She wanted this cake to be perfect, so after several frustratingly unsuccessful attempts she went to the crafting store to look at the painting tools. She bought several decorative rollers used to make designs in wet paint. One of them would probably do the trick.

Gran still wasn't back by the time she got home again, and feeling a bit restless, Sugar left a message for Noor. Noor didn't call back, but when Gran got home they all spent some time with Bridget selecting a housecoat to wear in the hospital to cover those chintzy hospital gowns. Then they fussed about how to relocate a few pieces of furniture to clear a better walking path.

"I won't be on my feet for weeks," Gran said. "There's plenty of time to decide all of this."

"But if we think about it now, when the time comes you'll have had a chance to reflect on it." Bridget was a calming influence and Sugar would try to convince Gran to let Bridget visit. "I'll ask my Eddie to help you move furniture."

"The hospital rental company said the people who deliver the bed will move a few things, including the old bed. That'll happen this Thursday while Gran's still in the hospital." They'd deliver the bed at about the time Sugar would have been presenting her entry to the judges. *Stop that*, she told herself. There was no point wishing the milk wasn't spilt.

She went back to working on the fondant. The paint roller with a basket-weave design was going to work, but it didn't create enough high and low to pass as wicker. She'd have to roll the fondant while on the marble, drape it over the cake and then deepen the pattern with a knife. She'd done it before. It was time-consuming, to say the least.

On Monday morning she opened her bleary eyes, her mind already spinning with the full details of the day. The refrigerator was supposed to be delivered at eight. Gran needed to see her own doctor again by ten. Since she wouldn't be up to baking for several weeks, Gran was determined to spare Sugar as much baking as possible by stocking up and freezing banana breads and pound cakes for the shelters.

While they baked there was going to be a precise and detailed lesson on the ins and outs of the Harvest Fair planning. Sugar knew that Bridget and others knew the details of when to place ads to encourage crafters to rent booth space, and where the rental contracts were kept, and was confident Gran's recovery would allow her to see to most of them. But it was also clear that talking about them relieved Gran from worry.

By three o'clock, Sugar needed to deliver the cake to the fire station near where she used to live, which meant she needed to be done with it no later than one to allow for a hour's firming up in the refrigerator. The basic creel was complete, but the leather lid and ties were yet to be done, and she wasn't happy with her first attempt to replicate the beloved fishing lure.

To start the day off to a really grand moment, she called the Seattle Eats organizers to withdraw her entry. At least she only had to speak to an answering machine, but it still hurt like hell for a few minutes.

Feeling tired and cranky, she expected the worse when her cell phone rang for the first time.

"Go buy yourself a laptop," Patricia said cheerfully.

"Why?"

"Because I think you can afford it now. I've got a fax of the insurance company's check. If you're willing to sign a nondisclosure agreement and that you agree they don't owe you dime but are giving you twenty-five thousand dollars out of the goodness of their hearts—"

"Holy shit!" Sugar groped for a chair. "Say that part again."

"Twenty-five thousand dollars." Patty sounded exceedingly smug, and for once Sugar could not blame her at all. "But remember, after taxes and the firm's cut you're only going to see about half of that."

"Patty, still . . . my goodness. It hardly seems fair that the house burned down and I'm better off financially."

"As Gran would say, the Lord works in mysterious ways. I take it you'll sign? It's a decent offer. Basically, they're afraid that you'll sue, claiming they ought to have discovered the illegal rental and the lack of building permits, and therefore in some way prevented the resulting losses to you. This is chump change to make a suit go away, but I know you don't want this to drag out."

"I don't. Of course I'll take the money. It's . . . a shock." She could buy a laptop today. And a printer. She could even start looking for commercial premises to rent for the busy holiday season. If the season was lucrative, a new car could be in the works without having to take on much debt. Don't get ahead of yourself, she warned. Money in the bank could sit in the bank. It didn't need to be spent today. There was plenty of time for that later in the week.

"You'll also get your deposit back from that ass. I'll see to that, gratis."

"Geez, Patty, thank you. Have I told you lately you are a fantastic attorney?"

"No, but feel free to bring me something tasty to eat someday."

"That's a deal." She knew of Patty's predilection for sour lemon squares, and Sugar thought she made them as well as their mother had. "Hey, I wanted to tell you that Gran's surgery is tomorrow. I meant to send you all a note. It got moved up. Isn't that a lucky thing?"

"Quinn knocked me in the head over the weekend, and yeah— it's a good thing it's so close. I'm glad you're there."

Sugar felt a definite lightening of her spirit. It was nice to be appreciated, even though she knew Patty's opinion ought not matter so much to her. But Patty was her big sister. No matter what, she always would be. She'd hoped to wave a competition medal in front of Patty's surprised nose, but this result was so much more satisfying.

She gave Patty the hospital details, and Patty said she'd send a note off to Quinn and Rose with the information. When she rang off, Sugar danced through the house with the big news for Gran.

"I think you should treat yourself to something nice to go with that hairdo," Gran announced. "Maybe after you've delivered that cake."

"The cake I need to finish," Sugar said enthusiastically. She practically bounced back to the kitchen, her tired eyes and weary back forgotten. She took the perfect loaves of pound cake out of the oven to cool. They'd drop them off on the way home from the doctor's office, giving Sugar a chance to meet the various shelter personnel. Busy day—it no longer mattered.

Of course by three o'clock Sugar ached all over. She'd been going nonstop, including a last-minute inspiration for producing the alabaster sheen on her edible fishing lure. Feeling harried and disheveled, she arrived at the firehouse with minutes to spare. She'd forgotten her chef's apron but supposed since it was an informal gathering it hardly mattered. A vaguely familiar fire-fighter was anxiously waiting for her so she had to be content with a quick pat to her hair in the rearview mirror. His uniform proclaimed him Ralph.

"Hey, you're the lady with the oven fire, aren't you?" He waved her in through a rear door, after inquiring if she needed help lifting the cake.

Knowing best how to manage the platter, Sugar had assured him she was fine. "That's me. This is really my way of saying thank you to all of you."

"I have to admit I'm looking forward to seeing it. Charlie's been on about it for the last week. She's got her dad distracted in the back. He's got a going-away thing later at the administrative office, but this is just for us guys, in his old stationhouse where his daughter now holds down the fort."

Sugar noticed lookouts a-plenty as she slipped through open doors to the communal dining room. There were paper plates and stacks of presents, one of which was obviously a fishing rod. Sugar grinned to herself, pleased that her creation would fit so well with the party's theme. She quickly unwrapped it, blushing with pride at the exclamations of the men gathering around to look.

"I can eat that?"

"Not all of it, you slob."

"That's amazing. Looks like the real thing."

Sugar whacked a hand that seemed to be aiming for a taste of the icing. "Touch it and die. I haven't taken photos yet."

They cheerfully gave her enough room to take a couple of long shots, then urged her to stay when she normally would have left them to enjoy the surprise. It didn't take much pressure. She wanted to see the look on Charlie's father's face when he saw the cake. Okay, she admitted honestly, she wanted to see the look on Charlie's face as well.

She didn't have long to wait.

"I think I left my coat in the mess," Charlie was overheard saying. "Help me look, would you?"

"Sometimes I think you'd lose your head if it wasn't tacked on—"

A hearty yell of "Surprise!" led to a rousing chorus of "For He's a Jolly Good Fellow." Sugar kept to one side, partially obscured by a pillar. She wasn't sure at all that Charlie had seen her as she led her father toward the presents and cake.

"Oh, this wasn't necessary. You guys are too much." Sugar was struck again by how much Chuck and Charlie Bronson resembled each other. Chuck's eyes were alight with humor as he surveyed the table. "Is that my old gear? I wondered why you were digging around in the garage last week."

"Nope, Dad, it's not." Charlie was grinning ear to ear. "Look again. I'm damn sure that's a cake."

"You're kidding."

"Somebody get a knife!"

When Charlie poised to cut the cake square down the middle Sugar could stand it no longer. "Please let me do that," she called out as she emerged from the little nook where she'd gone unnoticed.

"I wondered if you'd let me hack at your cake," Charlie said. Though her eyes were filled with delight, there was confusion there when she looked at Sugar. "It's really wonderful. Dad, this is the woman who made the cake for you."

"Miss Sorenson, I remember you. I didn't realize you were plotting with my daughter."

A voice from behind her muttered, "*Plotting*'s a new word for it if I know our Charlie."

There was laughter and Sugar fought back a blush. Did Charlie have some sort of reputation for sleeping with women she'd been out rescuing?

"Shut up, Ralph." Charlie bowed slightly, offering the knife handle over her arm. "Milady."

"An upright cake," Sugar said in her best imitation of Julia Child, "must be cut from the corners if one wishes to avoid disaster." She smoothly sliced away the edge where the faux lure rested, plated it quickly and offered the result to Charlie's father. "Congratulations. Working with this lot I'm sure you've earned your retirement."

There was a shout of good-natured laughter, and slices of cake were quickly passed around.

167

"Aren't you going to have some?" Charlie took the last piece Sugar cut, pausing with the fork halfway to her mouth. "Please do."

"I usually don't. I've tasted it along the way. But, yes, I'd like that." She abruptly felt teary, wondering if there was any way she and Charlie could get back to a better footing. Something about her was as easy to be around as Tree, and as exciting to fantasize about as Emily. A safe authority figure, she reminded herself, and she had to fight back a giggle.

Safe.

Right.

There were only a few pieces of cake left, and haggling over their dispensation had begun when Chuck was urged to open his gifts.

"I have to say, this was unexpected." He touched the package nearest him. "And unnecessary. You are the finest house I've ever had the pleasure to work with. Since I've got you all here, and she can hardly bolt out of the room, I also want to say how proud I am of my daughter. Most of you have watched her grow up and so have I, and I think she's one of the finest we've got. She's going to make a damned fine addition to the arson squad."

Charlie's cheeks were stained with color as she gazed proudly at her father. A tear trickled down one cheek, but she ignored it. "I'll miss working with you, Pop. But I'm looking forward to the fishing. Now get busy and open some presents."

Later, Sugar wasn't sure when she realized something was wrong. She didn't know Chuck well enough to recognize the odd way he patted his chest, but by the time she realized that the grimace of pain wasn't temporary, everyone around her was starting to move. She had the sense to get out of the way.

The table was shoved unceremoniously aside. A radio call for paramedic support was already being made and Charlie was out of the room in a matter of seconds. She returned before Sugar could make sense of anything, rapidly going through her father's coat pockets. "I've got it, I've got it," she shouted, passing over something that looked like a pen to one of the men leaning over Chuck.

Chuck was breathing in great gasps, his face contorted in pain. "Charlie, Charlie," he'd been repeating, then he simply stopped. Stopped moving, stopped breathing.

"He's arresting." Ralph pushed chairs over to clear space and Chuck was lowered to a prone position. "There's no response. Beginning CPR. Charlie, get out of the way!"

In the distance, Sugar could hear a siren's wail, and it was like the afternoon of the fire all over again. She was a helpless bystander while emergency personnel made decisions so quickly she couldn't follow what they were saying. Charlie was hurriedly describing something to one of the paramedics, and Chuck, a mask now over his still, lifeless face, was already being lifted on a stretcher. It seemed like only minutes had elapsed from the first indication of Chuck's distress to the sight of the ambulance door closing on the tableau of Charlie leaning over her father, one of his hands in hers.

Sugar turned to Ralph. "What happened?"

"Chuck's had a bad ticker since he was born. He's had these attacks before, but I don't think he's lost consciousness like that. Charlie's real worried. Damn thing to happen today of all days."

Sugar would have asked more questions, but a claxon warning sounded and the dispirited group of firefighters leapt into action. It was only another minute before Sugar found herself completely alone. The only thing she could think to do was tidy up the room, mop up the scattered remains of the cake and restack the gifts. She hoped Charlie and her father would get to see them opened soon.

169

Chapter 9

"Oh, the poor man," Gran said, her eyes alight with sympathy. "I'll add him to my prayer list tonight. What a shock."

"I hope he's okay." Sugar had called the firehouse twice, but so far no one had answered. "Charlie must be frantic."

She was trying to keep the alarm out of her voice, figuring that so close to Gran's own surgery, unnecessary thoughts of mortality weren't precisely helpful to Gran. Still, she could not shake the stricken look on Charlie's face from her mind. To this day she remembered the numb disbelief she'd felt when Patty had arrived to tell her their parents had died. Poor Patty, she suddenly thought, to have to bear that kind of news to a sister almost twelve years younger. Patty had mothered them all through the shock. She hoped Charlie wasn't having to face it, not when her father was on the edge of a new life where they could spend more time together.

"What would you like to do tonight, Gran? I finally have no

work to do. It's hard to believe." If she'd been entering the contest she'd have been still working on the placemat portion, but nearly done.

"Truthfully, I think I'd like to read and pray, dear. And you have a computer to buy, don't you?"

"Oh." Sugar had completely forgotten about her ability to spend money. "Are you sure?" She wasn't certain she wanted to leave her grandmother alone.

"Just get me to my bedroom and I'll take it from there."

"You'll use the walker while I'm gone?"

"Yes, of course," Gran said, irritated. "I hate that thing, though."

"I know, but you promise, right?"

"Yes, yes."

"Swear on a stack of Bibles?"

"Get on with you," Gran snapped, then she laughed. "Bring me a stack and I'll swear. I'd do nearly anything to get you to touch one."

"I'll carry yours for you tomorrow," Sugar promised. "Will that do?"

"It'll do very nicely. Oh, this is getting much too hard," Gran said as Sugar slowly lifted her to her feet. "The surgery is coming not a moment too soon."

After fifteen minutes in the megastore outlet where she hoped to find a good deal, Sugar decided the entire day had been too surreal to make up her mind about something so important. She wrote down some price information, glanced at photo-quality printers, then left, feeling more than a little overwhelmed.

Gran had wanted the evening to herself, so Sugar didn't want to return home so quickly. She had no idea what movies were playing, or if any of them were any good. She wanted to find out if Charlie's father was okay, but the firehouse phone still clicked over to an answering machine. Noor didn't answer her phone either.

171

She thought of Tree, then, and was happy to reach a real live human being. "I don't suppose you're free for a simple dinner?"

"Hey, I'd love one. I was just heading home. I'm in Issaquah. Where are you?"

"Bellevue, but traffic is starting to get bad. Want to meet halfway?"

They agreed on a salad bar off 150th, and Sugar spent the next twenty minutes getting there. She still made it ahead of Tree, so she gathered a plateful of healthy things she knew were good for her along with a large slab of cheese bread chosen precisely because it was not. She dug in, certain Tree wouldn't mind that she hadn't waited.

Tree joined her shortly, her plate also a balancing act between healthy choices and indulgences, like hot muffins. "This was a great idea, thank you. I love your hair."

"Do you? It still feels funny. The broccoli salad is good."

"It looked it. Did you see the shrimp bisque? That's my next stop. So what's up? Hair looks great but you look wiped out."

"It's been a heck of a day." Sugar started with the news of Charlie's father but hadn't even finished before Tree had her cell phone out.

"Let's find out. You just have to know who to call." She pressed a few buttons, then said briskly, "Dispatch? This is Gantry Racine, two-oh-oh-four-nine. I need a hospital destination for an emergency transit. Bronson, Charles. About three-thirty this afternoon. Oh, got it? Hope National? Can you give me the admissions desk number? Thank you."

"Hope National is where my grandmother will be tomorrow," Sugar said when Tree clicked her cell phone shut.

As she dialed again, Tree said, "I know he has a heart condition. Charlie must be beside herself. I can't tell you how surprised I was the day of the fire to hear her mention that her mother had called."

Sugar dimly remembered that. "She and her father seem so close."

"Like bread and butter." Abruptly speaking into the phone,

Tree said, "This is Gantry Racine from King County Social. I want to check on the status of an afternoon admission. Two-oh-oh-four-nine. Bronson, Charles. Really?" She looked up at Sugar with a hopeful smile. "Thank you. No, nothing for the file." She clicked the phone shut. "Critical but improving."

Sugar heaved a huge sigh of relief. "He was so lifeless when they left. I hope he recovers well. I'll see if I can visit him tomorrow."

They finished their meal as Sugar shared her worries about her grandmother. She also explained about the necessity of withdrawing from the Seattle Eats competition.

Tree was wonderfully sympathetic. "Wasn't that one of the things the producer was going to help with?"

"Well . . ." Sugar took a deep breath and found herself explaining all about Emily. Tree looked alarmed, then surprised, then most certainly a little bit angry.

"How could she not understand that your grandmother came first?"

"I'm not sure she does, even though she apologized. It made me realize that even though we have this real passionate thing between us, I couldn't see myself in a future with her that had any substance to it. It's her world, but I don't think I can live in it and still be me."

"Your grandmother's surgery likely saved you a lot of time and heartbreak, figuring that out now and not five years from now."

"I hadn't thought of it that way. I'm not sure that's what I was supposed to get out of it." Sugar gave a rueful laugh. "Anyway, when Emily was leaving, Charlie saw us kissing good-bye and she was—I don't know. Like she was disappointed in me."

"Really? Why would she be?"

Her face now flaming, Sugar explained about the blown-out fuse, the almost kiss and the unmistakable flirtation they had shared. "Maybe she thought that had set us up for more, and therefore my seeing someone else was against the rules."

"Stupid rules, then. She wants to date you, and be exclusive, she can say so instead of stalking around in those boots of hers."

Sugar actually laughed. "How did you know she was wearing boots?"

"She really was?" Tree grinned. "She's got it bad for you, then. She doesn't wear those boots for just anybody."

"Maybe she was headed for a date."

"That's my point, maybe she was."

Sugar was put out at the thought. "Well, if she wanted a date with me, she ought to have called. I'm not just available any old time."

"Now that," Tree said, her dark eyes twinkling, "is exactly what you need to tell Ms. Bronson next time you see her. Charlie's an intelligent woman, but subtlety is not her strong point."

"She must be so worried."

"I'll bet she is," Tree agreed.

Sugar kept fighting the urge to cry, but she didn't know why. Charlie's dad was going to be okay. She found herself reflecting on her parents' death again.

"Hey, where'd you go?" Tree looked at Sugar expectantly. "Are you going to finish that ice cream or let it melt the rest of the way?"

"Sorry. I don't know why I'm still so worried."

Tree tipped her head to one side. "Let's make a list, shall we?"

"Of what?"

"Reasons for you to be fretting right now. You've been on a roller coaster nonstop for the last what . . . ten days?" Tree held up a finger for each new item she listed. "Not one but two women are courting you, and I certainly confused things there for a few minutes. Now the woman you thought was all that and a kite proves to have a bit of clay in her feet. The other is undergoing a crisis of her own and you have no idea if anything between you will ever pan out."

"I get the picture," Sugar said.

"Oh, Sugar, I'm not done. I might run out of fingers." Tree grinned and Sugar realized that she'd not yet seen Tree look so at

174

ease. She had a knockout smile. "You've moved your life. You've moved your business. You might think the fire wasn't life-threatening but your body did, and that kind of adrenaline takes a long time to replenish. Your grandmother goes for surgery tomorrow, and it's risky no matter what the doctors say. You had to give up some dreams to make it happen, and that hurts, too."

"That's fairly comprehensive," Sugar admitted.

"So, are you still wondering why it is you feel overwhelmed and stressed out?"

She shook her head. "Any recommendations, oh therapist?"

Tree grinned. "If I thought you needed one, believe me, I'd drive you there myself. Just slow life down if you can. Don't spread yourself too thinly. Catch your breath. Stick to things that make you feel alive and safe."

"I don't even know why I'm upset about that stupid contest. It doesn't matter." Sugar finished the last of the small dish of ice cream and pushed it away. "Gran could die tomorrow. Look at what Charlie's going through. But right now I'm thinking about that silly contest and I want to cry. How shallow is that?"

"Let me tell you about shock." Tree patted Sugar's hand. "I've seen it happen time and again. A shock to the system pulls the scabs off things that weren't healed. Even little things we've told ourselves didn't matter. Charlie's dad collapsing was a shock, and you were already pretty stressed out. The contest mattered to you, of course it did. You made the right decision, but doing the right thing can be painful. That's not shallow. You'll feel better for admitting that it did matter."

"It did," Sugar said quietly. "I had a great idea. It was all in my head. I was ready to put it all together. Now I have to wait a year, and if it hadn't been for that stupid fire I might be working on the entry right now."

"One of the hardest things in life is learning to accept Plan B with style and grace."

"Is that what you do?"

175

"Oh, no," Tree said airily. "I never accept Plan B. Instead I'm a buttinsky, remember? I mean, you might as well blame me. I'm the one who made sure you knew your grandmother had been advised to have the surgery."

"Yeah," Sugar acknowledged. "Tree?"

"Yeah?"

"Butt out of my life in the future."

Tree laughed, pushing her hair back over her shoulder. It was sexy as hell the way she did it. "I'll try, but no promises. You know, Charlie pretty much said the same thing to me."

Sugar had to ask herself why it was she couldn't just fall in love with Tree. Was sexual passion all that important? Remembering how she felt with Emily, however, Sugar had to admit that maybe it was. "Did she? Is that when you two had your falling-out?"

"It wasn't exactly a falling-out. We'd been dating—"

"You dated?" Sugar's jaw dropped. It seemed to her that one of them could have mentioned the fact sooner.

"Well, sort of. It never went anywhere. It went kind of backward, even. Friends had set us up, and the first time we liked each other enough to arrange to meet again on our own. Left to ourselves, though, we discovered we disagreed more than we agreed on any number of things."

"Like what?"

"Sexual politics." Tree gave a chagrined sniff. "This was at least ten years ago, you know. We were both young and absolutely certain we were right. I was adamant that any sexual relationship that included pain, humiliations, et cetera, as part of the scene was unhealthy. She insisted that adults were allowed to consent to things that other people might think harmful. She even threw the Wiccan motto in my face."

"Which is?"

"If it hurts no one, do as you will. But I felt that hurting oneself counts as someone getting hurt. And in reality, in practice . . . the truth probably lies somewhere between our two positions. But it was just one of many, many things we sparred about. After the

176

third time we went out, she suggested we were only going out to fight, and life was too short for that kind of stress."

"Oh. Well, I knew there was something."

"The story doesn't end there." Tree sipped her tea. "I did a buttinsky thing. We were friendly, friendlier certainly than we are now. I thought I was right, but I was wrong. And she told me to butt out of her life permanently."

"So what buttinsky thing did you do?" Sugar decided that the second half of the mango-pineapple muffin she'd scorned earlier was edible after all.

"I got in touch with Charlie's mother and suggested that she attempt to reconcile with her daughter."

"Oh, wow." That, Sugar thought, was a *hugely* buttinsky thing to do.

"Yeah. Charlie was completely pissed off with me. Then her friend Devin got into an abusive relationship and I told Charlie that's exactly what I thought it was, and she tuned me out. I was right—Devin turned up on Charlie's doorstep in the middle of the night with a broken arm and a couple of cracked ribs. If Charlie had trusted me about that, she might have been the one that Devin listened to before she got seriously hurt."

Sugar mulled over the insights into Charlie's personality. Stubborn didn't surprise her, somehow. "So . . . the greater metropolitan Seattle-Tacoma area is a small place sometimes, huh?"

Tree shrugged. "We work in overlapping circles. I respect her and I think she respects me now. We've made our mistakes. We'll never be friends, but respect is a good consolation prize."

They browsed a nearby bookstore after leaving the restaurant, and Sugar acquired a couple of paperbacks and magazines to get her through the long waits at the hospital. It had been quite a long while since she'd had time to read anything but the culinary trade information online. Quality encounters with her favorite dyke detectives would be a welcome diversion.

The alarm woke her far too early. Gran had been asleep when Sugar got home, and Sugar spent a restless night with strange dreams of siren wails and crackling electricity. At least she didn't think she smelled smoke when she woke. The clock told her sunrise wouldn't be far off and there seemed no point, then, to going back to bed.

It was the first time since her arrival that she beat Gran into the kitchen, but it wasn't by much. She heard the awkward clunk of the walker in the hallway and was glad to have a light breakfast already made. Gran wasn't permitted to eat again after this meal.

She told Gran the news about Charlie's father.

Gran whispered a brief prayer under her breath before saying, "That's certainly a relief."

"I'll be able to check today, because he's at the same hospital."

"Maybe you'll be able to flirt with that tall, handsome Charlie again."

In a million years, Sugar would never have believed that her grandmother would actually be encouraging her to flirt with another woman. She peeked out the kitchen window, but the sun appeared to still be rising in the east. "It would hardly be appropriate under the circumstances."

"I met your grandfather at a funeral, you know."

"You never told me that."

"His uncle and my father were in business together." Gran nibbled fitfully at her breakfast as she settled in to tell the story. Sugar laughed and commented in the right places, but her mind was partially preoccupied with the idea that during the course of the day she would most likely run into Charlie.

"Alma? Alma Fulton?"

Sugar realized the nurse with the clipboard was asking for her grandmother. She was unused to hearing anyone call her grandmother anything but, well, Gran. "She's gone to the bathroom but will be right back."

"We're ready to get her into a bed when she gets back. In the meantime, there are these forms to complete."

"More forms?" Sugar's heart sank. She'd already written Gran's name and address fifty times.

"For Medicare billing," the nurse said.

"But we already . . ." She was talking to herself as the nurse padded away to take care of someone else. They'd spent an hour in the financial office of the hospital providing insurance and Medicare information, then two hours going over exercises to practice after surgery. Sugar was given training on how to lift and assist her grandmother in standing—she'd been doing it all wrong, apparently. Then there had been a battery of tests, blood samples, breathing measurements and an official weigh-in.

When no one was looking Sugar had stepped on the scale herself and sighed at the result. Emily was truly nuts to have said Sugar's body was what wet dreams were made of. She caught sight of herself in a mirror and didn't know why anyone would look twice. But, she reminded herself, Emily had looked twice, and so had Tree. And so had Charlie. They were all certifiable.

Or maybe she just looked sallow and lifeless in the hospital lighting. Everybody in a hospital looked half ill, even the nurses. The peach silk shirt was wasted, and she'd been a fool to wear it to a hospital, of all places, where the temperature seemed to range from Arctic to Saharan within a few steps.

"Is something wrong, Sugar Bear?"

Sugar hadn't heard her grandmother's laborious approach. "Oh no, Gran, just more forms. Don't sit, they're ready for you now."

"Might as well get this over with." Gran took a deep breath and turned resolutely toward the nurse's station.

Sugar signaled to the nurse that they were ready, then she gathered up their things in the waiting area. True to her word, she carried her grandmother's Bible along with her own reading. It must be a new world order, she thought, when neither she nor her grandmother had anything to say about the Good Book rubbing its cover against a dyke detective novel.

She helped Gran get undressed and into the inadequate gown, then took her jewelry, which was hospital policy. The nurse returned as Gran settled into the bed, bringing with her a resident who was going to start Gran on her intravenous drip.

"It's time for you to wait outside," the nurse said gently. "She won't be moved for about an hour."

Sugar waited in the hallway for a few minutes, in case her grandmother called for her, but in short order that seemed pointless. She consulted a hospital directory and determined where the ICU was, as well as the cardiac center. She'd take a stroll to those destinations once her grandmother was in surgery.

With a sigh she settled down in the waiting-room chair.

She woke with a crick in her neck. This time it wasn't Emily or Tree she was looking at when she opened her eyes, but Charlie.

"Oh, my goodness." Sugar sat up, looking at her watch.

"You've been out at least a half-hour. That's how long ago I spotted you. I wish I could sleep in one of these chairs."

Sugar rubbed her neck. "Be grateful you can't. Why are you down here?"

"Pop's having surgery. They think this last attack of angina damaged his mitral valve. Most people, that's not serious, but he's got a congenital defect. As he puts it, he was told when he was fifteen he'd wouldn't see twenty, so everything is borrowed time. He became a firefighter because he figured if he could die anytime, he might as well perhaps do it helping somebody else." She stretched her legs wearily in front of her. "Your grandmother's here today?"

"Yeah, there was an opening, so we grabbed it."

Charlie cocked her head to one side. "Isn't that big contest thing this week?"

Sugar shrugged. Charlie continued to look at her with those incredible light brown eyes and she found herself blinking back tears.

"Life had other plans, huh?"

"Something like that. Let me go check in with the nurse, okay? I can't believe I fell asleep."

The nurse assured her that her grandmother's transition to surgery had gone as planned, and the surgery seemed to be progressing normally. It would be several more hours before surgery concluded and there was any chance of her grandmother's being lucid again.

She walked back across the waiting area to find Charlie watching her. It wasn't the bold, flirtatious stare she had received in the past, but it held warmth. There was something else, though, that Charlie seemed to damp down as she smiled in welcome.

"All's well?"

"Yes, apparently. Are you hungry? I'm starving. Gran couldn't eat and I didn't want to eat in front of her. Can I bring you something back from the cafeteria?"

"I had something right after they took Pop in. I was on my way back when I spotted you doing that Sleeping Beauty thing."

Sugar found herself fighting down a familiar blush. She didn't even think Charlie meant it flirtatiously. She looked tired and drawn. She must have had a hellish night. "I've got a spare paperback if you want to read."

"Now that's tempting. I went home for clothes and forgot to pick up a book. I remembered some nutrition bars, if you'd like one. It's not a candy bar, but it's better for you."

"Fair trade," Sugar said. She offered the book she wasn't currently reading and accepted the foil-wrapped bar Charlie retrieved from the small backpack at her feet. "I think this is the latest in the series."

"I haven't read it. Thanks."

They settled in side by side, turning pages and making the occasional critical remark about what they were reading, which led to other topics. Sugar finished the nutrition bar and definitely felt less hollow. They talked so congenially that she found it hard to believe that Charlie and Tree hadn't been able to. They had just reached the engrossing debate of whether lesbians in the mainstream arts meant a loss of cultural identity when Charlie's cell phone rang. The nurse scowled as she answered.

"He's fine so far. I can't talk here. I forgot to turn off the phone. Gotta go." She clicked it shut, then switched it off with an apologetic look at the nurse. "My mother," she explained. "She's always had a horrible sense of timing."

"Tree told me how she'd been a buttinsky, by the way."

"Did she?" Charlie looked surprised. "One of these days I'll tell her that her being a buttinsky did lead to a cease-fire between my mother and me. Just a cease-fire, where we're happy to leave it. She still had no right to interfere, though."

"No, she didn't. I'm not sure she's sorry, though."

"That's the trouble with Tree. Your life needs fixing? She'll fix it." Charlie yawned and closed her eyes to rub them. "She's a good woman, just irritating as hell sometimes."

"She said you two dated."

Charlie's eyes flew open. "We did not. We met at agreed-upon places and argued."

Sugar grinned. "That's about how she described it."

"Are you seeing Tree now?"

"Depends on what you mean by that question." Sugar didn't know where she found the energy to flirt, albeit mildly.

"I mean exactly what you think I mean."

"Oh, in that case, no. We're not seeing each other except as friends."

"Oh."

"I thought you were dating that blonde woman you were with."

"Devin? Hell, no, that would be like dating my sister."

Sugar was about to lead up to admitting that she and Emily were not an item either when the nurse interrupted.

"Miss Bronson? Your father's out of surgery now."

"That was fast." Charlie scrambled to her feet. "He's going back to ICU?"

"Yes, he'll be up there in just a few minutes."

Charlie turned to Sugar. "Would you walk up with me?"

"Sure." Sugar wasn't sure she could read any more without falling asleep again.

Charlie was quiet as they waited for her father to be wheeled past them to his room. It was only a few minutes, and he was completely unconscious, his face covered by an obscuring mask. The surgeon stopped to talk to Charlie in a low voice, then smiled broadly before walking away.

"It went well?"

"Yes, yes it did." Charlie's voice cracked and she burst into tears.

Sugar drew her into an alcove and put her arms around her. They stood that way for quite a while, until Charlie found her composure again.

"I'm just so relieved," she said finally. "I was so scared."

"I know," Sugar murmured sympathetically. Charlie's body was as firm, lean and supple as she remembered, but now she could also feel the soft curves. "I know."

"I'm not the crying type."

"I won't tell." Sugar was relieved to feel Charlie laugh slightly.

"Thanks. God, I feel like I can breathe again."

"I think you could use some food."

Charlie nodded as she gently pulled away from Sugar's embrace. "And so could you."

Sugar was smiling in agreement when Charlie gently touched her hair. "I like this. Did you do this for that producer?"

"No," Sugar said honestly. "I think I did it for me."

"Best reason of all." Charlie's hand stilled for a moment and her eyes became hooded and intense.

Sugar found she couldn't breathe. It was as if Charlie was inviting her to do something but she kept missing the cue. Did Charlie want Sugar to be the one who made the definitive first move?

The spell of Charlie's gaze was broken when Sugar's stomach growled loudly. "Come on, let's feed that beast."

An hour later, stomachs queasily sated by cafeteria food, Charlie escorted Sugar back to the surgical waiting area. Gran was out of surgery by then, and in the recovery room, doing just fine, the nurse assured her. Charlie lingered while Sugar asked to talk to the surgeon but said nothing as the surgeon explained that everything had gone as well as could be expected.

"There was less healthy bone than I had hoped," he explained, "but enough to make a good bond. She will need to be reasonable in her physical activities to avoid dislocating it."

Relieved, Sugar couldn't help saying, "So no more high-jumping?"

Charlie smothered a laugh, but the surgeon grinned openly. "Exactly. She won't be conscious for several more hours, and frankly, she's not going to know you're there. If I were you, I'd get some rest and come back later."

"I want to be there when she wakes up so I can give her her Bible."

The surgeon nodded understandingly. "I think if you're back by six you'll be fine."

Sugar found herself walking to the hospital entrance with Charlie. "I'd go home, except traffic now would only give me an hour's sleep before I had to come back."

"Same here. I was thinking I'd set my watch alarm and sleep in my truck."

"Oh, it would be big enough for a nap, wouldn't it?"

"You could stretch your legs out, but I can't quite do that."

Sugar stopped walking. Maybe it was relief, maybe it was because she was so tired. She wrinkled her nose. "Are you offering me the opportunity to sleep with you in your truck?"

Charlie gave a surprised hoot. "Well, when you put it that way, yes, I guess I am. I have to admit, though, I've slept in my truck with guys."

"Have you now?"

Charlie led the way through the hospital parking lot. Her truck was parked very conveniently in the shade of the building. "Trust me, if you've been working a fire line for twelve hours, you don't care who else is in your truck with you. You just sleep."

"I can understand that."

She unlocked the cab with the remote, then leaned in through the open door. "Let me move some of my crap." She glanced over her shoulder a few moments later. "I don't usually do this for my fellow firefighters, though. The front seat flips back and the console lowers, so . . ." She stepped back from the doorway to let Sugar see the inside. "Is this okay?"

Sugar had been thinking they'd each take one of the rows, but the new arrangement would allow them to share the space. If she hadn't been so tired she might have entertained thoughts of the activities that would certainly be more than possible. But as it was, she simply said, "It looks better than heaven right now," and allowed Charlie to give her a boost up to the seat.

They stretched out side by side, carefully not touching. After a moment, Sugar said, "I feel like I'm sliding toward my head."

"Yeah," Charlie said drowsily. "Let's switch around."

In the subsequent rearrangement it somehow seemed completely natural that Sugar curl up in the crook of Charlie's arm. The steady thump-thump of Charlie's heart was reassuring. She was asleep in moments.

There was an annoying noise in her ear. She swatted at the source and someone groaned. It took a minute for Sugar to work out where she was, but when she did it seemed perfectly normal to roll over and find Charlie waking up next to her.

Her stomach lurched as she watched Charlie stretch awake. Typical, she thought, now that you've had some rest your mind is back in the gutter. "Hi," she said softly.

Charlie shut off her watch alarm, then relaxed again on the seat. "This beats those hospital chairs."

"You can say that again," Sugar agreed. "I'm not seeing the producer anymore."

Charlie blinked. "Why tell me?"

"Like you don't know the answer to that question."

Charlie pulled herself up onto her elbows. Sugar's mouth

watered at the long lean curve of her body. "Okay. Cards on the table. I thought that was what I got for being a gentleman. Snooze you lose."

"Huh?"

"She kissed you, right? The first chance she got?"

"Well, not the first."

"Close enough. Well, I wanted to kiss you really badly on the patio at your grandmother's. Really badly. It was hard not to. But I didn't."

"Why didn't you?"

Charlie made a noise like the answer was obvious. "You'd just had a big shock. I didn't think you were quite yourself. I thought I'd wait. I didn't know I'd get out-maneuvered by the redhead."

"Cards on the table?" At Charlie's nod, Sugar said honestly, "She didn't take advantage of me. We had a very mutual heat for each other, I guess I'd say. And it feels a lot like the way I feel when I look at you."

"A lot? Is that what we've got? Mutual heat?"

Sugar chuckled. "In spades, if we're talking about cards."

Charlie wouldn't meet Sugar's gaze. "I'm glad we're clear about that then. Mutual heat does cover it." Then she slid across the seat, opened the driver's door and got out.

Sugar briefly reviewed their conversation and tried to figure out how it hadn't ended with at least a kiss. She had not a clue. She followed Charlie out the door, trying to look something less than a major dweeb as she jumped unassisted to the ground.

Charlie said nothing as they went back inside. At the elevator Sugar said, "Thanks for sharing your mobile hotel."

"You're welcome."

"Did I say something wrong?"

"No. You put everything in perspective."

The elevator arrived. Sugar pushed three. Charlie pushed six.

"Thanks again," Sugar said as she stepped off at the third floor.

Charlie didn't answer in the whole time the doors slowly closed.

Fuming, Sugar stomped to her grandmother's room. It was an effort to calm herself. She sat down in the only chair very quietly, then remembered the Bible. She retrieved it from her bag and slipped it gently under Gran's hand. She didn't know if it was a reflexive motion, but Gran's fingers eased around it and she sighed.

A few minutes later, her eyes fluttered open.

"Everything went great," Sugar said slowly. "I'm here, Gran, and everything went just fine."

Her grandmother nodded, then winced. She brushed her dry lips with her tongue and Sugar knew she had to be thirsty. "I'll see if you can sip some water. Be right back."

She met the nurse at the door to the room. The nurse said small amounts of water were okay and went to get a pitcher and ice. Sugar fished a long-forgotten tube of lip balm out of her purse and carefully applied a very light coating to her grandmother's lips. "I hope that helps. Here's the water."

She lingered for a few minutes as her grandmother slipped back into sleep. The nurse reassured her that everything was as it ought to be, and that between the painkillers and residual anesthesia Gran would be comfortable throughout the night.

Realizing she had nothing more useful to do, Sugar knew she should head for home and get some real food and sleep. In the elevator she wanted in the worst way to push the button for six, but what would that get her? Another royal brush-off from C. Bronson, Firefighter Who Blows Hot and Cold?

She had better things to do with her time. She'd call her sisters the moment she got home. She'd prep ingredients for the morning's baked-goods production. She'd buy a laptop and a printer and call Noor to go on a clothing shopping binge. That's what she was going to do with her time, and damn Charlie Bronson and the fire truck she rode in on. Damn her for being understanding and seeming safe and oozing sex appeal and being able to walk away without so much as a good-bye.

Chapter 10

With at least a week to herself in her grandmother's house, Sugar set up her new laptop and printer at one end of the kitchen table. The first coffee of the day was brewing, the ingredients for the first batch of banana bread were set out, and she was going to check her e-mail surrounded by the comforts of home.

She liked the little laptop and had fiddled with its setup the night before, until her body had screamed for sleep. It had been mindlessly engrossing, and she only thought of Charlie a half-million times. She still didn't know what she'd said that was wrong, or even if it was something she'd said. Maybe there was something she hadn't said, but it wasn't as if Charlie was meeting her halfway in discussing their feelings.

She added more creamer to her coffee and was gratified to find an order from Julie, Emily's caterer, for the graduation party. Woo-hoo, she thought. It wasn't due for three weeks and they wanted a letterman's sweater and/or a rowing trophy. Photos were attached.

She also had a note from Patricia, saying she was going to be at the hospital today around eleven, and if Sugar was there she could sign the papers and get her check on the spot. The day was steadily improving, Sugar decided, especially when she got to that second cup of coffee. She had a brief pang as she thought of the fondant decorations she had planned to be working on this morning for the contest, but it slipped away without causing even a hint of tears.

She would not think about Charlie while she mashed bananas and measured vanilla. She wouldn't think about her as she picked out clothes to wear to the hospital. She most assuredly would not wonder if she'd see a mammoth silver truck in the parking lot. Absolutely not. She had a life to live.

Of course the scent of vanilla reminded her of the cake she'd made for Charlie's father. She couldn't wear the buttery yellow polo shirt again, because Charlie had already briefly seen her in it. And when she got to the hospital and saw a familiar silver truck parked in roughly the same place as the day before, she couldn't help but recall how right it felt to wake up next to Charlie.

She had a loaf of banana bread for the nurses and a shoebox full of tart lemon squares for Patty. To her surprise, not one but all three of her sisters were in Gran's room. Rose was chatting casually with a nurse, who didn't look as if he minded that at all. Men tended to have that reaction to Rose, and Rose wouldn't notice anyone else while a nice-looking guy was around. Noor had joked that Sugar's sisters could be categorized as the Smart One, the Nice One and the Slut. She'd never said what that left for Sugar.

"There you are." Patty gave her a big hug and then another when Sugar gave her the shoebox. She'd wrapped it in decorative paper and labeled the top with "Patty's Lemon Squares—Keep Out!"

"I didn't know you were here, Quinn, so I didn't bring you anything."

Quinn shrugged. "Sure, sure, a likely story. I only stopped in for a minute," she added. "I've got a class this afternoon."

"How's Gran doing?"

"I'm strong as a horse," Gran croaked in answer.

Peering around Quinn, Sugar was delighted to see her grandmother looking much, much better than Sugar had anticipated. "Why, yes, you are. I brought you an egg custard if they're letting you have solid food."

"They gave me something they claimed was a solid breakfast but I have my doubts. My throat won't stop being dry, though."

"That's the anesthesia," Sugar explained. "Are you in any pain?"

"A bit, but not bad. Just don't bump the bed."

"See you this evening," Quinn said to Gran after gently kissing her on the forehead. She was nearly to the door when it opened and Charlie peeked into the room.

"Hi," Charlie said directly to Sugar. "Is this a bad time?"

Sugar wanted to turn her back and put her nose in the air. She wanted to pretend that Charlie's presence was of zero consequence to her. But instead she felt herself blushing as her sisters, with a single set of eyes, glanced from Charlie to her and back again.

Sugar found herself making introductions. "Meet the Sorenson girls. Patricia, Quinn, Rose and of course me, Sugar."

If Charlie was daunted by meeting them all at once, it didn't show. Then Sugar noticed Charlie had her hands in her pockets. Was that because maybe she was nervous and didn't want it to show? "I just wanted to see how Mrs. Fulton was doing."

"Please come in, dear," Gran urged. "I'm doing well. And how is your father?"

"Much, much better today. He might get to go home day after tomorrow if he keeps getting stronger."

"What good news."

"It's a pleasure to meet you," Quinn said. "I really do have to go, I'm sorry. 'Bye all." Quinn left after a pointed look at Charlie, fanning herself elaborately as she went out the door.

"I've got those papers for you to sign and that lovely check," Patty said.

"You made out like a bandit," Rose said enviously. "How come nobody will burn my house down and give me a nice nest egg?"

Trying to hide her annoyance, Sugar said, "I don't consider what happened to have been a grand piece of luck, Rose."

"Seems like it to me."

"Charlie was one of the firefighters on the scene. She probably had better things to do with her time." Sugar signed the papers where Patty indicated.

"Is that how you met? Talk about the mother lode. That fire may have been the best thing to happen to you."

Charlie said quietly, "Or it might have killed her, but let's not worry ourselves too much about that." Rose started to interrupt, but Charlie dished out one of those bedroom smiles that Sugar was chagrined to admit was having the same effect on her as it was obviously having on Rose. "Besides, we'd met before then. I jogged past her house almost every day for four months on the sheer hope she'd be out getting her morning paper."

"Now that's what I call romantic," Gran said.

Charlie gazed at Sugar for a long minute. Sugar couldn't read the expression in her eyes at all. Was it a kind of apology for stalking off so rudely yesterday? Was it *I want you, I want to spend more time with you, so how come we can't figure out how?*

Charlie sighed abruptly, and Sugar could breathe again. "I need to get back to my father. I'm so glad you're feeling better."

She slipped out of the room before Sugar could think of a thing to say.

Rose said, "She could make me change my religion."

"Claws off," Sugar snapped.

"So it's serious?" Patty pointed to one last place on the paperwork to be signed.

"No. Yes. I'm not sure. Give me a break," Sugar muttered. "No, Rose, you cannot date her. She's not your type. First off, she's not a guy."

Rose pouted. "Pity. What a waste of all those muscles."

Sugar did not think Charlie's muscles were the least bit wasted, but she didn't say so. Maybe she was finally learning how to handle

191

her sisters. Do what Patty says, sometimes, and ignore Rose most of the time. Listen to Quinn darned near all of the time.

Patricia handed Sugar an envelope. "The grand prize. Don't forget to set aside taxes, and don't spend it all in one place."

"It's going directly to the bank."

"And now I have to run," Patty said. "Thanks for the lemon squares. I love these things." She, too, gently kissed Gran on the forehead. "I'm glad Sugar is with you, but call if you need anything, okay?"

"I'll keep it in mind," Gran answered. She abruptly looked tired and pale.

"Why don't I leave you the custard," Sugar said. "I'll come back in a little while, after you've had a chance to rest. Coming, Rose?"

Even Rose couldn't be so dense as to miss Sugar's intent. She trailed out the door after a dutiful kiss on Gran's cheek.

"You really do have all the luck," Rose said once the door was closed. "Maybe I should try women. I have no luck at all with men."

Sugar winced as she considered the swath of destruction in the lesbian community that Rose would leave in her wake. "I have to warn you, lesbians your age like to talk a lot." Talking had never been high on Rose's list of good qualities in a man.

"I suppose you heard I'm getting a divorce."

"I did. I'm sorry it didn't work out."

"Why do you suppose I think if I fuck them I have to marry them?"

Sugar turned toward the elevators. "I don't know, Rose. I do know that since marriage wasn't ever an option I thought I'd get to use, I never got confused about the difference between a good time in bed and a good time in life." But she nearly had, she realized. Emily had been one but likely not the other. Noor and she had had a good time in life, but only up to a point. Bedroom fun had been adequate but not mind-blowing.

Forever was such a complicated recipe, a recipe she hadn't given much thought to because the end result wasn't something she had believed was possible. It occurred to her that she'd been fairly contemptuous of Rose's failed relationships, but at least Rose was *trying*.

"Like I said, maybe I should try women. Oh look, there's that gorgeous creature again. Go get her, Sugar Pie, she's a dish and a half." Rose cheerfully waved good-bye, the click of her high heels and sassy walk drawing the usual complimentary attention.

Sugar noticed Charlie looking, too. "So now you've met my sisters," she said as she approached. "Rose got all the looks."

"She's got nothing on you."

Sugar shook her head. "Don't do that."

"Do you think I'm lying?"

"I've got an artistic eye. You look and walk like a model. Rose has got all the well-rounded curves. Tree is unbelievably gorgeous—"

"Oh, you got me there. She's easily the most attractive woman I didn't date."

Sugar didn't want to laugh. "So you can't tell me that there isn't a difference between all of you and me. I'm not in your league. I'm not even in the B squad."

Charlie looked amazed. "Don't you look in the mirror?"

Sugar sighed. "Why are we even talking about this?"

"Because I'm avoiding apologizing for being rude yesterday."

"Oh."

"I'd much rather spend the next several hours convincing you how lovely you are and how much I'd like to get acquainted with every inch of your body."

"Oh," Sugar said again. Bedroom voice, it was the bedroom voice. "Why were you upset yesterday?"

Charlie shrugged. "I wasn't myself. I mean, I don't usually let beautiful women out of my truck without kissing them first."

"You've kissed a lot of women in your truck?"

"Well, when you have heat, you have heat."

Even though Charlie's expression was as smoldering as Sugar could have hoped for, it annoyed her. They had more than heat, didn't they? Why was it so unbelievably confusing and frustrating to talk about how they felt? She settled for a falsely bright, "Yep."

Charlie's light brown eyes steadily darkened. "Is that a problem?"

"It wasn't with the producer." Sugar could have torn out her tongue the moment the words passed her lips. Was she trying to make Charlie jealous or something?

"I'm glad you had a good time." The look that had seemed to be removing clothes from Sugar's body was gone. Charlie patted her pockets. "I need to run some errands, but I'm glad I got a chance to apologize. We'll probably run into each other again."

"Probably," Sugar echoed. Her subsequent "See ya" was aimed at Charlie's back.

She stood in the hallway for several minutes, once again replaying their conversation in her head. Where had it gone wrong this time? They agreed they had heat and every time they did they got upset and said stupid things and somebody walked off. It was like a soufflé all puffed up and perfect but then somebody slams the oven door.

Though she felt thoroughly unsettled, Sugar went to the bank and then completed the delivery of baked goods for the shelters. Meeting Noor for an early dinner was a welcome prospect. Noor was positively glowing with her pregnancy and Sugar didn't have the heart to burden her with woes of her love life. Instead, it was a wonderful diversion to hear about exams and ultrasounds, sperm donors and Deenie's family's response. She'd never seen Noor looking so happy. Whatever the recipe was she and Deenie had found, it seemed to be working out for them.

After dinner they made a sweep through Noor's favorite store, looking for both maternity and after-maternity wear. Noor felt that Sugar's new hairstyle required softer colors. Sugar bowed to pressure for several new tops and even let Noor talk her into a bra that wasn't white.

Gran was glad to see her after dinner, but her strength quickly ebbed. Tomorrow she'd be urged to try sitting on the edge of the bed and Sugar only then began to realize how long the road to recovery would be, even for someone as healthy as Gran was. They'd manage, though. So far, they'd managed really well.

The house was quiet when she got home. Even the whir of the laptop didn't fill the space. She checked e-mail, read headlines, even tried to work up interest in a game of solitaire, but nothing settled her.

The restless feeling still lingered Thursday morning, and in the stillness of the house it was hard not to think about the contest. Somewhere out there chefs were assessing the humidity. Anyone who worked with delicate baked goods would fuss over the sharp upward spike in temperatures. It was nothing to her, she thought morosely. Quick breads, cobblers and crisps were, for the most part, foolproof.

The delivery of Gran's rented hospital bed was a flurry of activity. Sugar had the movers break down the existing bed and move it to the garage. After they left she spent some time with the lighting and side chairs, trying to arrange things so Gran's first reaction wasn't that she was returning home to a sick room. She'd buy a new sheet set, Sugar thought, in bright colors as far away from hospital moods as possible.

Loaves and other goodies packed for deliveries, she checked her e-mail on her way out of the house. The short message from Emily reading, "Nothing here even compares to your work," was depressing. Fine, Emily could think Sugar had made a huge mistake, but Sugar did not regret it. She was sad about it, but she wasn't wishing anything undone. Admittedly, she was curious about the outcome, but the message from Emily seemed like a big "I told you so."

It was easier to set aside her long-suffering feelings when she saw how cheerful Gran was. The doctor ate two of Sugar's low-fat, high-fiber oatmeal raisin cookies while explaining how pleased he was with Gran's progress. There was more postsurgical swelling than they liked, which could delay her physical therapy by a day or two, but overall, things looked good for a normal recovery period. Gran could be home in ten days.

She visited with Gran for a while, reassuring her that the baked goods would be delivered and that no, no one from church had called to say the Harvest Fair would be completely changed while Gran wasn't paying attention. She read the names of people who had called with best wishes and fussed about the pretty flowers that had arrived from the auxiliary. But she felt as if her brain was a computer processing a program in the background that she didn't realize was running.

It was ridiculous to think that she felt that way because Charlie Bronson might think badly of her, though for what reason she could not begin to imagine. And it was mere politeness that kept her inquiring daily about Charlie's father's progress. She was relieved when he was moved from ICU, relieved for his sake, not the sake of his bad-tempered daughter. And if she looked at the digital photograph she'd taken of the Bronson family's long-ago fishing trip, it was to send good thoughts through the ether for his recovery, not to gaze at the little girl holding his hand.

Admittedly, the days seemed long. Grant Street Bakery won the Seattle Eats Event Dessert grand prize. The photo Emily sent of the Art Deco-style wedding cake was titled, "No Contest." It was a very pretty cake, Sugar allowed, and the long, jewel-like accent decorations were difficult to make. But if she'd had the time and focus, there would have been no competition. Next year, she thought. Next year.

Her own orders kept coming in, however, and her calendar was filling up in a very encouraging way. The settlement nest egg made her business plan look not nearly so bleak. Within a day or two she no longer thought about the contest. It wasn't strange to wake up at Gran's anymore, either. The weather warmed sufficiently that

Sugar spent Saturday evening on the patio, reading for a while, then letting herself get lost in the glory of the rising full moon. She wanted to tell someone about how beautiful it was.

Be honest, she told herself firmly. *It's not just anyone you wish you were sharing the moon with tonight. So what are you going to do about it?*

Sunday afternoon she arrived at the hospital to find Gran enjoying a variety of visitors. Sugar's chewy, still-warm peanut-butter cookies were appreciated by all and nobody seemed to notice when she slipped out again, another box of cookies under one arm.

Given how she and Charlie had bumped into each other before, Sugar had been surprised not to have done so again, even though she was certainly not wishing for that to happen. She'd had enough hot and cold from Charlie Bronson to last a lifetime. That they might now have to encounter each other wasn't her problem, Sugar told herself as she carefully pushed open the door to Chuck Bronson's room.

Her first thought was that there was no sign of Charlie and the second was that firefighters, as a breed, were big. The three of them visiting Chuck took up as much space as five members of the church auxiliary.

"I thought by now, if your nutrition plan allowed, you'd be bored of hospital food," Sugar said shyly. She gave the other men, still in their work uniforms, a stern look. "These are for the patient."

Chuck looked about the way Gran did—strained but recovering, and tired but glad of diversion. "I'll have to share because they're not letting me eat that kind of thing until tomorrow."

"In that case, I will bring you more," Sugar said as she popped open the box.

Ralph, talking around a mouthful of cookie, asked, "Are you

married? Do you want to be married?" A buddy nudged him, hard. "What? Oh. Sorry, didn't mean anything by it. I forgot you were Charlie's girl."

A flash of extreme annoyance mingled with an undeniable flush of pleasure. "I'm not sure what gave you that idea," she said.

Even Chuck joined in the laughter of the three other men. Sugar was about to ask what was so funny, but they all sobered guiltily before she could.

Even before she turned she could smell Charlie's cologne.

"Hi," Charlie said, hands in her pockets. "What's so funny?"

"Nothing." Chuck quickly gestured at the cookies. "Have a cookie."

The men went into fits of giggles. Sugar would have glared at them if she could have torn her gaze from Charlie. Jeans were never meant to look so sexy, of that she was certain. A pristine white KCFD polo shirt was supposed to look official, utilitarian even, not luscious to the point of seductive. She told herself to stop staring but she couldn't. It felt wonderful to look at Charlie.

"So you finally got here," Chuck continued after Charlie silently chose a cookie from the box. "These guys have been here forty minutes. Your shift ended at the same time, didn't it?"

There was more giggling, but it quieted at a glare from Charlie. Not looking at Sugar, she said, "They might want to go around smelling like our last fire, but I don't. And after three days of the shower at the firehouse I was ready for my own."

"I need to get back to my grandmother," Sugar lied. "I just wanted to bring the cookies and tell you I'm so glad you're feeling better."

"Thank you very much for the cookies," Chuck said warmly. "I was afraid when they delivered my soup for dinner these guys would take it."

"You're welcome. See you." Sugar said it generally, not to anyone in particular, and made what she hoped was a dignified exit.

Charlie's cologne seemed to be in the elevator, in the hallways, even in Gran's room. It wasn't fair.

"Why there you are," Gran said excitedly. "You just missed her. What a shame."

"Who?"

"Charlie. She was just here. Said she'd been on duty for the last three days or would have stopped in sooner. Look at the gladioli she brought! Said she'd noticed the potted ones on the back patio and thought I'd be glad for the sight of some."

Charlie had checked in on Gran before going up to see her father. Had, in fact, stopped to shower and change beforehand. Her head spinning, Sugar was pretty sure she made all the right responses. The flowers were beautiful, and probably accounted for the smile that she couldn't get off her face. Somewhere deep inside a little imp was turning cartwheels. Okay, so today they hadn't really spoken to each other. But contact had been mutually made. Talking could happen sometime this century, perhaps.

The rest of the country called it Memorial Day, but it was just another Monday to Sugar. She popped up to Chuck's room and left an easy-to-digest egg custard. Sometime in the early afternoon, Charlie left Gran a travel magazine on the Holy Land. On Tuesday Sugar caught Charlie in the act of leaving peppermint tea, so she gave her the two-person spice cake for Chuck.

"I remember you said it was a favorite. Yesterday he thought he'd be allowed."

"And day after tomorrow he'll probably get sent home," Charlie added. They moved slowly toward the door of Gran's room, stepping out of the way of the visitors for the other occupant.

"We won't have an excuse to keep meeting like this, will we?"

"No." Charlie stared into Sugar's eyes for a long moment, so long that Sugar thought that surely Charlie was going to kiss her. Then she sighed, breaking the spell. "We won't."

Trying to control the quaver in her voice, Sugar suggested softly, "We could perhaps arrange to meet somewhere else. To exchange gifts for other family members," she added quickly.

"Probably should keep it public, or the heat will get the best of us."

Sugar wasn't certain what showed in her face, but she knew how her body felt on the topic. There was obviously some sort of aphrodisiac in Charlie's cologne, because her physical response to it was ridiculously Pavlovian. "Would that be such a bad thing?"

Charlie's eyes widened. "It would probably be fan-fuh . . . er, fantastic."

Sugar swallowed hard. "I don't understand, then." She really didn't. Why was Charlie keeping her at arm's length when their arms seemed to be aching to hold each other?

Very quietly, Charlie asked, "Are you seeing the producer anymore?"

"No." She would have added more, but Charlie stilled her lips with a gentle fingertip.

"That's why."

Feeling more confused than ever, Sugar watched Charlie walk away. Would anything ever make sense?

Wednesday brought the welcome change of pace in the form of baking for her own business again. For the next seven weeks she had two or three cakes on her calendar, including the large '55 Chevy for JaeLynn. The chrome would a challenge. It felt good to be back in the swing of things. By the end of the day she was more tired than she had been since moving in, but it felt good.

She realized she was staring blankly at her laptop screen and that the rumble of a large truck outside had been present for several seconds. She jumped, startled, when the engine noise died.

She was in a near panic when the doorbell rang.

Charlie looked so worn out in the porch light that Sugar immediately pushed open the screen door. "What's wrong? Is your dad okay?"

"Yeah, he's good. I just left. He's coming home tomorrow on schedule. I was on call and had to go to a structural fire for a while

200

earlier. I was going home and I realized I can't . . ." Charlie paused in the hallway, slowly shaking her head.

Sugar shut the door and put her hand on Charlie's arm. "Can't what?"

"I can't get through today without seeing you somehow."

Sugar's breath caught in her throat and her heart felt as if it would burst when Charlie pulled her firmly into her arms. Without conscious thought, Sugar went up on her tiptoes and Charlie stooped so their lips could meet.

I was hungry for this, Sugar thought, hungry for her arms and her mouth. Charlie made a small sound that could have been a moan of wonder—or of pain. Their bodies were finding the ways to melt together, to merge.

Sugar let her hands explore the smooth contours of Charlie's back. Scenes in her head were way ahead of where they were. She could envision giving herself to Charlie in a hundred ways and just as easily anticipate the moment she stretched out on top of Charlie, too. The heat was there and it was as sharp and hot and wild as what she'd felt with Emily.

Why, then, did she want to cry? Why were these wet, needy kisses almost painful?

Charlie pulled back with a gasp. They stared at each other in the low hallway light, then Charlie wound her hands in Sugar's hair and pulled her close again. Hungry, Sugar thought again. This kind of hunger could leave both of them utterly consumed. Her hands cupped Charlie's breasts through the thin polo shirt and she was more certain that Charlie's moan was pleasure.

"I'm so glad you're a woman," Sugar murmured into Charlie's mouth. "So very glad."

Charlie laughed softly. "Well, if I weren't I wouldn't get to sleep with lesbians."

"It works out well, doesn't it?" Sugar's heart was pounding, but it wasn't with passion. Parts of her were swimming with wetness, but her mouth felt dry with panic.

"Especially with all this . . . heat." Charlie lazily ran one finger down Sugar's chest, slowly approaching the swell of her breasts. "That's amazing."

"What is?"

"This," Charlie whispered as her fingers closed on Sugar's nipple. "You. Your body has been in my dreams since the first morning I saw you get the paper wearing nothing but a T-shirt."

Her nipple seemed to swell in Charlie's grasp. She wanted Charlie's hand on her directly, not through her clothes. "I don't remember that."

"Believe me, I do. I couldn't figure out how to talk to you."

"Then my house burned down."

"It didn't seem like the right time to ask you for a date. I'm funny that way."

Charlie's fingertips had not stopped teasing her nipple. Sugar trembled and felt near tears again. "So what do you propose we do now?"

"You know perfectly well what I'd like to do." Charlie kissed her hungrily. "Let's take care of this heat. Putting out fires is my specialty."

Sugar laughed, then something in her shifted and tears spilled over. "I want to, I really want to."

"What's wrong?" Charlie immediately let go of her and put some space between them. "Did I hurt you?"

"No. I just . . . I'm scared and it hurts to be with you like this. I don't know why."

"I thought you wanted this."

"I do." Sugar wiped her eyes.

"I tried to take it slow. I didn't kiss you the first night I was here. I thought you wanted it that way."

"I did."

"Then you went to bed with someone else because you had this thing with her. Which I'm not judging," Charlie added quickly. "You didn't need my permission. I felt like you were saying that was all you wanted with me, too. So you were with what's-her-name because of heat, then you stopped seeing her. And I couldn't stand the thought that if I slept with you I'd never see you again afterward."

"Oh." Sugar blinked. "So you didn't try to see me so you could go on seeing me?"

"Yeah." Charlie nodded as if it made sense.

Maybe it did, maybe it didn't, but Sugar didn't care. What mattered was that, given how hard it was to keep their hands off each other, Charlie must want to keep seeing her, a *lot*.

"Driving home tonight, I thought, well, if that's what you liked in a woman, good sex and no strings, I'd give that a try. It hadn't worked for me before but I'd do just about anything to see if I could be with you. I'd try to be some sexual superwoman if that would keep you wanting me around."

"Oh, Charlie," Sugar said, laughing. "I'm not a sex-focused free-love kind of gal. The thing with the producer was the first time I've ever been that casual."

"Must have been a pretty powerful attraction, then."

"It was." Honesty made her add, "And still could be, but that doesn't mean I'm going to doing anything about it. It was a hell of a forest fire, but it's not . . ."

Charlie moved slightly closer. "Not what?"

Not *this*, Sugar wanted to say, but her courage failed her. "Why me?" she asked instead. "You could be with anybody. All I can offer you is a good roll in the hay and a great birthday cake."

"Stop that," Charlie said softly. "I want to be with you because of the way I feel when I look at you. I was walking around thinking I was whole, until these past few weeks when I saw where my life could include you. Then I realized all the empty places I was carrying around. When I'm with you—okay, sometimes I want to scream because we never seem to be talking about the same thing and I realize later you meant something else or you didn't get what I said."

Sugar nodded emphatically. "I know that feeling."

"Then when I'm with you and everything is clicking it feels like everything I do makes you laugh, and I love your laugh. I feel new and sexy, and I have never flirted with anyone the way I flirt with you and I *love* it. When we were talking about books and passing the time together at the hospital I thought, holy shit, wouldn't it be nice to do that every day? Wouldn't it be nice to hold you and love you and talk to you all the time?"

Sugar hiccupped. "What about the mutual heat?"

"Good lord, Sugar, that'll be the easy part, don't you think?"

"Then why am I so scared to go to bed with you?"

"You weren't with the producer?"

"It was . . . easy." Sugar hesitated. Maybe, she thought with a flash of clarity, maybe she hadn't been scared because her heart hadn't been involved. "I'm sorry if that makes you jealous."

"It does, a little, but damn." Charlie cupped Sugar's shoulders. "Give me a chance to prove she was a one-night wonder."

"Well," Sugar said honestly, "there were two nights."

Clearly amused, Charlie said softly, "Then I'll stay at least for three so you can make up your mind."

"How do you do that? That thing with your eyes?" Sugar looked at Charlie in wonder.

"What thing?"

"Like you don't know. You have bedroom eyes, Charlie Bronson."

"Don't change the subject. You haven't said if you accept my offer. If three nights is what you want, I'll do my best to make them the best three nights of our lives."

Very clearly Sugar said, "I do not want three nights."

Charlie caressed the side of Sugar's mouth with her thumb and it was all Sugar could do not to give in to kissing it. "Then what do you want, Sugar? Let me at least try."

Sugar's heart was pounding in fear again. She was petrified, feeling as if her entire life was suddenly swaying over a pit of complete ruin. Say the right thing, she warned herself, find the right words or you'll ruin it all. The crossroads was scary. One path led to far more than three nights. The other had Charlie walking out of her life.

Charlie didn't do that U-Haul thing, she'd said so herself. She wanted a woman with brains, she'd said that too. Charlie was brave, not just in her career, but in coming here to try to see if they couldn't work something out. She wanted to know what Sugar wanted. What did Charlie want? What did Charlie need? Sugar had no idea if she could come anywhere close.

Charlie's hands had fallen to her sides while she waited for Sugar's answer. If she didn't speak soon, the moment would be lost. All the ingredients seemed to be present, it just took the confidence to combine them in the right order.

I don't have the experience, Sugar wailed inwardly. Not when it comes to love.

Then she realized that Charlie had put her hands in her pockets.

Maybe, she thought, Charlie doesn't either. If Charlie was as clueless as she was about how to make things work, then she wouldn't know when Sugar was making it up as she went along, would she? Maybe they could make mistakes together. They'd certainly done enough of that.

"I want a thousand nights," Sugar said, firmly. "You can't get me for a paltry offer of three."

Charlie grinned at her, but it didn't quite reach her eyes. It's not enough, Sugar thought. It looked like she was going to have to be the brave one.

"I think," Sugar added slowly, "I think I'm falling in love with you."

Charlie swallowed hard as tears seeped from the corners of her eyes. She shook with a half-sob. "I'm scared to death, but now I don't care. I think I'm falling in love with you, too. I think I might already be in love with you."

She pulled Sugar fiercely into her arms and Sugar no longer felt afraid.

There was no staircase, no pounding surf. Nobody carried anybody anywhere in a delirium of romantic passion. Taking her hand, Sugar led Charlie down the hallway to the room that was hers.

They found their way out of their clothes in a long, continuous dance of tangling arms and languid kisses.

Charlie nibbled her way down Sugar's throat. "I woke up this morning thinking about your shoulders. They're such a perfect combination of soft and strong. And I was sure they would taste—" Her tongue ran over the notch in one. "They would taste just like that. Your skin is incredible."

Sugar felt worshipped as Charlie's mouth explored her. She touched the curly black hair, eager to feel it in her hands, against her thighs, resting on her back. The delicious combinations of their bodies were parading through her mind. Charlie's hands were like magic on her body. She hadn't realized that her hips loved to be stroked, hadn't known that her calves would flex in response to a firm, warm grasp.

In response to the pressure of Charlie's hips Sugar spread her thighs so Charlie could slip between them. She felt small in Charlie's embrace, but treasured. "I keep trying not to laugh," she admitted. "It all feels so good."

"We're in no hurry," Charlie said. "We've got time to laugh."

"Good. Time to kiss?" Sugar pushed herself up against Charlie's body and ran her tongue suggestively over Charlie's lips. "I think kissing you could become my favorite hobby."

Their hips were moving in a rolling rhythm that was slowly increasing in pace. "Do you remember what I said, the first night you were here?"

"You said a lot of things." Charlie kissed Sugar thoroughly, pushing her down into the bed.

When Sugar regained her breath, she explained, "I said if I wanted you to do me, you wouldn't have any doubt of it."

"Oh, yeah." Charlie smiled into their next kiss. "I could do this forever."

"So could I."

"But I think I heard a request from the lady about getting done?"

Sugar breathed into Charlie's mouth a heady, "Yes."

"You're sure?"

"Yes," Sugar said again. "And then I'm going to do you, just so we're clear on that."

"Okay. Sounds good to me."

Sugar started to laugh in response but Charlie's hand was suddenly between her legs, firm and possessive. She stiffened as a wave of desire crashed over her.

The laughter in Charlie's eyes was gone, and that heavy-lidded, intense gaze seemed to cut Sugar open. She was completely exposed. She couldn't hide the way her body liked what Charlie was doing. They groaned long and hard together as Sugar arched in response. Sugar felt the flutter of fear as her climax grew rapidly, inevitabley. She'd fall to pieces and never be the same again.

Charlie's arm was tight and firm around her. It's Charlie, she told herself. It's Charlie and you love her. She gazed into Charlie's eyes, saw the heat there, but there was also wonder and strength. It's Charlie holding you so tight, and maybe you won't be the same again after she's loved you, but it's Charlie and she's not going to care. She loves you.

The love in Charlie's eyes melted the fear and Sugar could only hold on to the strong arms as her body threatened to fly away.

"If you think you're going to doze off, you're wrong," Sugar said after a few minutes. Her body was in one piece, of course, but what felt new and different was that her heart was no longer all her own. Desire was still stirring inside her, but it was mixed with tenderness, a combination she had never felt before.

Charlie opened one eye. "Am I?"

Sugar playfully pushed Charlie onto her back, then settled astride her. "I like this position. I can keep track of these long legs and arms of yours." It also allowed her to run her fingers lightly over the compact, defined muscles of Charlie's arms and stomach.

"Whatever makes you happy, my love."

Sugar fought down a wonderfully gooey feeling in the pit of her stomach. "Quit that lovey-dovey stuff right now. We're having sex."

"Can't we do both?"

"For a little while," Sugar said, bending to capture a tantalizing nipple between her teeth. She nibbled and teased it with her tongue, then looked up to see Charlie's response. "Which is it? Lovey-dovey or sex?"

"Sex, please." Charlie slipped a hand between Sugar's wet center and her stomach.

Sugar slapped it away. "Stop that. Don't distract me."

"Can you be distracted?"

Charlie's fingers made Sugar's legs threaten to collapse. "Yes, probably." It took all her strength to move away from that wonderful pleasuring touch. Grasping both of Charlie's hands, Sugar lifted them to the headboard. "You keep those right there. They're troublemakers."

Charlie grinned. "Yes, ma'am."

Sugar slithered down Charlie's body and licked her lips suggestively. She had the satisfaction of seeing the smile fade from Charlie's face. She submerged into the tight, sleek folds between Charlie's legs and heard Charlie's hoarse groan of response. Strong legs around her, Sugar gave herself over to pleasing Charlie and the wonder of Charlie's abandon. She wanted Charlie to feel beyond wonderful, more than fantastic.

Charlie cried out sharply, her hands still grasping the headboard. "Don't stop."

With an answering moan, Sugar slid fingers inside Charlie, sensuously enjoying the slippery heat. With another cry Charlie let go of the headboard, bringing her hands to the back of Sugar's head. They froze together for just a moment, then Charlie's hips bucked wildly and Sugar, with her own cry of pleasure, didn't stop.

Giggling like teenagers, they admitted hours later to being famished.

"How about toasted banana bread?"

"That sounds like ambrosia," Charlie agreed.

Sugar sliced the bread as Charlie stood behind her, holding her close. Their hips continued to rock together. The night was young, Sugar thought, though it was after midnight. They'd only just gotten started.

She dropped the slices into the toaster and pushed down on the lever. She gave herself over to the sensuous pleasure of Charlie's kisses on the back of her neck. After a minute she realized the toaster wasn't working.

"Oh," she said dreamily. "It's not plugged in." She pushed the plug into the outlet.

The lights went out.

Charlie laughed into Sugar's ear. "We can eat it untoasted, can't we?"

"Yes, but what about the lights?"

Charlie's hands smoothed Sugar's hips, then moved slowly up to caress her breasts. "Who needs lights?"

Publications from
BELLA BOOKS, INC.
The best in contemporary lesbian fiction

P.O. Box 10543, Tallahassee, FL 32302
Phone: 800-729-4992
www.bellabooks.com

SUGAR by Karin Kallmaker. 240 pp. Three women want sugar from Sugar, who can't make up her mind. ISBN 1-59493-001-5

FALL GUY by Claire McNab. 200 pp. 16th Detective Inspector Carol Ashton Mystery. ISBN 1-59493-000-7

ONE SUMMER NIGHT by Gerri Hill. 232 pp. Johanna swore to never fall in love again— but then she met the charming Kelly . . . ISBN 1-59493-007-4

TALK OF THE TOWN TOO by Saxon Bennett. 181 pp. Second in the series about wild and fun loving friends. ISBN 1-931513-77-5

LOVE SPEAKS HER NAME by Laura DeHart Young. 170 pp. Love and friendship, desire and intrigue, spark this exciting sequel to *Forever and the Night*. ISBN 1-59493-002-3

TO HAVE AND TO HOLD by Peggy J. Herring. 184 pp. By finally letting down her defenses, will Dorian be opening herself to a devastating betrayal? ISBN 1-59493-005-8

WILD THINGS by Karin Kallmaker. 228 pp. Dutiful daughter Faith has met the perfect man. There's just one problem: she's in love with his sister. ISBN 1-931513-64-3

SHARED WINDS by Kenna White. 216 pp. Can Emma rebuild more than just Lanny's marina? ISBN 1-59493-006-6

THE UNKNOWN MILE by Jaime Clevenger. 253 pp. Kelly's world is getting more and more complicated every moment. ISBN 1-931513-57-0

TREASURED PAST by Linda Hill. 189 pp. A shared passion for antiques leads to love. ISBN 1-59493-003-1

SIERRA CITY by Gerri Hill. 284 pp. Chris and Jesse cannot deny their growing attraction . . . ISBN 1-931513-98-8

ALL THE WRONG PLACES by Karin Kallmaker. 174 pp. Sex and the single girl—Brandy is looking for love and usually she finds it. Karin Kallmaker's first *After Dark* erotic novel. ISBN 1-931513-76-7

WHEN THE CORPSE LIES A Motor City Thriller by Therese Szymanski. 328 pp. Butch bad-girl Brett Higgins is used to waking up next to beautiful women she hardly knows. Problem is, this one's dead. ISBN 1-931513-74-0